Tempted by Trouble

Also by Eric Jerome Dickey

Resurrecting Midnight (Gideon series)
Dying for Revenge (Gideon series)
Pleasure
Waking with Enemies (Gideon series)
Sleeping with Strangers (Gideon series)
Chasing Destiny
Genevieve
Drive Me Crazy
Naughty or Nice
The Other Woman
Thieves' Paradise
Between Lovers
Liar's Game
Cheaters
Milk in My Coffee
Friends and Lovers
Sister, Sister

Anthologies

Voices from the Other Side: Dark Dreams II
Got to Be Real
Mothers and Sons
River Crossings: Voices of the Diaspora
Griots Beneath the Baobab
Black Silk: A Collection of African American Erotica
Gumbo: A Celebration of African American Writing

Movie—Original Story

Cappuccino

Graphic Novels

Storm (six-issue miniseries, Marvel Entertainment)

ERIC JEROME DICKEY

Tempted by Trouble

DUTTON

DUTTON
Published by Penguin Group (USA) Inc.
375 Hudson Street, New York, New York 10014, U.S.A.
Penguin Group (Canada), 90 Eglinton Avenue East, Suite 700, Toronto, Ontario M4P 2Y3, Canada (a
division of Pearson Penguin Canada Inc.); Penguin Books Ltd, 80 Strand, London WC2R 0RL, England;
Penguin Ireland, 25 St Stephen's Green, Dublin 2, Ireland (a division of Penguin Books Ltd); Penguin
Group (Australia), 250 Camberwell Road, Camberwell, Victoria 3124, Australia (a division of Pearson
Australia Group Pty Ltd); Penguin Books India Pvt Ltd, 11 Community Centre, Panchsheel Park, New
Delhi—110 017, India; Penguin Group (NZ), 67 Apollo Drive, Rosedale, North Shore 0632, New Zealand
(a division of Pearson New Zealand Ltd); Penguin Books (South Africa) (Pty) Ltd, 24 Sturdee Avenue,
Rosebank, Johannesburg 2196, South Africa

Penguin Books Ltd, Registered Offices: 80 Strand, London WC2R 0RL, England

Published by Dutton, a member of Penguin Group (USA) Inc.

First printing, August 2010
10   9   8   7   6   5   4   3   2   1

Copyright © 2010 by Eric Jerome Dickey
All rights reserved

 REGISTERED TRADEMARK—MARCA REGISTRADA

LIBRARY OF CONGRESS CATALOGING-IN-PUBLICATION DATA HAS BEEN APPLIED FOR

ISBN 978-0-525-95058-5

Printed in the United States of America
Set in Janson Text LT Std 55 Roman
Designed by Leonard Telesca

For Dominique

Tempted by Trouble

LANGUAGE TUTOR FOR HIRE
SPANISH, ITALIAN, LATIN, GERMAN, OR FRENCH

Reply to: D. Knight

I provide one-on-one language lessons tailored to your professional and educational needs at $25 per hour. We can meet at a local coffee shop, a library, or a bookstore anywhere in the Detroit metro area. I also provide group lessons for up to six people. The price differs depending upon the number of people.

I was born in Detroit and so were my parents. I attended college in Florida, but I graduated from Cass Technical High School. Autoworkers or former autoworkers will receive a 15 percent discount or ten classes for the price of eight. It doesn't matter if you worked on the line or were booted from a corner office overlooking the Detroit River. My wife and I are both out-of-work autoworkers, so I understand your hardships and can offer a payment plan, if that is what is needed. In this country being bilingual will give you a leg up on the regular Joes.

Every man has to pull his weight, so let me help you pull yours.

Dmytryk Knight

Prologue

Eddie Coyle had parked on the right shoulder of I-94 and left the engine running and the heater on low. It was below freezing in the Motor City. My seat warmer was on low, but the heat became too much and I turned it off.

Eddie Coyle said, "Back in '97 there was the Loomis Fargo Bank robbery."

His words pulled me out of my trance. His voice was powerful.

I asked, "Where was that?"

"Charlotte, North Carolina. They withdrew over seventeen million dollars."

"That's a lot of money."

"Seventeen million."

"Where are they now?"

"Jail."

I removed my black fedora, then reached inside my suit coat and pulled out my pocket watch, checked my time against the time on the dash.

He said, "Two minutes. That's how long it took Dillinger to rob a bank. When you're on the job, keep that number in mind. Two minutes. I'll cover the rest with you next week."

"Violence and injury occur in less than three percent of bank robberies."

"You did some research."

"Less than one percent involve murder, kidnapping, or hostages."

"I never did the research. The only numbers that matter to me are on the front of money."

"Well, I like to know my odds. They don't look good, but they're better than the odds in the unemployment line. I'm starting to feel I have a better chance of winning the lottery than getting a job."

Sheltered from the inclement weather, I was sitting at the crossroads with the devil.

Sometimes the only choices a man has left are bad ones.

Eddie Coyle asked, "How long have you been out of work?"

"Over two years."

"You speak a handful of languages."

"I do."

"Your wife said that you used to be an executive."

"I was. For a while, I was."

"And can't find a decent job."

"Welcome to America. The long line on the left is the line for the disenfranchised."

"A chicken in every pot and a car in every garage."

"Add that to the long list of lies."

"That's not the way it's supposed to be."

"I know."

"It goes against the grain of the American dream. Doesn't make sense to me."

"I worked on the line too. I was blue-collar too. Yep, I was laid off, lost my white-collar job, took a drastic pay cut, and ended up on the line for nine years. Seven years white-collar, seven blue-collar. I was willing to work wherever I could work, despite my education."

"Not many executives are willing to take a blue-collar job when things get rough."

"Not many."

He looked at his watch and I thought about my own future, a future as dark as the night.

I pulled down the visor, flipped open the vanity mirror, and when it illuminated I stared at my image. My father's image. My face was Henrick's face. The face of a real man, a face not made for billboards and magazines. I used his pocket watch, a timepiece that had been his father's timepiece, a pocket watch that had kept time for decades.

But the world had changed since Henrick walked on top of this littered soil, and not for the better. No one would say it was the best of times. It was bad for Wall Street, the housing industry, and law enforcement, and a travesty for the car industry. I didn't see another way out.

As the SUV hummed, I asked Eddie Coyle, "What's the cargo you have in the back?"

"I told you already."

"What are we waiting on?"

"Godot."

The man who had appropriated the name Eddie Coyle was in the driver's seat, both literally and metaphorically. Ice spotted the sides

of the roads and icicles hung from barren trees for as far as the headlights from passing cars would allow me to see; the same symbols of a
harsh winter hung from interstate signs. Detroit was in a deep freeze.
The chill that had crippled the Midwest and parts of the North sat on
us as we waited on the right shoulder of I-94, the engine running and
the lights off. It was twelve thirty in the morning. Five minutes later
another Cadillac Escalade pulled up behind us.

I kept my voice smooth, masked my nervousness, and asked, "Are
you expecting company?"

"My brother."

"So you didn't come from Rome by yourself."

"I haven't been alone all evening."

"You said you worked with two other guys, Rick and Sammy."

"From time to time."

"Which one is your brother?"

"Neither. My brother is Bishop. We call him Bishop."

"What's he doing back there?"

"He's going to be our lookout."

"You and your brother could've done this alone."

"If you want to make it to the next level, you'll do this, not him.
He's already in."

When there was a break in traffic, we stepped out into the cold and
moved to the back. Eddie Coyle popped open the rear of the luxury
SUV. The interior light revealed a man stuffed inside industrial carpet. He had been rolled up like a cigarette. He wore wingtip shoes
that were similar to mine. The man had been a professional. As we
grabbed the dead body and unloaded it from the back of the SUV,
one of Detroit's landmarks, the giant Uniroyal tire, towered on the

opposite side of I-94. A freezing drizzle tapped against my fedora like an erratic heartbeat, that same freezing water adding weight to my long wool overcoat. The ground crunched underneath my Johnston & Murphy shoes as I held on to the feet of the dead man. My breath fogged in front of my face and my lungs contracted with each frigid breath. We were about forty yards into the brush and debris when we heard a boom, then in the distance the sky lit up. It was a new year and fireworks brightened the suburbs. For three seconds, if anyone on I-94 had looked into the wooded area that served as a barrier between the interstate and a strip mall, they would have seen two men wearing suits carrying six feet of carpet off into the nether regions. The carpet moved like a giant caterpillar battling to become a monstrous butterfly. The man in the carpet kicked, his right shoe slipping off his foot. Startled, I jumped and caught my breath. I didn't yell, but inside my head my voice screamed, and I abandoned my end of the rug.

The dead man wasn't dead.

Eddie Coyle dragged his end of the carpet another ten yards before he let it fall hard. While the man kicked and fought until the carpet unrolled, Eddie Coyle reached underneath his suit coat and pulled out a handgun. The man wore black socks and wingtips. Nothing else. He was naked, pale, tall, and no more than thirty years old. His wrists and mouth were wrapped in duct tape. He struggled to get free. Traffic passed by on I-94, everyone intoxicated and unaware. As another late round of fireworks put beautiful colors in the dark skies, Eddie Coyle fired three shots, each shot lighting up his face. He was a CEO who was executing his business with a calmness that was terrifying. The man collapsed, fell back onto the carpet.

Eddie Coyle regarded me, his breath fogging from his face.

He said, "No witnesses."

I nodded.

He nodded in return.

I stood tall and firm, despite feeling that this frozen ground was about to become my grave as well.

He asked, "You ever heard of Yoido Full Gospel Church?"

"Can't say that I have. That's not in Detroit or Dearborn, is it?"

"It sits on Yeouido Island in Seoul, South Korea."

"Okay."

"It has over eight hundred thousand members."

"You thinking about going there?"

"I can only imagine how much money they bring in every Sunday. I can't imagine how much we could pull if we organized and hit a church that size."

"Are we robbing a bank or are you talking about robbing a church?"

"Banks. I'm a bank man. Banks are federally insured, so no one loses in the end."

Eddie Coyle's attention went back to the work at hand.

Eddie Coyle said, "The body won't smell for a while. It's below freezing and will stay that way for at least a week. It's cold enough to throw off the time of death by a few days. It might be weeks, maybe a couple of months before anybody finds what's left of him."

Another chill ran up my spine, a combination of coldness, fear, and hate.

Eddie Coyle said, "You're almost officially one of us now."

"Almost."

"You just knowingly and willingly participated in a crime."

"I guess this makes me a partner in your business."

"You don't get your name on the door, not just yet."

"I stand corrected."

"It gives me a bargaining chip in case you have other ideas. Mister Executive, so far so good. You didn't fall apart. You didn't freak out and run. You passed the test. You'll need nerves of steel."

I shivered from the cold. I knew it would have been futile to run. His brother was probably standing in the cold, waiting for me to panic and run out of the woods, his gun ready to fire.

Eddie Coyle took out a package of Marlboro Blacks, then tossed me his smoking gun.

He said, "It's your turn to put a few bullets in one of my problems."

"The man's dead."

"But he's not dead enough, Dmytryk."

He took out a plastic lighter and lit his cigarette, its tip glowing in the night.

Eddie Coyle smiled. "Any man who crosses me will never be dead enough."

Again in the distance, there was an explosion and beautiful colors that lit up the skies.

I handed the gun back to Eddie Coyle. "He was your problem, not mine."

"Be a man."

"I am a man. And putting a bullet in a dead man won't elevate that status."

Moments later the sound of feet crunching the ground came toward us.

It was Eddie Coyle's brother. He was a large man dressed in a fur coat that made him look like a bear stalking through the darkness. When he came closer I saw that he carried another rug over his shoulders. He dropped the rug and allowed it to unroll. The body of a woman rolled free and came to a stop next to the man who had been hidden inside the first rug. She was still alive.

Bishop regarded me. "You're the new guy that my little brother is vouching for."

His voice was thick, not as refined as Eddie Coyle's. Bishop sounded like years in prison, drug smuggling, and everything immoral. He sounded like crime personified. He was the type of man I loathed, the type of man I'd never wanted to associate with.

I said, "I'm the new hire."

"You look like a jerk who would do my taxes, if I ever paid taxes."

"You look like a man I'd hit in the mouth for insulting me, if he ever insulted me intentionally."

"Your wife said you had a chip on your shoulder."

"My wife isn't part of this, so I'd like to keep this between the parties involved."

"That's what the old wheelman said. And you see where that got him."

Eddie Coyle said, "Dmytryk is motivated and will fit in with Rick and Sammy."

Bishop asked, "You ever been employed in this line of work?"

"That's none of your concern. Eddie Coyle is the one I report to."

Eddie Coyle hunched his shoulders and turned to walk away. I followed Eddie Coyle, my wingtips crunching over ice and frozen grass as we headed back toward the interstate.

We left Bishop behind. Halfway to the interstate, behind us, a gun fired three rapid shots.

Those celebratory explosions sent a chill up my spine.

When we climbed back inside the SUV, Eddie Coyle turned his lights on and put the Cadillac in drive, pulled away, and said, "No witnesses left behind. That's my number-one rule. No witnesses."

"Even the woman."

"Breasts or balls, penis or poontang, spook, Jew, or wetback, a witness is a witness."

The message was clear.

Eddie Coyle said, "Megachurches are nothing more than tax-free symbols of greed and power."

"Back to talking about robbing God."

"Megachurches are the Walmarts of the religious world, one-stop shopping, pulling members away from all of the local mom-and-pop box churches."

"What's the issue?"

"Capitalism and how it has infected everything that was once good."

"Capitalism was all about big fish devouring little fish and never stopping to masticate their prey. It's a good thing when you're winning. When you're losing, you see its faults."

He nodded. "The country is devolving. The Tea Party is out there expressing their outrage over health care. If this is the outrage that comes from health care, it's going to be crazy when immigration is brought to the table. Bad economy and racism, the fear of a new labor pool coming from beyond these shores to do jobs in an already jobless country—it will be a Molotov cocktail. It will be the Detroit race riot in '43 and the Detroit race riot in '67 and the Watts riot and the '67 Newark riots and the Oklahoma race riots in every state, city, and town in America."

I didn't say anything else. He'd just murdered two people and was engaging in a casual conversation about churches and politics.

Eddie Coyle said, "I hope your wife feels better. When you get home, tell her I said that."

"You don't have to worry about my wife."

"Understood."

"Worrying about my wife is my responsibility."

"Again, I apologize for crossing that unseen line."

I tightened my jaw and held on to my fedora, a classic hat I had inherited from my father.

In my mind I was grabbing Eddie Coyle's gun and shooting him over and over as the SUV lost control and flipped over a half dozen times. As he sped down I-94, I should have killed Eddie Coyle right then. But I had known the man for only two hours.

DESPERATION

The state of being desperate or of having the recklessness
of despair.

0

Four walls closed in and I woke up wanting to scream at the universe.

Every man had a breaking point and I'd conceded to mine four seasons ago.

Before sunrise touched the iconic palm trees in California, palm trees that were not native to the region, those colorful fireworks had returned, only they were exploding behind my eyes and inside my head. I was caught in an ongoing war between stress and anxiety. The tightness in my chest slithered up to my throat, became a snake, and then I was being strangled. I gripped the edges of the sink and shut my eyes as the whole world closed in on me from every side. Head lowered, sweat ran down my neck and my body was racked with dread. Every now and then a man had to let his eyes spring a leak in order to remain sane.

I looked to my right, searched for something to focus on. I settled for the bathtub. The tub looked like it hadn't been cleaned since

Kennedy was assassinated and the toilet hadn't been treated to any harsh cleansers since Jack Ruby took out Oswald to cover up that conspiracy.

Almost a year had gone by since that frigid night I stood on the side of I-94 with Eddie Coyle, sealing a deal with a ruthless and congenial devil.

It seemed like it was yesterday. Maybe because nothing in the world had changed.

Money was still low. I found out that in this business the money was always low.

I had thought about that cold night on the side of I-94 every day and night since then.

I had on a Hanes T-shirt and the same dark pajama bottoms I'd worn when I was married. My wife had given these to me for one of my birthdays. I looked down at my wedding ring. It was a white gold wedding band that had cost a little less than six hundred dollars on Amazon, less than a tenth of what I had paid for my wife's wedding ring. Whenever I looked at my wedding band I thought about my wife too. I thought about Cora every day, sometimes all day long. Six months ago, without notice, my wife had walked away from our marriage, had packed up and left the way people across the country were walking away from bad mortgages. I had returned home from a business trip and everything she owned was gone. I knew that I would be the last one to find out the truth. The fool was always the last to know.

The panic attack held me prisoner and refused to set me free.

It was my third episode since I started working with a crew that robbed banks. Last night while I slept on the forty-year-old sofa, I tossed and turned and was unable to get comfortable. Not because of the flashing neon lights and the activity that was going on in Koreatown and the apartments around me. I never slept well during the two or three days before a bank job. Last night, no matter how hard I tried to rest, I'd tossed and turned on the old sofa out front. As soon as I had jerked awake, surges of heat trampled across my neck like a trail of anger and sorrow, and then those flames had made their way to my eyes and I battled with tears. I never shed tears as a boy. But when I was a boy there wasn't much to cry about. As a boy I never had the stress that came with being a man. Every man carried an invisible load. Henrick and Zibba had been the best father and mother a boy could ask for. Bits and pieces of the dream had stayed with me. I'd dreamed I was back home in Detroit.

In my dream I was falling from the seventy-second floor of the Renaissance Center, the Detroit River and Windsor in the distance.

This morning I shivered like I was naked on that frozen tundra in Motor City. I cooked every day to relieve stress, but I never ate much. I'd lost my appetite two seasons ago. I was twenty pounds lighter than I had been a year ago. For half a year, sleep has evaded me. I was up and down most nights. And when I looked in the mirror I saw a man who had a six-inch knife in the middle of his skull.

On the other side of the bathroom wall, the bed rocked as they sang hallelujahs and called out to the man above. There was no escaping their maddening sounds. My team and I were sequestered inside a one-bedroom safe house that was no more than 120 square feet of claustrophobia. The bathroom and bedroom shared a wall and the open area was the living room and kitchen, both so small that they reminded me of when I was in college and living in the cramped dorms my freshman year.

I threw cold water on my face and tried to control my trembling and shortness of breath.

It was Friday morning, payday for the part of the nation that still possessed gainful employment. Friday morning before noon was the most popular day of the week for bank robberies.

Always on a Friday.

When I stepped out of the stale bathroom, I saw the bedroom door was ajar, open about the width of my hand. That was wide enough for me to see Sammy Luis Sanchez. He was on a shopworn twin-size bed and his face was between his mistress's legs. The lights were off, the apartment was dark, but red and yellow lighting flashed in from their bedroom window. A neon sign that stayed on all night blinked across their bodies, allowing staccato glimpses of what looked like a psychotropic hallucination before sunrise. She was on her back, a shadow with her wrists tied to the metal bedpost; his necktie had been over her eyes as a mask. But the necktie had slipped away. His mistress saw me. She saw me and I knew she was gazing at me while Sammy held her legs and gave her his tongue. She stared at me, then closed her eyes and moaned for Sammy, begged him to come get on top of her, begged him to put it inside.

I backed away and crept toward the kitchen, opened and closed my hands, tried to strangle the invisible demon that had a hold on me.

I stepped over the silhouettes of my luggage and the board games we had left scattered in the cramped living room. The apartment made a Motel 6 look like the Charles Forte presidential suite at the Lowry Hotel in Manchester. My duffel bag rested at the end of a Knoll Charles Pfister sofa that had been made in the seventies. Beer cans littered the counter, along with empty wineglasses, a couple bottles of Smirnoff vodka, and two ashtrays that were overflowing with cigarette butts. Even in the dark, the place looked and smelled like a dump, but the darkness that came before sunrise hid some of its imperfections. The lingering scents from the dinners I'd cooked over the last week didn't mask the mustiness.

Rick Bielshowsky was sleeping in the middle of the floor with the plaid covers pulled over his head. I opened the refrigerator and grabbed a bottle of water. Jackie became louder. When I headed back to the bathroom, I paused in front of the bedroom door again. Sammy was on top of Jackie and she had her legs hooked around his ankles. Jackie's eyes stayed with mine. I frowned at her, held eye contact until I closed the bedroom door. I closed the door hard enough to let them know I was irritated.

I went back inside the bathroom, splashed water on my face, and ignored their moans.

Before every job we all stayed in the same space, remained interdigitated until the money had been divided. That was part of the ritual. Maybe it kept us from having a snitch. Or fostered camaraderie, like soldiers before a big mission. Whatever the reason, it kept us safe. Maybe it made us more like family than thieves. We'd sat up and planned and ate and watched DVDs. We always watched the same DVDs. *Snatch. Reservoir Dogs. Two Hands. Boogie Nights. Raising Arizona. Pulp Fiction. Heat. Dog Day Afternoon. Inside Man. Lock, Stock, and Two Smoking Barrels.* Everything we watched kept us attached to the realities of a grubby, violent, and dangerous world. I took a deep breath. The last of the panic attack, the last of the stress, hadn't abated, and the claws of anxiety were raking their fingernails up and down my spine in a way that let me know that it would return. I rubbed the last of the dampness away from my eyes.

When I stepped out of the bathroom, Rick was sitting up, yawning and rubbing his eyes. He looked like JFK Jr. with blond hair. His hair was naturally black, but he bought dye and colored his mane for each job. It was red for the last job. And now with the blond hair, he thought he looked like a California-born movie star and all he needed was Angelina Jolie at his side. He frowned and tsked as he used his thumb to motion at the hallelujahs coming from the bedroom, then he shook his head.

I shrugged and moved on toward the kitchen. "Second night in a row. All night long."

"Sammy must be on Viagra, Enzyte, a handful of L-arginine, and two cans of Red Bull."

"Probably."

Rick turned the television to CNN. Northside United Methodist Church had been robbed. Someone had stolen the safe and gotten away with one hundred grand.

Rick whistled, shook his head, and said, "Geesh."

"Yeah."

"It's an inside job."

"Has to be."

Rick moved from the floor to the sofa, where I had slept, and pulled the coffee table closer. He took his gun out, a .38, then opened a kit and started cleaning his weapon. I went into the kitchen and looked over my diagrams, the streets of L.A., the primary getaway route highlighted in yellow. I took my executive suit out of the closet, pulled on my slacks, did the same with a fresh Hanes undershirt, then pulled on a starched and crisp white oxford shirt. After I put my cuff links on, I took a deep breath and leaned against the counter and listened to the broadcast on CNN. Newscasters used faux concern to talk about the high unemployment rate, but the words that stuck with me were the fact that 40 percent of the unemployed had been out of work for over two years.

I asked Rick, "Did you ever tell me how you ended up in the bank withdrawal business?"

"Thought I already bored you with that long story. I know I bored Sammy with it a dozen times."

"Not that I remember. I'm not one to ask a lot of personal questions. But I'll tell you this, and this you already know. What a man tells me, this is the end of the line. So far as whatever conversation we have, or have ever had, the buck stops here."

"I had a business." Rick said that and looked out at the city, his lips turned down, as if heaviness was rising from his heart to his mouth. "It was an import and export business. Long story short, my business partner died all of a sudden. Heart attack and he hadn't made it to age thirty-five. Over two dozen creditors sued me. Not to mention the fact that my business partner had failed to pay the taxes on the business for three years. Between Uncle Sam and the creditors, the phone never stopped ringing. I was in over my head. I had a family to feed."

"So you did what you had to do."

"Did what I had to do. After I cashed in my stocks at a huge loss, I understood how people become homeless. I'd come here to Los Angeles and gone to meet with this guy who ran some cons. Guy named Scamz. I went to this pool hall to meet him, only to find out he had been killed the night before. Sammy had come here for the same thing. We put our heads together. So there you have it."

"You met Eddie Coyle along the way."

"Yeah. We met him along the way. Right after he had been kicked off the police force for taking bribes. He was working with his brother, this guy nicknamed Bishop, and they were hitting banks down south. We linked up with them and ran a four-man crew for a few jobs. Had a lot of fun."

"Robbing banks, a vocation that can get you up to twenty years behind bars, is fun?"

"Was being facetious. I never really cared for Eddie Coyle and thought less of his brother. But Eddie Coyle handles his business."

My mind drifted back to that night I'd stood in the cold on I-94. I said, "That he does."

"We can't all like who we work for, or work with, but so long as at the end of the day the checks clear and the bills are paid. . . . The bottom line is all that matters."

"That's what Eddie Coyle told me."

"That's what Eddie Coyle told us all." Rick checked his watch. "I noticed that you're cooking a lot, but you're not eating much."

"I eat when I'm hungry."

"Stress will put you in the ground."

"Nothing I can't handle. Stress is nothing new, not in my world."

"You're a real good guy, Dmytryk. Real good guy. Now, Sammy, don't get me wrong, he's my buddy, and I love and trust the man, but he's not worth a bowl of muddy cornflakes. But you, you're a real good guy. Maybe you don't belong here in this hustle."

I smiled. "But I'm here. Therefore, here must be where I belong."

He smiled in kind. "You going back to the Midwest after this job?"

"Yeah. I'm going back home."

"Why?"

I searched for a lie, but the truth came out. I said, "My wife might come back."

It was his turn to pause and become deadly serious. "You heard from her?"

"Not as of yet."

He pushed his lips up into a thin smile. "When did you say she disappeared?"

"After that job we did in Pasadena, Texas."

"That Wells Fargo on Spencer Highway was about six months ago."

"About, give or take a few hours."

"We're taking bets that you killed her."

I laughed a little. "Put me down for twenty. I'm betting I killed her too. I killed her and blocked it out of my mind. Better yet, put me down for forty."

He laughed for a moment, then rubbed his chin and became serious.

I smiled. "You okay, Rick?"

"So things were bad between you and the wife."

"We had ugly moments."

"Rihanna–and–Chris Brown ugly?"

"Mine wasn't like that. But things were said. We both did things that left us with a lot of collateral damage. Losing jobs, a lot of psychological changes come with that."

"I went through that with my wife too."

I said, "Losing your job is like having your identity stolen, like having what defined you run through a paper shredder. After a while the despair gets you, and it gets you good."

Rick nodded. "Yup."

"Financial problems led to stress."

"Me and my wife had it bad for a few years."

"Stress led to desperation and that spiraled into depression."

Rick nodded. "So, your wife was depressed."

"Me too. I was depressed too."

"I bet."

"Cora wasn't working a real job and my part-time gigs didn't do much more than cover the mortgage and put food in the refrigerator."

"She left you right after we did that job in Texas."

"Maybe Cora had wanted to leave before she vanished, but she couldn't afford to leave."

"Don't be so hard on yourself, Dmytryk. You did what you could to make it work."

I nodded. "So did she."

Rick paused. "It's been half a year, Dmytryk. She hasn't reached out to you. Your address is the same. She's moved on. So maybe you should just let the wife go."

"Would you let your wife go? Would you, Rick?"

"Well, we have three kids. Like it or not, when you have kids, it's a different ball game."

"Married is married, kids or not."

He yawned. "You said that the jobs in Detroit are gone and not coming back, at least not the same jobs."

"I did."

"Some women are like those jobs. Gone and not coming back."

The reality of his words put cracks in my wall of denial, added a hundred fissures to my heart. We sat on those words for a moment. I knew that Rick meant well. I respected his every word. As we paused, moans seeped into the room. Then the bed rocked and Jackie sang.

Rick motioned toward the bedroom. "Sammy is killing Jackie in there."

I smiled. "Like I said, we all kill what we love. We kill what we hate too."

Rick yawned again. "You all cleaned up?"

"I showered last night. Didn't want to hog the bathroom this morning."

"You're not going to shave?"

"I never shave before a job. Always shave after."

"Right, right. Your ritual."

"You could say that. Some people wear the same socks. I refuse to shave."

"We all have rituals. I clean my gun before every job. I've never had to use it, don't plan on ever using it, but I still clean it and carry it. Sammy, well, he's doing his pregame ritual right now. He's been through more women than I can count. They're all disposable to him. As disposable as used condoms."

"Except his wife."

"Yeah, and I've had my share of one-nighters. Takes the edge off being married, if you ask me. But I'd never do like Sammy. I'd never get into anything serious. I'd never compromise my marriage."

The sun started to rise and erase some of the shadows. I went to the kitchen table and studied the layout of the streets once again, playing it in my mind the way I had rehearsed and driven those streets the last seven days. By lunchtime this would be over and the anxiety and stress would lessen.

Rick came and stood next to me, looked down at the maps and checked the routes.

He said, "You're a decent man."

"Thanks. I feel the same way about you, Rick. You're a real good guy."

"I have to leave and handle one more job down south."

I looked at Rick. "Room for me on that job?"

"Sorry. The crew's been set for a while."

"Is something changing that will open a door for a man such as myself?"

"After breakfast, I want to sit down and talk with you."

I asked, "What about?"

"Just me and you. We'll talk then. You've become like a brother to me."

"Did I do something wrong?"

"Look, let's talk later."

I was confused. His tone was grave and shaky, unsettling, but I shrugged. "Sure. We can talk."

"Just me and you."

"The buck stops here."

Rick grabbed his toiletry bag, his suit pants and starched white shirt, then he went inside the bathroom. He wanted to get in there before Sammy's mistress went to shower. She would use up all of the hot water. The shower kicked on. I thought Sammy would come out of the bedroom, but I heard Jackie's soft voice pleading, telling him she needed more. She begged him for more. Said that he hadn't given her as much as he had promised. Not long after that, the moans started again.

While I was surrounded by noises that blended in with the bad news on CNN, I turned on my laptop and did my other ritual. I went to MySpace, Facebook, Twitter, Tagged, Hi5, Google, and a dozen other Web sites. I entered my wife's name, her social security number, her driver's license number, searched morgues and hospitals, pulled up missing persons sites, looked in the eyes of the living and the faces of the dead. Like a man obsessed with living in the epicenter of his own pain, I searched for my wife. While I scoured the Internet, Rick finished his shower, came out and put on his shoes, then grabbed his Marlboros and lit one before he gathered the garbage and headed out the front door. Jackie emerged from the bedroom, cellular phone in hand, deep in the middle of a hostile conversation.

"It's not right," she snapped into the phone. "How do you keep a child from her mother? How do you even sleep at night doing something like this? I don't need to talk to your attorney, I'm talking to you."

She had a white robe wrapped around her body, but her left breast was exposed to the nipple. The robe was short, barely hit below her backside and candy store. She was a tall woman. She had a small waist and plenty of very nice curves, a dark-haired, full-figured woman with a youthful girl-next-door face but a complexion that had noticeable acne. Her skin had a radiant glow, was actually shining while she held her cellular up to her face and argued with her ex-husband about their ongoing custody battle. She had a kid who she was fighting to see.

Sammy's mistress ended the call, then closed her cellular hard and shot me a nasty frown.

She asked, "Did you lose something?"

"You really should dress appropriately in an apartment this small that is filled with men."

"I'm not a daisy chain kind of woman, if that's what you're implying."

"I'm just saying take into consideration that other men are present and be mindful and respectful. Despite pretending that you're Sammy's wife, you're not his wife and this isn't your honeymoon suite."

"Screw you."

"That's Sammy's task, not mine."

"I hope you enjoyed the show."

"I've seen better on YouPorn, but that's not the point."

"In case you didn't hear me the first time, screw you."

She broke her stare and headed inside the bathroom and showered, then came out about twenty minutes later, the scent to her perfume leading the way, her hair wet, wearing pink Reeboks, tight jeans, and a SOY LATINA IN THE EEUU T-shirt. Sammy had given her that T-shirt as a gift, had bought it for her two days ago in Santa Monica.

She was part Latina but couldn't speak or understand more than a handful of words in Spanish. Sammy told me that she had grown up ashamed to be Latina. The woman had many issues. She had put makeup on top of her acne, had piled it on so thick her oval face looked as pallid as a ghost.

She said, "Keep looking at me and I'll tell Sammy to put his fist in your piehole."

She grabbed a small duffel bag, left without saying good-bye, high heels dangling from one of her hands, her face in a deep, harsh frown despite the riding Sammy had given her. Sammy called his wife, talked with his kids, made plans to go snow skiing next week, got back on the phone with his wife, told her he loved her, then hung up, showered, and put on his business suit.

Rick came back inside and saw I had the browser open to a Web site for earthquake victims.

He said, "I don't think she's hiding out in Haiti."

"I'm not looking for her."

"Yeah, whatever. Look, nobody runs away *to* Haiti. People run away *from* Haiti."

I gave him a short smile. "Told you, I wasn't looking for her. I was checking the news."

Rick put his loaded gun inside his holster, one he wore underneath his suit coat. Sammy did the same, holstered his gun before he adjusted his tie. A small version of the U.S. flag was pinned to his collar, like he was a politician. Sammy reached inside his pocket and took out a Mexican switchblade.

I asked, "Where did you get that toy?"

"Bought it yesterday afternoon when me and Jackie were in Hollywood."

"Prop knife or the real deal?"

"This six-inch blade is sharp enough to leave your head hanging."

A moment later I picked up my thirty-year-old black fedora and slid my silver pocket watch inside my pants pocket, eased it inside by its silver chain, then I took out my iPhone. I slipped on earphones and turned on an app that tied me into scanners for the LAPD and the Los Angeles sheriff's department. I pulled on my suit coat and grabbed the keys to the stolen car we had left parked down the street.

Sammy asked, "Dmytryk, man, you cooking again tonight?"

I said, "Tell your mistress to put on some decent clothes, make herself useful, and cook."

Rick chuckled. "If he can get her to stand up that long."

Sammy said, "She thinks I'm going to leave my wife and kids to take care of her and her kid."

I said, "You're joking, right?"

Rick said, "Sammy, tell Dmytryk about her big scheme."

"She's planning on kidnapping her kid and hiding out in South America. I'll help her get her kid, then I'm done. I worked for five years and saved enough to pay a coyote ten thousand to get me out of South America when I was seventeen, and going back would defeat the purpose of spending ten grand and walking across three deserts and sleeping in the wilderness for three months so I could get bussed up from San Diego and work in sweatshops and cut yards and build houses and wash dishes and cook and labor and send money back to bring up my brothers and sister and educate myself and get a better life than the one I had when I was a kid."

I said, "Sammy, you and those long, run-on sentences."

He went on. "I know how it would go and I'm not stupid. She'd get knocked up and I'd be trading problems for problems, end up having to support two households. So yeah, I'll take her out tonight. Sure, we'll have fun, then go balls to the walls. But at the end of the day, I'm a married man with a family."

Rick interrupted. "Okay, boys, adjust your panties and let's go make some money."

Sammy said, "Two twenty. I'm betting we're in and out in two minutes and twenty seconds."

Rick said, "Two minutes. This feels like a two-minute job."

"Put your money where your mouth is." Sammy yawned. "Dmytryk, what's your bet?"

"I'm betting on two minutes thirty seconds."

Rick said, "You're on. Five hundred a bet as usual and winner takes all. Anything over three minutes goes back in the pot. I'll have both of you ladies' monies before we eat breakfast."

Then we left together, three men in suits and wearing the same brand of shoes—the Johnston & Murphy Bandits—and stepped out into the din and early-morning pandemonium. It was an area that had over three hundred forty thousand registered people in less than five square miles. Might have been close to a half million when the illegal immigrants were added in.

Sammy said, "*Mad Men.* We look like those cats in the TV show *Mad Men.*"

Rick said, "People trust men in suits. Especially women. It puts them at ease."

Sammy said, "Makes their legs open like doors."

Rick nodded. "That too."

A stolen four-door Chevy was waiting on us. The car was ten years old. The type of car no one would look at twice. I walked around the car like I was inspecting a private plane before takeoff. The tires were good, the lights worked, the engine ran smoothly, and we had gas.

My personal automobile was parked half a block away. I owned a Buick Wildcat. It had been my father's car. Like my father, I kept the car's exterior looking top-shelf. I'd used money from the first two jobs and made the Wildcat look the way it had looked when my father drove it off of the lot in Michigan. Only a fool would drive his own car to go rob a bank.

After I finished looking over the stolen Chevy, I climbed inside and took to the wheel while Rick took the backseat. Sammy always rode up front with me. He had that Mexican switchblade in his hand. He kept opening and closing it, made the blade click out, that sound like the click of death.

From Koreatown, across Wilshire Boulevard and over to Crenshaw Boulevard, the radio was off. My ears were tuned in to the scanner. It was almost Christmastime, and during morning rush hour in Los Angeles people wore Lakers baseball caps and scarves and drove around with the tops dropped on their convertibles. Back east and in the Midwest everyone was shoveling snow and bundled like Eskimos, but out here the people stood at bus stops dressed in T-shirts and gloves. A few women were dressed in shorts that barely covered their backsides, shorts that were highlighted by fashionable, furry, knee-high boots; a few of the others wore sandals that matched their gloves, scarves, and sunglasses. We looked at the strangeness as we rode to our destination.

There were no smiles. There were no jokes. Our game faces were on.

Rick and Sammy were professionals. All jobs had been walk in and walk out, not a shot fired, people terrified, but not a person injured. They'd made a lot of tax-free money over the last decade, but not enough to rival Wall Street. Family and women on the side were expenses that required a man to have deep pockets. Soon the quick money was gone and it was time to make a few more withdrawals.

I'd worked with Eddie and his crew on five jobs. I was in an unwanted and dangerous occupation that was a long way from the simple life I had planned for myself back in Detroit. In high school, I'd mapped my life out to the other side of grad school.

But as they said, man planned and God laughed.

God must've been sipping a Corona, doubled over and slapping his knees right about then.

Baldwin Hills appeared on our right, behind one billboard for a local radio station and another billboard for *The Leonard DuBois Story* on HBO. The area didn't look like much, but Rick and Sammy had said this neighborhood had million-dollar homes. What a man got for a million dollars out there in Botoxville was nothing to brag about. Thousands of L.A.'s hyperinflated properties were being foreclosed on. Every man who had been inspired by free enterprise and greed was tumbling down the hill like Jack, dragging Jill and their tofu-eating rug rats along with them, silver spoons flying from mouths as they busted their crowns on oil- and urine-stained streets populated with the poor and the unknown. The rich had the most to lose, and the people at the bottom of the hills probably took joy in watching all the Goliaths fall.

I entered the parking lot on Santa Rosalia, just as we had planned. The street ran parallel to Crenshaw at this end but curved and gave us a great escape route. I parked outside the bank and watched the flow of traffic between there and the Baldwin Hills Crenshaw Plaza.

Sammy stepped out first, adjusted his suit coat and tie, then put on his killer smile.

He tossed me his Mexican switchblade. "Hang on to this for me, Dmytryk."

I dropped his souvenir inside my suit pocket.

Rick nodded, then he stood next to Sammy and took in the surroundings.

All was clear. Everything was perfect. This small crime would be over in a few minutes.

Rick and Sammy didn't walk inside the bank like they were the

Sons of Anarchy. They entered the bank at a casual pace, heads up high and confidence strong—not stick-up men, but businessmen making an early-morning transaction, two chisel-chinned CEOs stepping into a Fortune 500 meeting. They walked in like gentlemen and would exit the same way.

Anxiety moved up my spine like ice, gave me a chill that rivaled the coldness I had felt in Detroit.

I whispered, "Two minutes."

1

Twenty seconds had passed since Rick Bielshowsky and Sammy Luis Sanchez eased out of our stolen Chevy and strolled inside the Wells Fargo bank.

I adjusted my earphones so I could hear the broadcast from the police scanner, then inhaled the arid and sweet fetor of Poverty and her traveling companion Desperation. John Dillinger. That criminal knew that there were only two ways to get money in the land of free enterprise: You earned it, or you took it at gunpoint. That was about as American as a man could get in the land of red, white, and the blues.

Inside Wells Fargo, the teller would be terrified. She'd be afraid to look in Rick's eyes, afraid that he would blow her brains out. She had been trained to surrender the cash on demand. The girl was probably pretty. Rick loved sexy women. He would go to a sexy woman's window before he went to rob an ugly woman. And a few of the tellers he'd robbed actually had a smile that told him they loved the bad boys, had grins that said they were stimulated by the crime.

Cars stopped in front of the bank. People too arrogant or too lazy to park and walk ten feet blocked the exit that led to Stocker. Fifty yards beyond that was the Baldwin Hills Crenshaw Plaza and one of its anchor stores, Walmart. Beyond the Baldwin Hills Crenshaw Plaza was a strip of vanity shops and low-end businesses that lined this end of the Crenshaw District, the land of the underpaid hardworking man and woman, the people who went to bed with aching backs and swollen feet, then woke up before the sun warmed the palm trees.

The wail of sirens jarred me from distraction. LAPD blared down Crenshaw Boulevard, sped toward a different crime scene.

One minute and thirty seconds. They should have had the money in the bag by now. The people should have been facedown on the floor, following Sammy's instructions. Sammy would give the instructions in English and in Spanish, the languages of America. The bank managers should have been following procedures and surrendering every dime without hesitation. Sammy should have had everything under control while Rick loaded up the cash. Twenty more seconds went by, each tick of my watch reverberating like a mallet striking a gong. There was a popping sound, like a firecracker exploding. Then there was another popping sound. There was a commotion at the entrance to the bank. People who were about to walk inside looked startled at first, then two older Asian men became terrified and backed away from whatever horror they saw.

Rick hurried out of Wells Fargo first and Sammy was right next to him. I saw Rick's black three-button suit, then caught a better view and saw his crisp white shirt open at the collar. He had taken off his golden tie since he'd stepped inside. Rick had the bag in his left hand, but he was damn near carrying Sammy, and Sammy had his loaded .38 down at his side, exposed to the public. A bright red spot had opened up in Sammy's chest. My breath shortened and my heart enlarged, drummed against my chest.

Customers queued at the ATM witnessed what was happening. A few reacted immediately, some ducked, but it took most of the crowd seconds to register that they were standing in the back end of a bank robbery. We were eight miles from Hollywood. Some probably thought they were watching a Tinseltown blockbuster being filmed. People craned their necks like they were expecting to catch a glimpse of Robert De Niro or Brad Pitt.

Car in drive, teeth clenched, I knew we had to get the hell out of there before we ended up in hell.

Rick dragged blood-soaked Sammy toward the car, but too many cars had pulled between us. Sammy held on to Rick like he was lost at sea and gripping a life preserver.

A Latino security guard staggered out of the bank. He was overweight, wore a dingy white shirt and pants that were as dark as this situation. His white shirt was covered with blood, new holes in his left shoulder and stomach. The loyal employee yelled, stumbled after my coworkers, raised his gun, and fired. Sammy fired back at him. The security guard returned fire like he wanted to prove he could dish it out as good as the next man. People ducked behind stucco columns. Traffic screeched and cars stopped. Horns blared. The guard used the stucco wall to hold himself up. Sammy fired again. The wounded guard grimaced, made a determined and diabolical face, then he fired another round. Sammy's head opened up like a watermelon being smashed with a sledgehammer.

His face erupted. Half of his face was gone, blood and gray matter all over the pavement.

It was a nightmare.

Rick let Sammy's body slam to the ground, two hundred pounds of warm flesh that had become dead weight. The security guard kept firing. Rick reached to pull his .38 from underneath his suit coat.

The bag with the money exploded and shot bright red dye all over Rick's hands, suit, and face.

The root of all evil took wings and flew into the sky, went as close to heaven as it could, then, like Icarus when he flew too close to the sun, began to fall, rained down like confetti at the Thanksgiving Day parade. Rick stood in the middle of a crimson cloud of money being blown away by a gentle L.A. breeze.

The freaking money had a dye pack. The pack had been activated by a perimeter alarm that caused it to explode seconds after the pack made it outside. That explosion stupefied Rick. He dropped the red-tinted greenbacks and stumbled. Over one hundred thousand dollars took to the air and scattered across the pavement. My cut of that treasure was going to reverse the curse and change the course my life had taken, get me out of this business. With each windswept bill went a piece of my heart, my future blowing away.

The guard had broken the bank's rules, kept yelling and coming like it was his money being stolen. He fired again and the bullet hit Rick in the back. Rick's eyes widened as his teeth clenched with the pain. Hot lead spiraled through his body and kept going until it struck the passenger window of our stolen getaway car. The window shattered, glass spraying everywhere, then the hot lead kept going and hit the driver's-side window. By then it had lost its power. The lead hit the window and bounced away, fell into my lap. I looked down at the spent bullet. It was still hot and decorated with a dying man's blood.

Rick collapsed, went down hard, and tumbled on the blacktop.

The car that had stopped between us accelerated and left the scene, the driver terrified.

A crowd of people dashed beyond the wounded guard and ran toward Rick. People bolted from cars, from trucks, from the ATM, all with their eyes wide, all with desperation.

The crowd clutched the fallen money, some trying to snatch cash that wasn't stained and others who didn't care. The young, the old, Caucasians, Latinos, African Americans, Africans, they all rushed, grabbed what they could grab, pushed each other out of the way, lips pulled back, growling with vengeance.

What I witnessed was like watching vultures pick at the carcass of what had been left behind. Everyone grabbed money like they were robbing the system that had stolen their dreams.

This madness was the common man's corporate bonus.

Rick looked up at me, his face scratched and bloodied from his fall, his expression panicked and desperate, pleading for me to help him before the parade of sirens came. His hand reached for me the way the poor reached out for their savior. Blood pumped out of his wound as his eyes begged me to save him. I trembled, put my hand on the door's handle, had to risk it all and get out and help him.

But I paused when I spotted at least three opportunists capturing the bloodshed with iPhones and BlackBerrys. Eyewitnesses would get descriptions wrong, as most did, but video cameras didn't lie. This would be broadcast on television, would become breaking news in ten minutes, or on Twitter and Facebook within two. The Internet was a beast that John Dillinger never had to worry about.

I took a horrified breath, a breath that played out how this could end, for Rick and for me, both of us being caught right here in this parking lot. I played the unfavorable odds that were getting worse with every passing millisecond, and I frowned and shook my head. There was no way out for him. There was no way I could get to Rick and drag him inside this stolen car. And if I couldn't stanch that wound, I'd end up covered in blood, fishtailing out of there, trying to escape the police with a dead man at my side.

Hard choices had to be made. My life had always been one hard choice after the other.

My foot punched the accelerator and I sped off, left Rick on the pavement, his image fading in my rearview mirror as Sammy's spirit rose above me. I cut a hard left, took to Santa Rosalia, accelerated down the two-lane street that ran by Debbie Allen's dance studio. Horns blew as I rocketed through the light at Marlton, battled potholes, and passed by more strip malls, most of the businesses abandoned.

I blew through stop signs and intersections, sped by a group of runners who jumped out of the way when they saw my uncompromising pace. The pack scattered and cursed me for ignoring California's law that proclaimed pedestrians owned the right of way. Then, as I approached Hillcrest, a black SUV rolled through the red light without stopping, broke the law and did what they called a California roll, made a goddamn right turn less than ten yards in front of me, then galumphed well below the speed limit.

I was going too fast to slow down.

I hit a dip that snatched the car to the left. That cavernous hole grabbed the front tire and I lost control; I shifted and my foot pressed down on the accelerator.

My eyes widened while my hands gripped and battled with the steering wheel.

Sirens punctured the atmosphere as I slammed into the back of the slow-moving SUV.

Fiberglass met fiberglass as I crashed harder than Black Monday.

2

The airbag exploded and the impact catapulted me back in time, hurled me into the dark skies and frigid air of the Midwest, back into the land of Butch Jones, Maserati Rick, and the Chambers Brothers. The explosion of lights inside my head faded like stars at sunrise. I battled to regain focus. My face was numb and my nose felt like a middleweight boxer had hit it with a knockout punch.

Stunned, I fought with the deployed airbag, struggled to get oriented and shove it out of my way. Horns blared. People yelled. Each noise echoed a thousand times. In front of me, over the front end that had folded like tinfoil, beyond the hissing steam from the fluids, was the SUV I had rear-ended.

It took most of my strength to shove the door open. It took just as much energy to pull myself out of the wreckage. Eyes peered into the rearview mirror of the SUV I had hit. It looked like the driver was a woman. I broke free of my pain and hurried to her window. She was shaken, her eyes wide open. She was shocked, but there was anger too.

She had been thrown forward as her neck snapped backward, and her seat belt had locked and held her captive. It was still clamped across her sternum. A powerful violence had attacked her world without a sliver of warning.

I had taken the fedora with me when I limped away from my car. The brim was tilted down. I'd become Humphrey Bogart, disheveled and wounded, in a dark city trying to hide his injured face.

I asked, "Are you okay?"

"I . . . I think so. My . . . oh my God . . . my cappuccino . . . my seats . . . my clothes . . ."

A venti-size Starbucks cup had ended up on the passenger seat; most of the contents were on the leather seats and across her pin-striped suit. She grimaced like the cappuccino had burned like acid. She reached for her seat belt, tugged it over and over and was unable to get it to unlock, that simple movement making her cringe with pain. She moved in slow motion, as if her life were underwater.

Horns screamed in a dozen octaves and the *kindhearted* yelled for us to move the SUV.

Her BMW X5 was damaged, the bumper knocked askew, but the damage wasn't enough to debilitate her vehicle. Mine was dead. Steam rose from the front end of an American-made car that was mangled. Every exit we had planned had been by car, not by foot. Everything was upside-down and I'd fallen into a worst-case scenario. Eddie Coyle had said that there was always a way out. People were on the sidewalk, but not many. A pregnant teenage girl was pushing a baby carriage. She kept going. A few old people did the same.

Police were all over town and that wrecked vehicle would be on the most-wanted list in a matter of seconds. I needed that car moved and

I couldn't do it myself. I limped toward a handful of Latinos, speaking in Spanish. I told them I'd pay them to push the car. They were all day laborers, more than likely heading to the nearest Home Depot so they could hustle for work. For five dollars each, one climbed inside and guided the car while two more shoved the scrap metal to the side, pushed it off the streets and into a parking space.

Now each man was five dollars richer and their fingerprints were all over the car.

Again I looked around. Sweat streamed down my face. I was less than a minute away from Wells Fargo. I hurried back toward the wrecked SUV and limped up to the driver's window again. I needed to pull her out and commandeer her SUV, needed to throw her onto the asphalt and speed away before it was too late. Sweat ran down from underneath my fedora, trickled across my forehead to the stubble on my face. I held the iPhone in my aching hand, the earphones dangling to the filthy ground, the echo from the police scanner rising up from the headphones and being swallowed by a multitude of noises. Her eyes focused on my face and followed the trail of sweat to my lips.

She said, "Your bottom lip is busted. Your nose is bleeding too."

I didn't care about the blood that was staining my white shirt. I needed to rip her out of the SUV now, but when I reached for the door handle, I grimaced with the pain. The airbag had exploded and hurt my arms. She'd been rear-ended, assaulted from the rear, so her airbag didn't deploy. She was shaken up, but she wasn't wounded, at least not on the outside.

She panted, every motion frantic as she dragged both hands through her mountain of hair and said, "I need your insurance information."

"Did you call the police?"

"I was sending a text to . . . someone . . . and . . . and I'm . . . I'm about to call the police."

"You don't need to." I put an earphone inside my left ear. "I'm calling now."

"Oh, okay. This happened so fast. You hit me from behind really hard."

She wanted to see the damage, but I shook my head, stopped her from getting out.

I said, "It's not safe to get out right here. You should pull over so traffic can get by. Let me get my insurance card and I'll come back and we can exchange information."

She regarded me with apprehensive eyes. Maybe it was the way I had instructed the immigrants to push my car off the street or the way I had handed them money that had made her fears rise. Or it could've been the panicked way I had kept my fedora tilted downward as I limped to her SUV. My gut told me that she should have known then. She should've locked her doors and sped away sounding her horn.

But she didn't.

She had been rear-ended by a man wearing a classic suit and wing-tip shoes.

I opened the passenger door and saw that she had her red insurance card gripped inside her trembling fingers. She raised her head from sending someone a text message, her lips tight with hostility. Her frown deepened when she didn't see any insurance card in my hand.

She shook her head and groaned. "Please, tell me that you have insurance."

I knocked fallen books to the side, threw her Starbucks cup out of the door, then climbed in and sat on the wet leather seat. I slammed the door, removed my fedora, let it fall and land at my feet. I reached inside my suit pocket and pulled out the Mexican switchblade. It wasn't open, but she knew what I was holding. Urgency was engraved in my face and my gentlemanly smile was gone. Her fear came alive. Instant fear. I pushed a button and the six-inch blade popped out like death.

Her lips parted and said one word: "No."

Her cellular was inside her right hand. The panic in her eyes told me that she was about to dial 911. It pained me, but I reached over and gripped the cellular, snatched the phone out of her hand. She yelled and reached for her door handle. The door opened, and she had time to get away, but she couldn't leave. Her seat belt was still on. Again, she reached to try to undo the buckle, but I intercepted her hand, then I grabbed her body and pulled her back. Terror gripped me and my heartbeat accelerated. She opened her mouth to scream, but I jerked her hard, forced her to look at me. I shook my head in a way that told her there would be no screaming.

She was a small woman, manageable even with my injuries. I gripped her and made her sit still. I held the blade in my hand, held it like I was Jack the Ripper. More police cars and emergency vehicles zoomed by us in a blur. Her eyes went to the police cars, then gradually came back to the switchblade, her horrified expression telling me that she was adding things up, and the pandemonium revealed I had concerns more monumental than a totaled car and a ticket for tailgating. My desperation danced with her fear, and our lips trembled. A man wearing a Don Draper suit had become the bogeyman in her world. Face bruised, nose bloodied, distressed, I clenched my teeth and grimaced. She still had her insurance card clenched inside her other hand. I took that from her too.

I read her name. "Abbey Rose Brandstätter-Hess."

She regarded the six-inch blade, shivered, and whispered, "Please … don't kill me."

A fear worse than death trembled in her voice.

My face burned. My hands throbbed. I swallowed pain and told the woman to be still.

I said, "Close your eyes."

3

My hostage closed her eyes with fear and defiance, more of the former than the latter.

She was tense, body tight, waiting to feel the Mexican switchblade dig into her body.

I held my inner panic at bay and evaluated the situation. She had keen features and a head of thick hair colored springtime blond and auburn. She wore a business suit. And for a moment I thought she might have been an undercover cop, but a cop never would have allowed things to get this far.

Her SUV was filled with dozens of books. One of the books was turned over on its face and I saw a picture on the back. It was a picture of the terrified woman, only she was dressed in faded jeans and a white blouse, her face in makeup, and her smile was wide and joyous. In the photo she was sitting on a yacht, clear blue waters and an island behind her, smiling like she owned the world.

I kicked the book out of the way, then I looked at her. She wasn't breathing. She had frozen, hadn't moved or inhaled since I told her to be still.

I said, "Take a deep breath."

She did.

I did the same as blood dripped down to my shirt.

I said, "Now take another one."

She did.

"Now I want you to open your eyes and drive."

She hesitated, then her eyes eased open.

"Drive."

She pulled her lips in and nodded, too terrified to utter a sound.

I told her to move from blocking traffic, make a U-turn, then turn and cut up Hillcrest, a street that ran toward the million-dollar homes. I told her to drive up that two-lane street and stick to the right side of the speed limit.

She trembled and asked, "Where are you taking me?"

I pointed toward Hillcrest, motioned for her to be quiet and drive. I needed her to move me through the hills, then come out facing Kenneth Hahn Park and drive down the hill headed toward La Brea. I looked back to make sure the SUV wasn't being followed.

She turned on Hillcrest and rode past apartments, pounds of litter, and the smell of fried bacon mixing with the stench of marijuana, those aromas mingling with the funk of government-assisted living. She slowed down as she passed Hillcrest Drive Elementary School. When she slowed I tensed because I thought she was scheming to bail out. But her seat belt was on and both hands were on the steering wheel. A chubby kid was crossing the street eating a corn dog. She had slowed to let the obese kid run jiggling across the street. I looked behind us again. I didn't see LAPD or the sheriff coming this way.

My frightened chauffeur hit a speed bump and everything in the SUV bounced. The back end rattled. She was going too fast. I touched her shoulder. She cringed, jerked like she had been stabbed.

My touch was gentle. And with a slight turn of her body my soft touch was rejected.

I said, "Slow down."

She nodded, took a few curt breaths, pulled her lips in tighter, and eased off the accelerator.

There was coldness between us. Coldness and a heated fear.

As we climbed the hills, apartments gave way to houses. We crossed into the area called the Dons, where all the streets had exotic Spanish names, like Don Zarembo and Don Quixote.

Sweat drained down my face like a salty river in search of an ocean.

I looked at my getaway driver. She sweated just as much. It was a brisk morning in L.A. but we sweated like we were in the Bahamas under the midday sun. Her lips remained tight as she drove through an area that had homes with panoramic views, some hanging over hills and supported by metal stilts. It was an older section of the city, and after seeing Beverly Hills, Bel Air, and the beaches, nothing in this zip code impressed me. We passed Mexican lawn keepers. The people who maintained the yards were as south-of-the-border as the street names. The people who cleaned the toilets were probably from Mexico or another part of Central America too. My terrified chauffeur slowed at speed bumps. I looked back down the hill. LAPD had a chopper up high, circling the area we had just left. At least two news choppers were in the area too, circling skies painted with gloom.

My heartbeat deafened everything.

Everything ached, but I could drive now, so I had to figure out what to do with her.

My hostage kept both tense hands clenched on the steering wheel and her eyes straight ahead.

A ring sparkled on her left hand. I looked in the backseat again, didn't see a child seat, just more of the same book and some scattered CDs, but that didn't mean she didn't have kids.

Sweat rained across her forehead and upper lip. Her labored breathing told me she was terrified. I'd earned a kidnapping charge. If I had been able to run away from the accident, the two-second glimpse she had of me wouldn't have mattered. But fate had derailed our operation.

Sammy was dead.

Rick had been shot.

I'd been forced to leave them both behind.

This wasn't supposed to happen, not like this.

No one was supposed to die. I wasn't supposed to take a hostage to get away. But all had gone to hell and now this woman named Abbey Rose had seen my face.

She was what stood between me and living the rest of my life behind bars.

Darkness rose up and told me that in order to remain free, I'd have to kill her.

4

I opened my hostage's glove compartment and found tissues.

It hurt, but I dabbed my bloodied nose and split lip. Abbey Rose twitched whenever I moved. My skin burned. I touched my damaged face with the tips of my fingers and cringed, then reached inside the glove compartment and searched for more tissues.

I said, "I need you to relax and look normal while you're driving."

She nodded. "I'm doing my best."

"Do better."

Then I turned, and in pain I reached to the backseat and snatched her purse off the floor. She jumped like her first instinct was to reach and stop me, to claw at me, but I gritted my teeth and shook my head. Her eyes and facial expression told me that she was praying for either LAPD or the L.A. county sheriff to come this way. My prayer was the opposite. Blade at my side, I went through her wallet.

I fumbled around and removed her driver's license. The address on the insurance registration card matched the address on her license.

She swallowed and shook her head, made a terrified sound when I took her driver's license and stuffed it inside my coat pocket.

I said, "Abbey Rose."

"Yes."

"I know who you are. I know where you live."

Lines gathered in her forehead as she pulled her lips in tighter.

Police helicopters continued circling the area we'd just left.

I said, "Abbey Rose."

She didn't say anything but her paranoid eyes were glued to the rearview mirror.

Something was back there. I looked in my side-view mirror and saw law enforcement.

"Abbey Rose, maintain your speed. If they turn their lights on . . ."

Tears ran down her face as if that was her last hope of surviving. When the police turned left at Don Lorenzo, I took a deep breath.

Abbey Rose cried a little harder.

A Maserati was parked in front of one of the homes we passed. The next-door neighbors had Toyotas and Nissans. After that I saw a garaged Lamborghini and a fleet of Mercedes.

I sighed. "Everybody up here has two imports per person in each household. For every one car we export, they import three hundred to our soil, and all the imports are up on this hill."

"What?"

"Nothing. Just drive."

Drops of sweat dripped from my chin.

She asked, "What did you do? Why are the police after you?"

I licked my lips and felt pain. I said, "I can't chance you calling the police."

She whispered, "I won't."

"You will."

"I promise I won't."

"If I let you go, you will."

She wiped her eyes. "You said *if.* Not *when. If.*"

I took another frustrated breath. My heart beat faster.

I said, "You're married."

She paused. "Yes. And my husband is looking for me right now."

"What day was your wedding? And where did you get married?"

She clenched her teeth.

I said, "You're not a good liar."

She snapped, "You're not a good driver."

Fear and frustration blistered my mind and I was about to detonate, but I put the switchblade down at my side, then I rubbed my temples and shook my head before I regarded the streets, my pained movements nothing more than controlled nervousness. I was distressed and angry, and that anger was almost explosive. I wanted to scream and pummel her German-made dashboard with my hands.

I motioned for her to stop driving.

I said, "You've seen my face."

She wiped her dank hands on her pants, then she pulled her mountain of hair back as best she could, but her mane remained strong, rebelled and bounced back to its circular form.

I motioned for her to drive again. She didn't hesitate to pull away from the curb.

That told me she felt safer with us moving. I felt the same way.

She said, "You were speeding."

"You ran the red light. Is that how they teach people to drive in

L.A.? My guess is you were on your cell. You were distracted. Am I wrong?"

She trembled. "I was reading a text message. I slowed in front of you because I was reading a text message. My fiancé was breaking up with me. Days before Christmas and he broke up with me with a text message. So, that's why I slowed down. I was in the middle of breaking up with my fiancé."

I said, "Makes sense now."

"What makes sense?"

"Most people get out of their cars right after an accident. It's a natural thing. You didn't get out right away. You didn't scream about your BMW being wrecked. Something else was on your mind. And now it makes sense."

"What are you going to do to me?"

She had driven Hillcrest Drive to Don Milagro Drive to Don Felipe Drive to Don Miguel Drive. Right before Don Miguel touched Don Lorenzo, I instructed her again to do her best to look normal. We were in the section where the houses started to become smaller and old apartment buildings began to reappear.

I motioned for her to turn right and we came to La Brea. Again, I motioned to the right. Then she was stopped by the red light. It was a no-right-on-red light. I pointed that out and told her to obey the traffic laws. Some people crossed the street while others jogged up a dirt hill that led to hiking and jogging trails at the park. When the light turned green she turned right, drove down the pathway that cut between Baldwin Hills and Kenneth Hahn Park. We were heading north at close to fifty miles an hour, a little over the speed limit but a lot slower than the rest of the traffic. I motioned for her to turn left onto Coliseum Street and pointed up ahead. We were behind the Village Green, a seventy-acre wooded area that was a maze of tropical confines, a place I could vanish into and never be found again. First I looked beyond palm trees toward the village of condos. To the left were single-family homes rising into a different set of hills and more million-dollar residences that would never make the cover or centerfold in *Architectural Digest*.

Abbey Rose, my reluctant getaway driver, parked next to the curb, across the street from a single-family home. A van was parked along the curb too, one car-length away. I saw the driver look in the rearview mirror when we stopped. The engine on the van was running and the driver had a foot on the brakes.

My skin burned, salty perspiration dampening my face like blood from an open wound. Abbey Rose sweated the same way. I smelled her sweet perfume and looked at her diamond ring. She saw me staring at her ring and motioned like she was going to give it to me. I shook my head. I dug inside her glove compartment and found the last of her tissues, wiped my nose, dabbed my forehead. I closed the switchblade, then opened it again, repeated that over and over, the clicking sound making Abbey Rose shudder, take curt breaths, and blink a hundred times.

"Abbey Rose, close your eyes again."

"No."

"Don't test me."

"Please . . . I'm begging you."

"Last time. Close your eyes."

"I don't want to die."

Every part of her body trembled. She put her palms on her stained business suit, ran her hands across her globe of hair. Then she took another deep, trembling breath and closed her eyes.

I took a deep breath too. "Let your seat back, Abbey Rose. Recline like you're sleeping."

"If I don't?"

"You said that you don't want to die. Now's the time to start acting like you want to live."

5

The Wells Fargo job was supposed to be a two-minute job that ended with a four-way split. Sammy, Rick, and I were three of the crew. Sammy's mistress was the fourth. She was in charge of the stage-two getaway van. This was where we would've dumped the first car. I had already closed my switchblade and dropped it back inside my pocket by the time I had made it to the passenger-side window and read Jackie's face. She read my tense expression like it was a postcard from prison, the blood on my shirt the ink used to write a long letter, the injuries to my lips and nose the postmark and stamps. Her surprise magnified exponentially.

"Where is Sammy?"

"Dead."

Her eyes widened, then she swallowed. "Dead?"

"Took one to the head. He was gone before he hit the ground."

I expected a flicker of pain, maybe tears. The death of a lover made many people cry. She waited because she wouldn't leave Sammy behind. Now there was nothing she could do for him.

She asked, "Rick?"

"Rick might be dead too."

"You left them?"

"Had no choice."

"Sammy's dead. No way."

"He's dead, Jackie."

"What about the money?"

With the blink of an eye she had moved from the death of her lover to the primary objective of this trip. I shook my head to let her know this job had garnered no cash, not one dollar.

We paused and listened to the cries from police vehicles.

"You were in the passenger seat." She motioned behind her. "Who's driving that black BMW?"

"Somebody cut in front of my damn car. Car crashed and totaled. I had to improvise and carjack."

Her mouth dropped open. "Man or woman?"

"Woman."

"Kids with her?"

"She's alone."

"We can't leave any witnesses."

Jackie was former military. Her husband had divorced her during her third deployment and her kid had been taken away from her while she was in Afghanistan. In the eyes of the court, serving her country and protecting these shores had made her an absentee and unfit parent. But Jackie said her husband was an unfit parent. If she hadn't deployed and had stayed home to take care of her kid, then the military could've locked her up for two years and given her a dishonorable discharge. Jackie had abandoned all allegiances, except to her child, her soul blackened by the government's betrayal.

Jackie's lips curved downward. "Get in and be ready to drive. I'll put her down."

"You're going to shoot her right here?"

"No, I'm going to take her on a date and buy her a drink first. I'll do whatever needs to be done and you need to do the same. Look, get in the driver's seat. When I signal, mash on the gas and let the sound of the engine revving cover the shots. Mash hard. Then be ready to roll out."

I shook my head. "Go. The woman is my problem."

"Your problems are our problems."

"If anybody saw me at the bank, and I doubt it, but just in case, they didn't see you. So think about your kid. I'll handle it and you go and we'll connect down the road. You know the drill."

Without any more hesitation, she raised her hand and extended a disposable .22, handle first.

She frowned. "No witnesses."

"Okay."

I repeated what I had said, told Jackie to drive away from this heated area.

She shook her head, sweat forming on her brow. "I'm not leaving you behind. That's not how this works. You do this and you do this now and then I'll get you out of here. You do it or I do it."

Her tone was filled with grief, anger, and angst. Her expression owned the same. It reminded me of my wife's tone. It reminded me of a cold day in Detroit when choices were made. It reminded me of a day when my manhood was challenged, when my marriage had been threatened. I took the gun and eased it underneath my coat. Guns weren't my way of life. I went back and stood outside the SUV and spied down on Abbey Rose. She remained reclined with her eyes closed. She had her hands folded across her midsection. Liquid anxiety drained down her face; that trickling had to feel like torture, but she didn't move.

I took the gun out and held it in my hand.

All sins spiraled and escalated. All sins ended with murder, the crime of all crimes.

When I opened the passenger door to the SUV, Abbey Rose opened her eyes and saw me standing in the door holding a gun. I held the door open but didn't climb back inside.

I said, "Keep your eyes closed."

"Please . . . please . . . please . . ."

"Close your eyes."

Abbey Rose trembled and closed her eyes tighter. I had never seen so much fear.

I wondered what it was like to know that you were about to die and have no control.

Then I looked at the getaway van, made contact with Jackie in the rearview.

I nodded and she mashed the gas, revved the engine hard, made smoke rise.

I raised the gun and fired twice. Those two rapid pops sent energy and regret up my arm.

It was hard to live but so easy to die.

Then I closed the door to the SUV, lowered my head, walked to the van, and got inside.

Jackie pulled away from the curb and drove past the Village Green, then entered an area filled with modest homes. She drove through an alley and came to La Cienega. That was where we were about to blend with what looked like a hundred thousand cars, not many manufactured on this soil. Gray skies covered us as she pulled out on La Cienega. Instead of going straight toward Hollywood and Koreatown, Jackie turned right on Rodeo Road, and that right was taking us back in the direction of the bank robbery.

I asked, "What the hell are you doing?"

"We're going back."

"Are you crazy? We're not going back there."

"Sammy's not dead. He can't be dead."

"He's dead, Jackie."

"I need to see for myself."

The horrid songs of traffic surrounded us as Jackie sped down the front side of the Village Green in the direction of KFC, then was caught at the light facing a strip mall that housed a shopworn Mc-Donald's. A torrential downpour of fear came out of my pores like it was hurricane season. There were hundreds of sounds, maybe thousands, but there was only one sound I cared about. The sirens. And those sirens punctuated the crisp air the same way bullets had punctuated the life out of Sammy.

I put my hand up to my head, reached for my fedora. My fedora wasn't on my head. Again my heart tried to break out of my chest. I had left the fedora inside Abbey Rose's SUV.

More anger and trepidation manifested inside my gut, became a raging ball of fire that boiled my blood. That fedora held DNA that was better than the fingerprints I had left inside that SUV.

Jackie asked, "What's wrong?"

"Drive. Slow down, keep to the speed limit, and drive."

That black fedora had belonged to my father. That had been Henrick's Sunday fedora.

I had imagined that my father's most prized hat would one day belong to my unborn son. Now it would end up mutilated and stored inside a dusty evidence room.

Jackie drove back toward the bank, went up the back side of Santa Rosalia.

The closer we were to the bank, the stronger my heart thumped inside my chest. The parking lot had been taped and an officer directed traffic and blocked the southwest entrance to the mall. Two dozen policemen and firemen and medics were in the parking lot.

And at least three local stations were on the ground, one of them a Spanish channel.

One body was down on the parking lot, covered up and waiting on the coroner. That was Sammy. All that could be seen was that the body was facedown, his shoes showing.

There wasn't a second body. Rick was gone. He had already been transported. Jackie paused and glimpsed the circus, her eyes wide with disbelief as she stared at what she never should have seen.

She said, "That wasn't Sammy, that was Rick."

"That was Sammy."

"You got it wrong, Dmytryk. Rick might be dead, but not Sammy."

"He's dead, Jackie. I'm sorry, but Sammy is dead."

Then she sped away, her lips trembling and tears falling. She made a hard right onto Stocker, then sped uphill doing thirty miles over the speed limit.

My face burned and I felt blood in my nostrils, but I asked, "Want me to drive?"

She mumbled, "You got it wrong. You had to get it wrong. An hour ago Sammy was laughing and joking and we were making plans."

Hell was a mythical place where people suffered for eternity. But I knew hell was real because I'd been living with the devil's breath on my neck for a long, long time.

I closed my eyes and went back to then.

6

Then.

I was one of the few men who had worked a white-collar job, then lost that cushy, salaried position and ended up on the assembly line at GM. Working in the offices and working on the line; those had been my jobs for fourteen years strong. My salaried job had topped out in the six figures. After that white-collar job had ended abruptly, I had worked the line, ended up shoulder-to-shoulder with people I'd gone to high school with. I was degreed and working with people who had GEDs. There was a joke in there somewhere. Sometimes my friends on the line teased me about my downfall and tried to help me find the humor in my situation, and many times they made me laugh. Working on the line wasn't going to make me the next Donald Trump, but it kept me living an above-average lifestyle. But that came to an end. Being laid off twice within a decade, the second time felt like it was déjà vu. One day I was on the line making seventy-five a year and the next I was unemployed and trying to save my home.

The bubble had burst in Detroit; the middle class was being dismantled thousands of jobs at a time. And in a land far, far away, the Japanese smiled. Bailouts and bankruptcies and job losses and foreclosures and exporting one American vehicle for every three hundred that were imported had left Americans starving on the pothole-filled streets.

That was back when it all began, back when I had been susceptible to anything the devil offered. While Jackie sobbed and drove us through L.A. and Hollywood, while we passed tourists and Chinese theaters and dealt with never-ending traffic, my mind drifted.

My mind took me back to the night that I was near Ford Field and the MGM Grand Casino, ten minutes from the airport and less than two miles off I-96 at Michigan Avenue.

It was a gentlemen's club that had no gentlemen as patrons.

While a dancer named Daisy Chain performed, looking like she was worth ten dollars for twenty minutes, I stood near the bathrooms and searched for a different dancer, one who was too beautiful to be in a place like this. I hid out in the rear of the den of lust, drink in hand and holding up the wall. It was Down and Dirty Thursdays at Club Pasha. The night customers were promised they'd be spoiled the moment they came inside. It was the night that three shots of overpriced Patrón cost twenty-five dollars. A fool's bargain. There were over forty-five dancers in the room, most already topless. Women were imported from Atlanta, Miami, and California. Most were in heels so tall they looked like their fake hair could touch the ceiling.

Men in sagging pants and shirts adorned with convoluted and outrageous hip-hop and thug-inspired designs competed with each other, moved to the front lines like warriors, and positioned themselves close to the dancers. Tonight men who were behind on alimony and child support were splurging, throwing money at women who were behind on their rent and had small children at home. The customers spanked the women and baptized topless dancers with money.

I'd wanted to become invisible, but everyone noticed me. I was the only man in the club who wore a business suit and shoes by Johnston & Murphy. When I had walked across the room, some reacted like they thought I was an undercover cop; panic sprouted in the eyes of the men who were wanted or on parole. I carried a black fedora and wore a three-button dark gray suit that fit the way a suit should fit, not oversize like the suit of a ringmaster at a circus. That made me feel both out of place and out of time, an anachronism, because all of the other patrons wore outfits so large they hid all of their obesity. Women with cosmeticized faces were swinging from the bars in the ceiling. Others were working the poles at either end of the stage, stretch marks barely noticeable under the dim lights.

Then the DJ announced that the dancer who called herself Trouble had arrived.

I stared at Trouble as she took to the stage. Her beauty was uncommon and her unique appearance drew eyes. She was born in Brooklyn, but going back three generations, she was Dominican, Canadian, Jamaican, Chinese, and a few other exotic lands combined. Her heritage gave her a distinct look. Her hair was dark brown with golden highlights. She had an erotic face that, from some angles, reminded me of Maria de Medeiros Esteves Vitorino de Almeida. Soft, youthful

features, round and doelike eyes, making her appear childlike and seductive all at once. Outside these walls the dancer was a conservative
dresser, usually wore low heels and had an appearance as innocent and
gamine as Natalie Portman, Norah Jones, Robin Meade, and Audrey
Tautou.

She was my wife.

The heat in my heart and aching inside my chest confirmed that
these were our hard times. The financial pressures we lived under felt
like a mountain on our backs. But I was the man in the relationship, so
inside I carried the onus of having to live up to being a husband and
a provider for my wife.

Society had conditioned me to feel the lion's share of the shame
when things fell apart, and standing in a room that provided entertainment for the lowest of the low put pain in my heart.

Heat raced up my back and across my neck. I held a thin smile but I
wanted to scream. Stress and anxiety did their best to break me down
and drive me insane.

My wife took to the silver pole with energy, every move reeking of
confidence. In her sparkling thong and glittery bra, she went up the
pole by spinning in circles, looked like she was defying gravity. In a
flash she was upside down in a split, then she took the split to the pole,
had her body in a sideways Chinese split. She used her legs to hold
the pole and came down inches at a time, flipped before she made it
to the floor, then landed in a dramatic full split. She landed so hard it
made men groan.

This was the result of her mother struggling to send her to gym-
nastics and dance classes from when she was a child until she graduated from high school and joined the navy.

My wife saw me lurking in the shadows and lost her painted-on smile for a moment.

I wanted her to see me. I wanted to see how she would react when she saw me.

There was a pause that lasted no more than half a second. I knew my wife. I knew her every expression, no matter how subtle. She wanted me to leave. She didn't want me there. But I was there.

She could have motioned to a fat bouncer, and the fat bouncer would have asked me to go, but she knew better. She knew me. She knew my every expression as well. She read the look on my face. If a bouncer touched me, we'd come to blows. I'd lose the fight, but there would be a fight.

I backed up a step, but not in retreat. That step reassured her that I wasn't going to cause a scene. Not that night, but I wanted to. The love inside me made it hard to not hate what I saw.

Each dollar that was thrown her way felt like a flaming whip lashing across my ego.

Women went over to her throwing dollars, ugly women who had girl crushes and let it be known they wanted girl kisses as they leaned over and whispered in my wife's ear. My wife smiled and flirted. I wanted to hear what was being said. Liquored up, women were as aggressive as men. Some of the women dressed in oversize clothing, talked with their mouths twisted, had hair cut short, and looked like men.

Desperation's heated breath singed my neck, its jagged teeth prepared to devour my flesh. Poverty growled too, waiting its turn, famished yet patient, a beast that dined on the bones of men.

My wife finished her routine and stopped to gather the dollars that had been thrown at her feet. She bent over and hurried to get her dollars. It looked sad. It looked disgusting, the desperate way my wife picked up the money that had been thrown at her like she was the slave of the moment. She grabbed stray dollars that had fallen off the stage, pulled what she had garnered into one vulgar pile. I saw no dignity in what she was doing. I saw lust but no respect for her as a woman as she left the stage. She held her smile and flirted with customers until she vanished into the dressing rooms. Ten minutes later she came back out and walked over to me. She took my hand and led me to the back, away from all the eyes.

My wife lost the phoniness she had given the customers.

She whispered, "Go home, Dmytryk."

"Don't talk to me like I'm a child."

"Why are you here? You promised to never come here."

"We've both made promises, Cora."

"What do you want?"

"I want this to end. I want you to leave with me."

"I can't. We talked about this. We can't afford . . . we'll talk when I get home."

"Cora—"

"This kills me too, Dmytryk. This is killing me too. And I know you don't approve."

"This is supposed to be short-term. Only a few weeks, then we move on."

"It is. I'm not one of these girls. I don't do the things they do for money."

My eyes went beyond my wife, watched dancers lead men into the private area.

She said, "I have a few regulars out there and I have to . . . I have to . . . go talk to them."

"Regulars."

"Customers. They spend a lot of money to talk."

"To talk."

"They do all of the talking. All I have to do is smile and pretend I can't smell their bad breath and act like I'm interested. Stop shaking your head, Dmytryk. This is why you're not supposed to come here. I need you to leave. Baby, go home."

I reached inside my pocket and took out a ten-dollar bill. I slipped it inside her garter.

"Dmytryk . . ."

"Since you're talking to me."

"Stop it."

"I can't touch you?"

"Why are you acting this way?"

"You're so nice to these men. At home, you hardly smile."

"Please. Go."

"You're mad? I'm a paying customer."

"That isn't called for."

"Strange men do that and you smile like you're in love. Your husband does that and you frown."

"Don't raise your voice, Dmytryk. Please, don't."

"You touch them and I have to beg you to touch me."

"Don't do this here."

"Give me a few minutes. Then I'll go home."

I walked away. I didn't leave, just walked back into the main room.

My wife passed by me a few moments later, went to walk the floor, flirting with customers.

She was made up. As beautiful as she had looked on our wedding day, only instead of being dressed in white she was prancing around the room in honeymoon clothing. Her ring finger was as barren as our savings accounts. She wasn't the prettiest woman in the room, nor the sexiest, nor the one with the biggest backside, nor the one with the largest breasts. If a man judged on those standards alone, she wasn't the best in the room. But that didn't matter. She was my wife. What I saw when I looked at her, no other man would be able to see because there was no love in their hearts for her.

She used to labor on the assembly line at GM too. After she had graduated from Mumford High School, she had worked less than a year at GM, then joined the navy and did two years on the *Shenandoah*. My wife had been a lithographer; rank E4, petty officer, third class.

She had said the navy had been a good experience, but in the end, financially, she had been no better coming out of the navy than she had been going in. Her high school friends who had stayed behind were spending money and living the life; people who had gone to Henry Ford, Pershing, Mumford, and Cass were all side by side, working on the line, driving new cars and owning homes.

In the end, despite the training from Uncle Sam and training at GM, she was swinging from a pole with the rest of the women, half of whom were likely cut from the same cloth as the men and women who showered them with wrinkled dollars—the classless, the felons, and the undereducated.

That night I sipped dark alcohol and tortured myself, watched lustful animals throw wrinkled and stained offerings at my wife, watched animals touch her flesh like they knew her in a biblical way, watched her move like a gazelle as she smiled and flirted and laughed and acted like a woman who was less than a stranger to me, watched those uncouth animals slap her flesh like she had no value as a woman.

It was punishment.

Some dancers led high-paying customers to the back area, behind the magic curtain. Some nights I knew my wife did the same. Knowing that made my head throb. Made my heart ache.

The room was crowded, but the club used to have three times as many customers. People who were making it rain twenty dollars at a time used to make it storm two hundred dollars at a time.

Another man walked to my wife, threw two wrinkled dollars, and slapped my wife's backside. That was when I picked up my fedora and headed for the front door.

The night felt like a form of self-flagellation and I'd suffered enough.

That was around the time I heard about the man who had flown in from Rome. He wasn't in the club that night, at least not while I was in the room. I would've noticed him because, like me, he would've stood out from the rest of the patrons. My guess was that as I walked out to go to my car, that career criminal had pulled up and was walking into the den of ill repute from the opposite direction. The career criminal was the man they called Eddie Coyle. My wife had met Eddie Coyle at the gentlemen's club and later on she'd told me that he'd been in the club that same night. Maybe that was one reason she'd been uncomfortable. He was one of her top customers, and if I had remained in the club, I wouldn't have appreciated how he had earned that status. I would have viewed everything through the eyes of a jealous husband.

I'd promised not to ask her about her job, about what she did, about whom she met. But I wasn't stupid. I knew what happened at gentlemen's clubs. I knew what I had paid for when I used to go to the ones in Miami, back in my college days. But sometimes living in denial was the only way to keep a man from going on a killing spree. In my mind I was capable of walking inside that club and shooting bouncers, shooting dancers as they screamed to the god they had forgotten about the moment they had walked through the doors carrying their clear heels. I should've. That club was where Eddie Coyle had entered our lives and changed our world. Eddie Coyle had come into Detroit, spread stolen money around, and was treated like a rock star.

He had stolen from the rich and was distributing the cash to the disenfranchised.

Eddie Coyle had paid Cora to spend quality time with him during the daylight hours, had leased her services and wanted her to escort him around the Motor City starting at nine in the morning. He wanted to go on a tour, see the banks in the suburbs, check out Oakland, Birmingham, see the connected areas, and wanted to be done with his tour by noon.

He was going to pay her fifty dollars an hour.

I told my wife to text me every thirty minutes and let me know where she was. I told her that it was about safety, that I wasn't jealous. She complied, for a while. The tour of Detroit was completed by noon, but fifteen additional hours passed before I heard from my wife again.

My calls had gone unanswered. The same went for three dozen text messages.

That Sunday, she'd come in right before sunrise, had staggered in the house too drunk to talk. She was wearing a fur coat that looked like it had been stolen from a movie star. She had wrapped herself in it like a caterpillar inside a high-end cocoon. I asked her questions but she was too drunk to engage in conversation. I'd gone to church, had to leave before I went insane, and when I came back home six hours later, she was still sleeping. I cooked. I cleaned. I walked from room to room. I waited for her to wake up. But as soon as she opened her eyes I was there, standing over the bed, dressed in a white shirt and deep-blue slacks, golden tie loosened, a deep frown engraved in my face.

I fumed, "Where were you?"

"Don't scream. Please. Don't scream."

She struggled to her feet and went to the bathroom. I followed her and banged on the bathroom door. She came out of the bathroom with a bottle of Pepto-Bismol in her hand. Her hair was half pulled back, half down. Her illness had her sweating like she was standing in the rain. Her makeup had blended with her sweat, liner darkening both of her eyes.

She looked like a dying raccoon.

I repeated my question, demanded to know where she had been for those fifteen hours.

After she'd taken the Pepto-Bismol she said, "We went to church."

"On a Saturday?"

"It was a Seventh-Day Adventist Church."

"Church lasted until five this morning?"

"After church, Eddie Coyle took me to the Whitney for brunch."

"So, he spent a hundred dollars on a buffet."

"I didn't look at the bill."

"Then what? Brunch doesn't take all night."

"We went to the casino in Greektown."

She told me that her benefactor had blown a thousand playing poker. My wife lived for poker, and he had been kind enough to give her gambling money. Then they had headed back downtown to Tom's Oyster Bar for another expensive meal.

My anger had me ready to shout. I was at my wit's end, but I bit my tongue and listened.

I swallowed my growl and asked, "Then what?"

"Dmytryk. Please, not now. I'm sick as hell."

"I don't care if you're dead. Answer my questions."

"Don't scream. My head can't take it."

I snapped, "You were gone all night. Then what?"

She said they drove through the Detroit-Windsor Tunnel and landed in Canada, five minutes from the Marriott and the Ren Center in Detroit. That meant that Eddie Coyle had come to Detroit bearing a passport. He was probably an international criminal. And that meant that my wife had taken her passport, something that she rarely did. Again, it wasn't adding up. She said that Eddie Coyle had to meet a business associate on the other side of the tunnel at Shawarma Palace, a small eatery that sold Lebanese cuisine.

I said, "Explain the fur coat."

"I told Eddie Coyle I was cold. He bought me a coat."

"How much did that fur cost?"

"Fifty-two hundred."

She looked into my eyes and pulled her coat tighter, that reaction telling me she was not going to give it back, that no matter what I said or did she was keeping that present from another man.

I was about to say some things, some horrible things, but she spoke before I did.

She said, "Times are hard, Dmytryk."

"We have a new president."

"But our realities haven't changed."

I told her to be patient, reminded her that the president had made promises to us all.

My wife rubbed her temples and told me where I could stick any promise made at 1600 Pennsylvania Avenue. She cursed in Spanish and I responded in the same language, only with greater venom.

I pulled back, bridled my outrage the best I could, let her win the verbal war. We didn't need that volcano to explode, didn't need to get trapped in an avalanche of rage.

"Dmytryk, we can't keep living like this."

I nodded, then I waited. She was my wife and I knew her words, I knew that look in her eyes. This conversation was going somewhere, down a treacherous road she had already paved, but I just didn't know where that road went. Everything inside me went numb.

I waited for her to bring up the D word.

She said, "There is no future for us here, because as far as I can see, Detroit has no future."

"Detroit has a future."

She reminded me that the Silverdome had cost fifty-five million to build but was sold for less than six hundred thousand. The stadium was situated on 127 acres, had been the home of the Detroit Lions, the Detroit Pistons, and the Michigan Panthers, and it had been sold for less than the cost of a one-bedroom flat in New York. It had been sold to a company in Canada.

She said, "It was practically given away. So, what do you think the rest of the city is worth? They want to shut down neighborhoods because they are already ghost towns."

I couldn't argue with her.

My wife said, "Eddie Coyle can save us."

She said his name like he was a savior. I looked at my wife, a serious question in my eyes.

My wife shook her head. "He's nothing to me. But he can help us get back on our feet."

"How can he help me and my wife get our dignity back? How can he do that?"

She rocked, held her aching head, and said Eddie Coyle needed what he called a wheelman. He needed a getaway man. The last one had run into trouble, had killed his wife and was doing time at a prison right outside of Greenville, South Carolina. He'd asked her if she knew anybody he could use.

I said, "He's a bank robber."

"Eddie Coyle is a creative man who needs a getaway man. All you have to do is drive."

"You want me to rob a bank."

"Listen to me, Dmytryk. If you are the driver, you aren't actually robbing the bank."

I screamed that I would put hot daggers in my eyes before I stooped that low.

The fur coat was too much to look at.

My voice had become a deep growl. "Explain what you did to earn that coat."

"Nothing. I was cold. I said I was cold and Eddie Coyle bought me a coat."

"That's it? You said you were cold and this *Eddie Coyle* guy just bought you a fifty-two-hundred-dollar coat? Just like that?"

"It's just a coat. Look, Eddie Coyle has means and can help us get back on our feet."

"You say his name like he's the man that baptized Jesus."

"Stop it."

My jealousy exploded. While I went off, her skin tuned pale, then she held her stomach and raced for the bathroom. I stayed where I was. Served her right to suffer. For the next few minutes my wife was in the bathroom, her hangover out of control, on her knees praying to the porcelain god. I looked down the hallway and saw her agony had painted the wall before she made it to the bathroom. I went to the kitchen, found a mop and bucket, found Lysol, and cleaned up behind her.

When she had thrown up as much as she could, she staggered out and sat on the sofa.

I stood in the doorway watching her, anger darkening my eyes.

My wife sat there, eyes red, moaning, kept rocking and grinding her teeth. That had been a new problem that she had developed. Grinding her teeth. Unemployment had created problems beyond the checking account. We couldn't afford health problems, couldn't afford to catch a cold, but health problems were coming at us. She'd gained at least fifteen pounds. The weight didn't concern me as much as watching her pop Motrin like she was addicted to drugs. She complained about jaw pain, oversensitive teeth, facial pain, neck pain, and muscular pain.

"We've made too many bad decisions, Dmytryk. All the right decisions have been bad decisions."

"What do you mean?"

"Our town house was worth three hundred twenty thousand when we refinanced it and two hundred thousand when it foreclosed. We'd lost over a hundred thousand and we were working and paying on a mortgage when we should've walked away."

"I wasn't okay with that. I pay my bills. That's what a man does. A man pays his bills. I wasn't okay with walking away. I've never walked away from *anything*. This was my parents' house and I'm not okay with losing this home. No, we don't have the best zip code anymore, and we don't have a brand-new town house, but I'm doing my best to make sure we have food and a roof over our heads."

"*Husband,* your parents are *dead. Your wife* is alive. You have to do right by *your wife.*"

"How about doing right by your goddamn husband? How does that sound? For better or for worse. Do those words sound familiar? We signed up for better or for worse. Not for better or for best."

Disturbed and powerless, I sat down and broke the household rule. I turned the television on. I bit my lips and watched CNN. I wrung my hands and changed to the local news, searched for a way out.

The only thing that made me pause was a story about a brazen thief who dressed up as a Walmart supervisor, emptied a safe inside a Florida store, and walked out with more than two hundred thousand. Walmart's nonunionized employees applauded the outlaw. They were being paid less than the national average while CEOs took home almost thirty million.

Cora said, "If we had that much money, we could fix all of our problems."

That bandit had done what thousands of employees wished they had the guts to do.

Cora said, "The only way out is to make your own way out."

Dangerous emotions steamed from my pores. That same harsh energy emanated from my wife. She said, "Marriage is about compromise."

"Don't you know I know that? I was in grad school and now I'm delivering pizzas to people I went to high school with. People who barely made it out of high school are giving me two-dollar tips. Then laughing. You know how humiliating that is? Yeah, I'm compromising my friggin' dignity too. But I'm here. I haven't left. I haven't walked away from this hard life. I haven't walked away from this marriage. I'm compromising my ass off."

"Are you listening to me? We need action, not talk. Nobody cares about your degrees or how smart you are. Nobody cares but you. That paper does nothing. Are you listening to me?"

I lowered my head. There was an invisible fire in the room, stealing all the air.

She said, "It's your turn. You need to man up and make sacrifices like I have."

That barbed wire swiped at my ego and left an impenetrable silence between us.

I asked, "What have you done?"

"More than you."

"What?"

"Don't ask again. Please. Don't ask again."

My wife cried soft tears and told me that she had done all she could do for now. And there was only one thing left she could do to boost our pathetic income. My heart caught fire and my eyes watered.

She choked. "Men offer me *that* every time I go to work at that place. I was at the mall and a man who had been to the club recognized me. He came up to me, in the mall, and offered me money to go to a hotel with him. I smiled at him, but something inside me died. This is what I have become. Once you become . . . one of these women . . . once you do this . . . they never see you as anything but a whore."

She told me about the dancers who left with men, some with women who looked like men; some serviced customers who paid for acts of sadomasochism that rivaled the most disgusting Siffredi film. She repeated her question, asked me if I wanted her to cross that line.

She sounded destroyed.

And she wanted me to feel her pain, wanted to destroy me with her words.

I looked down at my callused hand and then looked up at the wall and saw my framed degrees. My wife complained about her life, but this wasn't the existence I'd mapped out for myself either. This life wasn't even close to what I had mapped out. I thought I'd end up with a sorority girl, a decent woman with a Ph.D. I wanted children who were White House–bound. I wanted a house filled with lawyers and leaders. Everybody fantasized until reality came along and knocked us flat on our rear ends.

I should've abandoned Detroit and my wife and her brand-new fur coat, my mind double-daring me to leave at that moment, my heart telling me that neither Detroit nor my wife would miss me. There was only so far a man could get when cash was low and credit cards had been maxed out. Only so much gas a man in my economic position could afford to burn.

The only thing I knew with any certainty was that my love for Cora hadn't changed.

In a hardened tone I said, "If your friend can use me, I'll be his getaway man."

She paused a long moment before she whispered, "I'll call Eddie Coyle."

7

Now Sammy was dead and Rick might be speeding down that same road.

Numbness had covered Jackie and me. We'd kept moving from morning until evening. We'd passed our hideout several times but put off going inside. We wanted to be sure that it was safe. Los Angeles had the world's largest population of Mexicans, Guatemalans, Salvadorans, Filipinos, Koreans, Samoans, and Armenians outside their native countries, and I think that we had seen every one of them at least twice since the fiasco at Wells Fargo. The darkening of the day had helped to lessen my fears, but not enough for me to feel at ease. Jackie and I lurked in the shadows of the safe house in Koreatown. Over a thousand bars, karaoke spots, spas that offered happy endings, pool halls, and clubs were alive and it sounded like I could hear the overlapping din from each and every one of them. Jackie parked on the crowded streets and we monitored the area. The earphones were in place and my iPhone was running the app that kept me in touch with both LAPD and the sheriff's department.

Jackie said, "You hear anything?"

"Nothing."

"It's safe."

"Why are you so sure?"

"Rick isn't a snitch. He has kids and a wife he loves."

"That's enough to make a man snitch."

"Not on this crew. Rick knows if he snitches, he'll be buying coffins for his family."

Jackie had changed clothes a few hours ago, back when we had dumped the van and traded it for the four-door Pontiac she'd rented from Hertz when she had arrived at LAX. She had lost the T-shirt and jeans, traded up and become a woman adorned in clothing by Givenchy, Calvin Klein, and Marc Jacobs.

Jackie went back inside the building first. The building that we were holed up inside was a dull edifice and all of its tenants were from south of the border. Thundering Spanish music shook the neighborhood as Jackie clicked the lights on and off three times. That meant everything was clear. She left the lights off after the signal was given.

Jackie clicked a small table light on when I entered the apartment. The place looked as tacky and unorganized as when we had left. I stepped inside the cold apartment and turned on the wall heater, then I hunted for something to rub on my face, anything to alleviate the swelling. Outside of deodorant and Band-Aids, there wasn't anything. I rubbed the stubble on my chin and that ached. The apartment was dark, but the neon lights of Koreatown yielded just enough colorful brilliance for me to be able to maneuver without needing additional illumination.

Jackie was in the living room, her lips pursed as she shook her head. She was in a trance, staring down at the things Rick and Sammy had left behind.

She cleared the pain from her throat, took a breath, and said, "Eddie Coyle called."

"When?"

"When I was coming up the stairs. I told him to call back in a few minutes."

"He's here in L.A.?"

"He's out of the country. There is another job coming up. He needs a crew."

"Now is not the time to think about another job."

"Court fees have drained me. Attorney fees have drained me. Now Sammy's dead."

I took a breath. "I'm in dire straits too."

"You have a house. You don't have any kids. What could you possibly need, Dmytryk?"

"Right now I need about four thousand."

"Well, I need ten times that, at least. I need at least ten times that to pull off what I'm trying to do, or I'll never get my kid back. Never," Jackie snapped. "I need to figure out a way to get some more damn money. Sammy and Rick were in on this next job and now—"

"Stay focused. You need to stay focused and I have to do the same."

"I am focused. I need to get my kid and get to South America, just like we had planned."

"Sure you want to do that? That might draw a lot of attention."

"Sammy told me I could get away with it, and I trusted Sammy with my life. He said that if a man kidnaps his child, it's news. But if a woman takes the child she bore, you'll never hear about it. My ex has used the system to his favor, and I'll take advantage of the rest. It won't even create a ripple in the news."

Jackie blinked and cleared her throat. She broke away from her trance and hurried across the worn shag carpet into the kitchen, then raided the cabinets and found some vodka.

Drink in hand, Jackie came into the living room and snapped again, "Everything has gone bad."

"Turn the television on so we can see if there's any word on Rick's condition."

She didn't respond. I found the remote and turned the television to the local news. They were in the middle of a story about a viral video of an old white man beating a young black man on a bus.

Jackie was dazed, eyes wandering around the room, shifting in and out of focus, moving from wall to wall like she was confused.

A cellular started ringing again. The same Spanish song that had played before. When the call ended unanswered, as if on cue, the second cellular started singing the Dean Martin ringtone.

Jackie caught her breath. "Their wives are not going to stop calling."

"They don't know."

Jackie took a deep breath and shook her head. "Sammy would want his wife to know."

The cellular phones started ringing again, first the Mexican song, then the number by Dean Martin. It made me wonder if Rick and Sammy were dead and calling us from the other side.

Jackie went into the bedroom and came back with the phones of our fallen comrades. After she stared at it with watery eyes, she handed Sammy's phone to me. She took Rick's phone. I answered Sammy's phone with reluctance, while Jackie answered Rick's phone in the same manner.

In a nervous tone Sammy's wife asked, "Is he there?"

"No." I paused and searched for words. "And he won't be coming back here."

"Not tonight?"

"Not ever."

"Oh, God."

"I'm sorry for your loss. My condolences to you and your family."

Grief filled her voice. I heard Sammy's kids laughing and playing in the background. The news of a bank robbery gone south wouldn't reach their local news. She'd had no idea that she was a widow.

Nothing else to say, I hung up Sammy's phone.

Jackie finished talking to Rick's wife about the same time.

I asked, "Rick's wife knows?"

She ran her fingers through her hair and whispered, "She knows something is wrong. Rick was supposed to call her ten hours ago. He's never late. I told her to not make any dinner plans because it might be twenty years before she talks to him again."

"Does your blood always run cold or do you keep it on ice?"

She broke Rick's phone in half. I did the same with Sammy's cellular.

She went to the kitchen and poured another glass of vodka.

Then the early-morning bank robbery at Wells Fargo hit the news. It was a thirty-second report. The security guard was former military. They showed his grieving wife and let her talk about how her husband had served in Afghanistan and left there after three tours of duty only to return home and struggle to find a job, and end up gunned down his first week working at the bank in Baldwin Hills. Half the cash had made it out of the parking lot in the hands and pockets of the opportunistic. The anchor said one of the robbers was on life support.

Jackie stared at the driver's license photo of Sammy Luis Sanchez that was being broadcast on KTLA. It was a chilling confirmation of Sammy's horrible death.

I'd fallen into a trance watching the report. Rick hadn't been identified. They had no idea who the second man was.

Then I heard something that I never expected to hear. Laughter. There was a soft chortle. It sounded distant, but it was inside this room. I looked at Jackie and her right palm was over her mouth, muffling what sounded like misplaced amusement. What I saw disturbed me because I'd seen that wide-eyed look on the face of many people who'd lost their jobs. Her eyes were wide open. She was shaking her head and she wasn't blinking. That laughter wasn't the kind of hilarity that came at the end of a joke, but the kind of laughter that came at inappropriate moments, the laughter of pain and disbelief, the frightening kind that ballooned and turned hysterical and sounded like the opening bell to the release of the madness within. All day she had held everything in. Now, while we were in this space and away from the rest of the world, she couldn't hold it in anymore.

She laughed and laughed and laughed. And when the laughter had moved beyond maniacal, it became so deep that she lost her breath. Jackie inhaled so deeply it looked as if she were suffocating, as if she were drowning in sorrow, and when she threw her head back and gulped air, when she could exhale and inhale, the laughter was gone, replaced by a series of curt screams that shattered any residual echo from the laughter, the screams icy and hot all at once, each scream reverberating and sending chills up and down my spine, that shrill the eruption of the inner volcano, the releases of pent-up denial and disbelief. She doubled over and when I went toward her, she moved away from me, stumbled into the kitchen, and picked up a plate. She threw the plate against the wall, and before the last bits of the plate had settled, she was grabbing everything in sight, began throwing glasses and knives and spoons before she turned over all of the food on the kitchen counter, threw things until there was nothing else to throw, and when that was not enough, she fought to breathe again, then went down on her knees, collapsed on her backside, and gave her angry and irate tears to her hands. My instinct was to try to hold her; that instinct to protect a woman was a man's flaw that had proven deadly to many. I wanted to contain her rage, silence her before people came knocking on the door, but I went to her, and as I said her name over and over and tried to quiet her, she fought with me, lashed out at me with both her hands and her words, as if it was my fault that Sammy had been shot.

"*You* should be dead, *not Sammy*. You should be dead."

Her depraved words almost sent me into a rage, but I held back. I stepped away and she hurried and got back on her feet. Her words echoed. She wished me dead again. Whatever she saw in my face and body language made her take a step back and scramble through things in the kitchen in search of a weapon. She picked up a steak knife and gripped it inside her hand, held it the way a solider holds a knife, her body ready. The news had brought the truth and the truth was too much for her to bear and now I was the epicenter of all faults.

She faced me and growled, "*You should be dead, Dmytryk.*"

I reached inside my pocket and took out the gun she had given me, the same gun that had been used back at the Village Green.

She snapped, "Is that supposed to scare me?"

I firmed my voice and snapped, "Just put the damn knife down."

We faced each other for a short part of eternity. The anger in her face changed, her bottom lip trembled, and her anger moved aside and allowed her sorrow a front seat among her litany of emotions.

Her words changed from fury to a frantic plea. "Shoot me, Dmytryk. In my heart, shoot me. Get this pain out of my chest and if you can't get the pain out, kill me and make it go away."

"Geesh, Jackie."

"Shoot me. Please, just shoot me. Get me out of this miserable world."

Her hair draped her face, came loose and covered her psychosis, fell across the makeup that failed to mask her troubled skin, and she gnarled her lips, bared her teeth, and gave me a rabid stare that was as grotesque as it was powerful. She snapped again, said words that made her sound no better than a feral, dirty-mouthed hooker, cursed and told me to shoot her like she was a dog, like they had shot Sammy.

"Think about your kid, Jackie."

Those simple words widened her eyes and pulled her away from whatever evil place she was visiting. She looked down at her hand, stared at the knife she held, then closed her eyes. The knife slipped from her fingers and landed on the tattered linoleum in the kitchen.

I put the gun back inside my pocket. It had never been pointed at her.

After that, I backed away from her.

Food decorated the walls and run-down shag carpet, the dinners

I had made over the last days thrown a pot at a time, then whatever she had spilled on the counter being slung a handful at a time, food that ran down the walls and made it look like the room was melting or like an abstract exhibit that should be at a museum in London or Germany. I kept my distance and looked at Jackie, her hair flying about her face as she released her angst. She stood before me, fuming in grief, bewildered, fraught, tormented by bad times, bad marriages, lawsuits, economic madness, and the death of a lover she needed.

Outside, the din from Koreatown piped into the room as red and yellow neon lights flashed across insanity.

Jackie leaned against the kitchen wall, winded, her chest rising and falling at a rapid pace. She evaluated the mess she'd made, then picked up the bottle of vodka, one of the few things that she hadn't thrown. She found a paper cup and filled it, then drank it like it was Kool-Aid.

She whispered, "I didn't mean it. I'm not crazy, if that's what you're thinking."

"You meant it. And I should leave before another tragedy happens inside this room."

"Not right now."

"I'd hate for another one of us to end up dead. And I'd hate for that person to be me."

"Don't go."

"Then take it easy on the vodka."

She asked, "Mind giving me that gun?"

"What are you going to do with it?"

"I'm not going to shoot you."

"If you're contemplating a reunion with Sammy, think about your kid. And if you still feel compelled to act like a loon, let me know and give me a twenty-minute head start before you pull the trigger."

We stared at each other for a moment, then I reached in my coat and handed her the weapon.

She held the gun and stared at me, her eyes dark, red, and swollen.

She said, "You should've had a gun, Dmytryk. Then you could've saved Sammy."

"We can't turn back the clock."

"You could've saved them both if you'd had a gun."

I said, "The way you're holding that gun, Jackie, it's making me a little uneasy."

She put the gun down on the counter and turned around, bumped into the kitchen counter, almost lost her balance, then stepped over the mess she had made like she was negotiating a minefield. She sashayed away, threw her hips side to side, and headed to the window, stood there drinking and shaking her head like she was struggling to not let her thoughts drive her crazy, releasing the occasional chuckle of disbelief, the neon lights making her appear and disappear, like the problems inside my head.

She whispered, "Sammy's dead. Sammy really is dead. I can smell him in this room, smell him on my skin, can feel him inside my body, and he's dead. I have the scent of a dead man on my body."

"We need to worry about Rick."

"Turn that television off. I can't handle seeing Sammy pop up on the news again."

"We need to get updates on Rick."

"I don't care about Rick. Something went wrong inside and I bet it was Rick's fault."

"If Rick isn't dead, if they hold his family over him and get him to talk, we're screwed."

"Rick would never talk. Look, Sammy's dead and I have to stay focused. You're right. I have to think about my child. That's what this is all about. I'm not robbing banks for kicks. I'm on a mission. Every dime counts. Every dime. This job was just a small job. And this small job was going to lead to a bigger job. Then me and Sammy . . . Sammy . . . Sammy's dead."

I let the conversation end on her words.

She whispered, "Turn the television off, Dmytryk."

I ignored her.

Jackie adjusted her skirt and moved her out-of-control hair away from her face, tried to summon some sophistication but failed miserably. I went back to monitoring the television. She finished her drink, went into the kitchen and picked up the gun, then came toward me, made me back away.

Jackie shot the television three times. She killed the newscasters as they smiled.

The television died as every other noise in Koreatown magnified and covered her insanity.

Then Jackie went back to the kitchen and made herself another tall glass of vodka.

8

Legs crossed, Jackie sat in a plaid chair and maintained conversation with Mr. Smirnoff. I turned on my laptop and searched for the same news that Jackie had destroyed, but what I found wasn't real-time. All I had was the app on my phone, so I let anxiety lead me around the cramped apartment while I monitored police bands. An hour later Jackie's cellular rang and she staggered inside the bedroom and took the call. I stopped pacing long enough to spy out the window at the row of dingy apartments on the street. Jackie came back and extended her personal phone.

Her eyes told me who was on the other end of her cellular. I knew it was her savior. My hand went up in a motion that told her to hold on. I turned off my laptop before I took her phone. I wanted her savior to wait for me the way others waited on him. Jackie ran her fingers through her hair and walked away, sashayed to refill her glass, her four-inch heels taking her tipsy sway across the claustrophobic room.

I said, "Eddie Coyle. The man from Rome."

"Well, if it isn't the blue-collar executive with no vowels in his ugly name."

Despite the fear and tension in the air, I played along and said, "I have two vowels."

"Either way, long time no talk to."

"Long time," I said in agreement. "Where are you?"

"Vancouver, but I'm loading up."

"Working a job?"

"More like vacation. We're preparing to fly back toward Rome."

"I heard the weather was pretty bad in that part of the world."

He asked, "What in the world happened out there in L.A.?"

Teeth clenched, I relived the nightmare, described the horror, and told Eddie Coyle about the morning, about the moments when Rick and Sammy had exited Wells Fargo.

Eddie Coyle said, "No way you could've saved Rick or Sammy?"

"No way. It was unexpected."

"We have to expect the unexpected."

"They came out shooting. Sammy was already hit."

"They were down when you pulled away?"

"Sammy's head was open and the bullet that went through Rick's chest, it shattered the car window. His chest was opened up. Sammy was dead."

"Sounds like it was really bad."

I rubbed my eyes. "The bullet that hit Rick, I have that bullet in my pocket right now."

"Glad you made it out. I'm sure Rick or Sammy would've done the same if the roles had been reversed. We don't leave anyone behind unless we have to, and I'm sure you had to, because you did."

"You said the driver never leaves the car."

"The driver never leaves his passengers either. But if Sammy's brains had been blown out and Rick had taken one like you say, you had no other options, I'm sure."

I didn't know how to take his last statement, so I held the phone and bottled my temper.

"Jackie said you handled some woman today, Dmytryk."

First I touched my busted lip, then I touched my tender face.

I whispered, "No witnesses."

"A witness is a guaranteed ride to jail."

"Guaranteed, Eddie Coyle. Guaranteed."

"She said that you did it and walked away like it was nothing."

I let his words hang.

Eddie Coyle said, "I know it's a bad time, but, well, if you're interested, of course at the risk of coming across as being insensitive, I have another job coming up fast, real fast, and I really need another man."

"Where?"

"Georgia. That's why I was calling Jackie. She just told me about Sammy and Rick. I send my condolences and prayers, but despite that situation I need a crew, people I know and trust."

"What's the take?"

"One hundred thousand. That's low end. Guaranteed. Five-way split."

"One hundred thousand."

"You'll get twenty. It's not much, but it's better than peanut butter on crackers."

I paused for a moment and looked down at my well-shined Johnston & Murphy shoes. There was a point in my life when one hundred grand would have been laughable. Now twenty thousand was the life preserver that would keep me from going under, maybe keep me afloat until the next ship came my way and saved me from drowning or drifting at sea.

I said, "At the risk of sounding insensitive, I need the money."

"If you make it to exit seven in the next four days, we'll take it from there."

He'd said *if*. Not *when*. A sinking feeling consumed my body.

We ended the call. Eddie Coyle was in a hurry. He was a man who was always in a hurry.

A savior never had time to rest.

I tossed the cellular to Jackie. Despite being toasted, she caught with her left hand.

Jackie whispered, "Dmytryk, you said you needed three grand?"

"Four. I need to get my hands on four thousand as soon as possible."

"Gambling debt or you plan on spending the night with a couple of hookers?"

"None of your business. I just need it."

Jackie stood and paced the room, her turn to walk the worn carpet.

I went to my duffel bag and opened it up. Off to the side were applications for grad school. There were job applications as well, only the latter seemed like a waste of good trees in a bad economy. Most companies did online submissions, but a few still used paper.

She paused a moment. "I'm really surprised that Eddie Coyle invited you in on his job."

I closed my duffel and faced her, my expression terse. "You think I can't handle it?"

"Did I say something to upset you?"

"Don't question me and what I'm capable of."

"That's not what I was doing, but maybe somebody should."

"If anyone can't handle it, it's you. You lost it before. You were ready to face off with LAPD with a .22. You held a knife and wished me dead. You went Elvis Presley and killed the television, and now it feels as if I'm being questioned here. I've worked with Eddie Coyle. What he is and how he is are nothing new."

"Sammy, Rick, and me were supposed to go alone. You weren't invited."

"I am now. So, if the job and the payout was a secret, I'm on the crew now."

"Relax. It's not that we were keeping the job a secret from you. It's just that, well, sometimes it's better to not speak about everything we do."

"I think Rick was about to tell me. He said he'd wanted to talk to me about something. Maybe he was backing out, going home to his family, and plugging me in on the job."

She nodded, then asked, "You said that you need four grand?"

"Why? You plan on robbing a few liquor stores tonight?"

"Can you relax for a moment? Loosen your collar and listen to what I'm about to offer."

I nodded. The alcohol had her humming, bouncing her leg, and smiling to herself.

She said, "Maybe I could float you that baby bankroll until the next job is done."

"You have access to that kind of money?"

"Say the word and I'll make a call and make it happen. Provided you agree to the interest."

There was always a catch. I took a breath and asked, "How much interest?"

"I usually take forty or fifty percent, but I can do thirty this one time."

"You're the bank."

"Yeah. I'm the bank."

"Thirty percent is outrageous. You're another predatory lender."

"Look, I have a kid and I'm trying to increase my funds tenfold so I can fix my situation. Every dime helps. This job has left me with nothing but a headache, heartache, and a bad taste in my mouth. So, I'll go out on a limb with my money and take a chance and loan you part of my nest egg, but only if it is lucrative for me and my kid in the short run."

"It's been a long day. Both of us are on edge. Let me sleep on it."

"No, I need to know now. You have five minutes. Then the bank is closed."

She went to the kitchen and poured a little more vodka. This time she opened the refrigerator and found a carton of orange juice, used it to cut the liquor. She sipped, then said, "Five minutes are up. Do you want to borrow four thousand or not?"

"Don't want to, but have to." My voice was harsh and just above a whisper, yet it filled the room. "Lower the interest rate and *maybe* we can make a deal. You have a kid, but I have to take care of a few things too. We all have lives, Jackie. I empathize with your child-custody issues, but your problems are not the center of my universe."

"Thirty percent. Take it or leave it. Tomorrow, if you ask, it will be back at my usual rates."

"I wasn't trying to offend you, just wanted you to know that I have my own issues as well."

"Thirty percent. That's all we have to talk about right now. Thirty percent."

I accepted her predatory interest rate and asked her how soon she could get me the money.

"In a few. Let me wash down your insults and insensitivity and calm my nerves."

I walked away from her and stood in the window, my arms folded.

She said, "Riddle me this, Batman."

"What?"

"You wear a wedding ring, but there isn't a wife around. No text messages, no sneaking off to call and check in. Sammy told me that you and the wife aren't together, that she left while you were doing a job."

I nodded and left it at that.

When my feet began to throb and the heaviness from life took hold of me, I sat down on the sofa and initiated the app that connected to the police monitors. I hoped Jackie would go into the bedroom, but she came over and sat down on the sofa. I struggled to get comfortable on one end and she relaxed on the far end, pulled her feet up under her body, took a very feminine position, and faced me. It was awkward being there with her. Over the last six months, it had always been four of us hiding out. And she had always ended up drinking and resting in Sammy's lap after a job was done.

She finished her vodka, then poured another tall glass of the same and sat next to me. This time she positioned herself on the worn pillow next to mine. Her skirt rode high and she undid another button on her blouse. She sipped her drink and rested her left hand on my leg. When I looked in her light brown eyes, she didn't move her hand away from my thigh. Her smile widened. She winked and rubbed my leg.

She asked, "When was the last time you were with a woman?"

"Let's not go down that road, Jackie."

"Maybe we could help each other out."

I moved her hand away. "Let's go get that four grand, Jackie."

"What's the problem?"

"I'm not Sammy."

She gave me an unembarrassed smile. "Give me twenty minutes."

"Then you're going to make that call and we're going to go get the four thousand."

She took her cellular, staggered into the bedroom, and slammed the door.

My duffel bag rested at the end of the sofa. I grabbed my toiletries and hurried inside the bathroom. I threw a ragged towel down in the tub and stood on top of that while I showered, then I wrapped a towel I had brought with me around my body. I borrowed a lime-green plastic bowl from the kitchen, one of the few things that hadn't been destroyed during Jackie's rage, then filled it with hot water and added shaving powder, stirred it until I had made a decent amount of foamy shaving cream. I always shaved after a job. Always showered and shaved. It was my ritual. I didn't need to break that now. While the lather was hot I used my shaving brush and swirled the wet tips of the brush, used the same motions my father had taught me, then I painted my face, again emulating the strokes he had used. I used a straightedge razor and shaved the way men had shaved for hundreds of years. I'd used Noxzema Lather Shave Cream, and this was a pow-dered version of the same, had the same scents, a mixture of coconut, eucalyptus, clove, and peppermint oils. When I was done I rinsed my face, inspected my injuries, packed up my shaving tools, and went back into the living room.

It was possible for a man to clean his body and not remove any filth from his soul.

I reached inside the bag and found a pair of black boxers, a white V-neck undershirt, and a fresh white shirt that had been starched— the way Henrick used to wear his shirts. I went back to the bathroom to dress and assess my reflection in the mirror. My face was Henrick's face. And I'd always used the same brand of shaving cream. I used his watch, a timepiece that had been his father's timepiece, a pocket watch that had kept time for decades.

I thought about my father. I thought about killing. I thought about Abbey Rose.

I whispered, "No witnesses."

Once a man killed, he was never the same. One death changed a man's world forever.

After I dressed, I went back into the front room. Jackie hadn't come out of the bedroom yet. I stepped over the destruction and dropped my duffel bag near the front door, raised my antique watch and stood in the window, found enough light and checked the time. Twenty-five minutes had gone by. It was late by L.A. standards, a loud and traffic-filled city overpopulated with bad actors and deadly thugs. Last call was at one thirty and L.A shut down by two, but it was still early enough to handle a few things.

The bedroom door opened and I expected to see Jackie swaying in her skirt and high heels, expected to see her hair pulled back or done in some presentable way, but she was dressed in her panties and her bra. Her heels were off and she had on a pair of thick white socks. Sammy's socks. She looked a mess. She stood in the door frame, struggling to balance herself and gripping what I assumed to be four thousand dollars inside her left hand. Looked like she had just robbed a liquor store. Something told me that she had gone through Sammy's luggage, appropriated whatever cash had belonged to her dead lover like a vulture.

Whether she burglarized the living or raided a tomb of the dead, money was money. I accepted the loan and counted the wrinkled bills before shoving them inside my pocket.

She said, "Now you owe me five thousand two hundred."

Her words slurred. She could barely stand. The vodka had finally taken control of her.

She said, "I'm going mad. My face is breaking out like I'm a teenager. Look at me."

"It's not that bad."

"I have to kidnap my own kid, get fake passports, take my kid to South America, and change our surnames. Sammy was going to help me work that out."

"So I guess all bets are off on that one."

"I can still make it happen. But I'd need enough money to last at least six years, maybe seven. I can build a house right outside of Tegucigalpa for fifty thousand. I'm talking about a mansion with six bedrooms. Sammy was going to leave his wife. He was going to leave everything behind and come with me. He was going to help me build that house and help me learn to speak Spanish and get my kid and me acclimated to Honduras. It was all mapped out. I had concocted the perfect plan. Now Sammy is dead."

She collapsed on the sofa and cried again.

Her tears came on strong, like she was a baby. She cried until she was exhausted. I brought her tissues and she blew her nose over and over. I helped her back toward the bedroom. She'd become dead weight and I had to drag her. I dropped her on the bed and struggled to flip her over on her stomach. She asked me if I was about to sex her. I told her no.

She chuckled. "You've been wanting to get inside me since you first met me in Rome."

"Turn over, Jackie."

"Are you gay or something?"

"I'm married."

"You're married. That's a joke if ever I heard one. You might be married, but she's not. She left you, Dmytryk. Everybody knows she split. Sammy joked about it and so did Rick. They laughed it up, the way you keep looking for her online and going back to a crappy house in Detroit. Eddie Coyle and his brother laughed about it too, and they laughed harder than Rick and Sammy."

"Stop it."

"The nerve to insult me. Yeah, my kid is the center of my universe. Your pathetic problems are no concern of mine either, Mister High and Mighty. Sit back, ugly shoes, I have a few insults of my own."

"I'm being a gentleman, and with you that is a challenge, so don't push me, Jackie."

"The best way to get over somebody is to get on top of somebody else." She laughed. "And your wife is probably on top of somebody else every night. Don't you feel like a fool right about now?"

"Shut up."

"She's naked and bouncing on top of somebody else and you're still wearing a stupid wedding ring." She kicked her heels and cackled harder. "Losers. That's all we are. Pathetic losers, nothing more and nothing less. So, come on, since this day's been so bad, let's give each other some pity sex."

It was hard to flip her over on the twin-size bed, but I managed. She put some arch in her back and pushed her backside up in the air. She dared me to mount her. In her eyes, if I entered her drunken body, then my worth as a man would be validated.

I needed Sammy's mistress to pass out facedown. That way if she regurgitated, she wouldn't drown in her vomit and end up dancing the salsa with Sammy as they waited on Rick to join them at the same cantina in West Hell. Then they could share a good laugh on my behalf.

She laughed a drunken, irritating hyena laugh, but the laughter became sorrow, both eyes rivers of never-ending tears. Her body quivered and her chest rose and fell as she struggled to breathe, her nose again stuffy as she panted, "Sammy left without saying good-bye. Just like your wife did."

I didn't say anything and hoped she would do the same. Everything felt eerie. I was standing in the bedroom where, hours ago, Jackie had made love with Sammy. His carry-on suitcase rested in a corner. It stood up like a well-traveled tombstone made by Samsonite. His belongings rested next to Rick's suitcase. Another bag that the frightened part of me hoped would become a grave marker.

Jackie asked, "Do you think Sammy really loved me?"

"Rest, Jackie. Close your legs and eyes and try and get some rest."

Jackie took a deep breath. "Losers. We're two pathetic losers stranded on an island."

A man like me could only take so much. I shifted and battled with a massive headache.

She said, "Any other man would take advantage of me right now. I'm sorry I said I wished you were dead. I don't wish you were dead. I just wish Sammy wasn't dead."

I didn't say anything.

"Oklahoma," she whispered. "When I'm sober I think that I'm going to tell you about Oklahoma."

"What happened in Oklahoma?"

She kicked her legs awhile, but that slowed down, then stopped, and she was gone. Her breathing was thick and choppy for a few minutes, but it smoothed out and she slept like a child.

I went to the dirty window, pulled the tattered curtains back, and looked outside at a filthy town that had endless traffic on the streets. As engines revved and horns blew and mixed in with Spanish music and American curses, neon signs flashed and assaulted me with primary colors, God's angry eyes blinking at us over and over. Head lowered, I gazed at my wedding ring and remembered the last nights I'd spent with my wife. She had left like a thief in the night. She had fled like a coward.

If we'd had a kid, if she had stolen our kid the way Jackie wanted to abduct her kid, and then vanished, I would've gone insane. I couldn't find it in my heart to respect her for the way she left.

For all I knew she was sitting on the white sands on the isle of Hispaniola watching the constellations. Or she could have been killed in an earthquake and buried in a mass grave.

Sirens continued to sound all over Koreatown. The smells, the sirens, the carpet, it all had become too much. An abrupt wave of fear rose up and did its best to strangle me out of this world.

Like Jackie had done, when images of Rick and Sammy surfaced, when seeing their belongings got to me, when I inhaled the scents they had left behind, when that danced with thoughts about my wife, I lost it, felt the same heat and surges I had felt this morning, only I let them get the best of me. I grabbed whatever I could grab, turned over suitcases, pushed over the television Jackie had murdered, let out primal grunts, and released as much tension as I could. When I was done, sweat drained down my forehead. Jackie's drunken words had pushed me over the edge.

I picked up the gun and went to her, stood over her with the gun pointed at her head.

For a long while I looked at Jackie. A woman who knowingly slept with a married man who was a thief of the worst kind. And I was no better than the company I'd been keeping. I'd become one of them.

It took minutes, but I calmed down, straightened my suit coat, and regained control of myself. I wiped the gun down, then put it on the dresser.

"See you in Georgia, Jackie. I'll see you when we get to everybody's savior."

I packed my duffel bag, took everything I had brought with me on this unprofitable trip, and left the unkempt hideout as fast as I could. I used my remote and started my car before I left the building. The remote upgrade had been added last year. When I made it to my Buick Wildcat, it was warmed up and ready to leave. My wife and I had owned two brand-new vehicles three years back. She had driven a Cadillac and I'd had an Expedition. Now both were gone. All we had was a car my old man had left behind, a 1969 Buick Wildcat, a four-door hardtop that was green inside and out. My wife called the car old. I chose to call it classic. My Buick was forty-three hundred pounds of U.S. history that had a cracked dashboard and crank windows to go with its three-hundred-sixty-horsepower engine and twenty-five-gallon tank. I loaded my Wildcat and took to the road, mixed in with hundreds of new cars built in other countries.

I took to the dangerous streets of L.A. with between five and six thousand dollars smoldering inside my suit pocket. I had a little money of my own. Soon that would be gone.

Out of habit, I checked the time on my pocket watch, then I reached to adjust my fedora, but it wasn't on my head. My father's prized fedora was no longer in my possession. It felt as if my brain swelled, doubled in size, and pressed against my skull.

After I had driven about seven miles, I was back in the area where things had gone wrong. The Crenshaw strip, Baldwin Hills, everything I had witnessed that morning owned a new face. I drove through the Wells Fargo parking lot, a parking lot that now felt haunted, maybe some sort of Valhalla for Sammy, and I parked where I had parked that morning. I took the same spot, as if I were trying to do the day over again. I sat there in the dark, sirens humming in the distance, an occasional car pulling up and the driver or passenger running to withdraw money from the ATM. I tortured myself, let this morning's tragedy replay in my mind a dozen times. Rick felt betrayed, that last look in his eye. I had failed him.

I clenched my jaw, wiped away a few burning tears, and left the same abrupt way I had done this morning, sped down Santa Rosalia until I made it to where I'd had the accident. The wrecked Chevy was gone. That made my heart accelerate. It was just a matter of time.

We could only be betrayed by the people we trusted.

Instead of taking the freeway east, I turned around and went back to the safe house.

I hustled back upstairs and grabbed everything that had belonged to Rick and Sammy and carried it to my Buick. One by one, I dragged their Samsonite tombstones to the car and tossed them inside the trunk with my traveling bags. Then I did the same with Jackie's carry-on luggage. I shook Jackie awake, then dragged her to the bathroom and threw cold water on her face until she was able to open her eyes. After that I waited for her to empty her bladder before I did my best to help her get dressed. I dragged her drunken frame down a set of concrete stairs and loaded her dead weight in the backseat of my car. When I opened the door, the side of her head banged the metal door frame as she fell back across the backseat. I had to go to the other side of the car and grab her arms in order to drag her body inside. After that effort, I grabbed some covers I had in the trunk, blankets I carried in case my car broke down in the cold, then propped her up in the corner behind me and covered her up the best I could.

She was a dead man's mistress. She wasn't my friend. She was the type of person I had no love for, but I couldn't abandon her the way my wife had abandoned me.

She was part of the team.

As I took to the streets, I wondered if I could've saved Rick. I wondered if I could've made it to him and pulled him inside the car. That action would've changed everything that had happened after.

Maybe I had been the weak link. Maybe I had been incompetent. If I had moved the car closer to the door about one minute and thirty seconds into the job, then, regardless of the fact that Sammy was wounded, they could've made it to the car and fallen into the backseat before the guard had staggered out the door. But then the money bag would've exploded inside the car and left that red dye all over the inside of the windows. It would've blinded us all and whoever didn't die would've been shackled within five minutes. I searched for another way I could've saved the men who had called me their brother. Tears fell and my hands trembled. I had been traumatized. Seeing Sammy's head blown open was like a bad dream that I couldn't shake. I despised this world and every living being on this planet. Behind my eyelids, I saw the opportunistic people jumping over Sammy and Rick, no regard for the dead or the dying, chasing dye-stained money as it flew away like confetti. Beneath smog-covered skies that were devoid of any real humidity, I had watched the world lose its humanity.

9

Last December.

My meeting was on the seventy-second floor at Coach Insignia, a bar that had a panoramic view of Detroit, the Detroit River, and Canada. That was where the man called Eddie Coyle was waiting. I found him seated at the swank bar, his eyes moving from the television to the well-dressed women as they exited the elevator and sashayed into the dimly lit area. Some wore open-toed high heels and short dresses. Those women were with men who wore Rolexes as symbols of success. The wives of executives wore the same brand of watch to symbolize they had latched onto the paychecks of wealthy men. I took a breath and reassured my battered ego that one day my wife and I would belong to that club, the one for people who had access to wealth and were given all the love that money could buy, people who had Panglossian temperaments and lived inside a gold-lined bubble where all was the best in this best of all possible worlds.

I took off my wool coat, then removed my fedora. Eddie Coyle had on a dark suit and tie. He was clean shaven and looked like he was trying to pass himself off as a businessman, but he had the face of a laborer. In a room filled with gastronomes with deep pockets, he was eating pretzels, drinking a glass of red wine, and reading a book. He looked up from his book, saw me watching him, evaluating him, and put the wine down as I snaked through the crowd. The bar was stocked with over eight hundred wines, but after we shook hands I ordered a Hennessy and Coke. Eddie Coyle ordered another glass of wine. On this floor and the one below everyone was beatific and dressed in expensive clothing, mostly tuxedos and gowns. On the seventy-second floor of the Ren Center the world wasn't in turmoil. People ate exquisite meals and drank the best wines like they were Roman gods.

My wife had told me that the man was from Rome, so I greeted him in Italian, said good evening, and then apologized for keeping him waiting. It had been a long time since I'd had a conversation in Italian, and part of me looked forward to that aspect of the evening. I asked him if he'd been waiting long. He looked confused and had no idea what I had said.

He moved his book to the side and said, "In English. This is America, so, if you don't mind, please speak in English."

"My wife said that you're from Rome."

He laughed. "I'm from the Rome in Georgia, not the one in Italy."

I asked, "What's the book you're reading?"

He slid it toward me. It was a nonfiction number titled *The Myth of Male Power*.

I said, "I've never heard of that book."

113

"This is my bible."

I nodded. "You're from the other Rome. I've never heard of Rome, Georgia."

"It's near Atlanta. Ever been there? To Atlanta?"

"Outside of a layover at Hartsfield, never been. How is that city?"

"Atlanta is nice, used to be nicer twenty years ago, but now it's on the verge of becoming another Paris. The people in France said that Paris was the city of love, but you should see their ghettos. I was there for a month. I wasn't impressed. Their ghettos are worse than the ones over here. Worse than the ones here in Detroit, if you ask me. And now, since Katrina washed its lovely canaille and destitute and drug dealers into Atlanta, it's become the same with Atlanta. I'll never live in the city. I own property there, but I'll never live in Fulton County. I'm stuck renting my properties to fags, jigs, and wetbacks."

"Before you go any farther, being the type of man I am, a man who says what is on his mind, I have to tell you that I protest the use of racial slurs and I'm not a fan of the disease known as bigotry."

"Common language in parts of the South."

"Understood. But despite the commonality of your colorful language, this isn't the South. And the way I see it, minus the revisionist history, if you're neither indigenous Mexican nor Native American, regardless of how you ended up in the country, voluntarily or otherwise, you're the ancestor of an immigrant."

"And as you will see, if you come on board, most of my associates are minorities. Whether they came here through Ellis Island or arrived on slave ships, that don't matter to me. So if you're implying that I'm racist, you're wrong. And the colorful language my associates use is twice as creative as mine. This isn't corporate America. Where you're going has nothing to do with white collars. We don't have to be politically correct. We're not forced to lie. We speak our minds and let the chips fall where they may."

"I wanted you to know where I stood." I said, "So, you're not keen on the populace in the city of Atlanta."

"I'd raise a family in a zoo before I let them live in Atlanta. Rome has history and values. And they have the right kind of parades."

My eyes went to the restaurant, taking in its architecture. Most of the hard hats and steel toes who had slaved their callused fingers to the bone building the half-a-billion-dollar edifice had ended up on the unemployment line. I saw Caesars standing tall across the river, its red marquee beckoning the down-and-out Americans to come into Canada and gamble away what they had left of their dignity.

I scowled at Windsor. That was where Eddie Coyle had taken my wife and bought her a fur coat.

He said, "Tell me a little about yourself, Dmytryk."

"What did my wife tell you?"

"Your wife said that you needed the money. That's about it."

I sipped my liquor and smiled. "You were with her a long time. Almost twenty-four hours."

"We were busy with business."

I nodded. "Well, next time you plan on keeping my wife overnight, make sure you invite me."

"Understood."

"And sending her home as drunk as she was, that doesn't sit well with me."

"She did that own her own. She's an adult. Still, I apologize for returning your wife to you in such a state."

I nodded. "Again, tell me what she told you about our situation."

"She told me she used to earn almost a hundred thousand a year operating heavy machinery and then she was laid off. Six months later the same had happened to you."

"Yeah, it was a one-two punch."

"And after she was let go, she moved from part-time job to part-time job until she ended up being a waitress at a gentlemen's club. She saw how much money the girls were making onstage, then gathered her nerves, went behind your back, and danced so your bills and mortgage could get paid."

"We were making it."

"Barely."

"But we were making it."

"I'm just repeating what she told me, that's all."

"I apologize for my hostility." I nodded. "She lowered her standards out of necessity. She's a better woman than that. I didn't know at first, but I found out weeks later. A high school friend had gone to the club and had seen my wife dancing, then he sent me an embarrassing message on Facebook. He'd taken her to the private room and seen my wife in a way only a husband should."

I paused right there because Eddie Coyle had seen my wife in the same state of undress.

"I hated it and she knew I hated it. I cursed and protested; things turned very ugly between us, but in the end, I didn't protest strong enough. The money. We'd been out of work long enough. We were destitute. That money has forced me to compromise my values."

"You're feeling powerless."

His words hit me deep. It took me a moment, but I nodded. "You could say we all are. Everything we do is an attempt to gain or create power. Or to restore some sort of balance."

He nodded. "How did a smart guy like you end up here, if you don't mind me asking?"

I told him that for me, this was the back end of four years in college and one in grad school. Work had stolen all of my time, money had become spotty, so I didn't finish grad school, and that remained a thorn in my side. I'd deferred my dreams and my white-collar career had tanked within a few years. That was eight years ago, and like a shark that had been flipped over, I'd been unable to turn myself back right.

He asked, "What happened to the white-collar job?"

"Budget cuts. Corporate restructuring. Me and about a thousand were let go the same day. Attorneys were taking minimum-wage jobs in Motown, doing their best to not lose their homes and failing. The unemployment line was filled with people with more education than I have, and it still is to this day."

"Why didn't you leave and go to someplace that had a little more sun?"

"By then I had a mortgage, car note, other bills. I did what I had to do to stay afloat. I followed the footsteps of my old man and his old man, put my tail between my legs, and went scampering to the blue-collar and unionized sect. I ended up working on the line. Maybe I would've left after that, but I met this girl on the line and one thing led to another. Marriage has a way of keeping a man where he is."

"Oh, I understand." Eddie Coyle nodded. "You stayed here because of Cora Mature."

"She told you her real name."

"Her maiden name."

"She's Cora Knight now."

He nodded. "I couldn't call her Trouble everywhere we went."

"She could've given you another phony name."

"She could've. But she didn't." Eddie Coyle said, "Dmytryk Knight."

I made myself comfortable on my barstool. "What brings you to Detroit?"

"I think your wife told you."

"Since this is our first date and this is our first drink, humor me."

He smiled. "I came here last week to go to church, then go out and see the city."

"You don't seem like a religious man."

"I went to visit a couple of megachurches. Where a man can get lost in the crowd."

"So you're a religious zealot who frequents gentlemen's clubs, then goes to pray."

Eddie Coyle checked his watch. "Well, why don't you tell me why you are here?"

I looked at my pocket watch and raised my drink, washed down some nervousness, nodded, then said, "So, my wife tells me that you're in the banking industry."

"Withdrawals only."

I paused before I lowered my voice. "My wife said you could use me in some capacity."

He sipped his wine and paused. "You sure you want to work in this industry?"

"I want my wife to stop working in the industry she's in now. Thanks for buying her a coat, but that was crossing the line. For me, as a married man, a fifty-two-hundred-dollar full-length fur coat was too much."

"I understand. But at that moment, I didn't know she was married. She told me after."

A moment went by. I was with a man who had seen my wife in a way only a husband should see his wife. My ego didn't feel good, not at all. But many men had seen my wife in the same way.

I said, "Now, Eddie Coyle, your turn. Before this gets too deep, tell me about yourself."

"Nothing to tell."

"There is always something. Besides, you know who I am. What's your birth name?"

"Eddie Coyle."

"I watch old movies."

"We have something in common."

"So you can do better. You could've at least called yourself Mr. Majestyk."

"Charles Bronson. He was damn good in that movie. The man had morals. But I'd have to say that I was more like Frank Renda. Only I have more self-control and common sense."

"So, Eddie Coyle, give me a better name or I take a walk."

He took a moment, then he said, "Lew."

"Lew what?"

"Lew Hunter. But that's all you get. But you can call me Eddie Coyle, like everyone else does. Just call me Eddie Coyle."

"You know my story, Eddie Coyle. You know where I live. And you know my wife."

"Fair is fair."

"Exactly. I'm at a bit of a disadvantage here. And I've always been a fair man."

"I was out of this aspect of the banking business for a while, for almost five years."

"What brought you back?"

"Well, I try not to talk about it because I'm not the kind of man who likes to complain when life has dealt him a bad hand, but I do think about my ruined home in Austell, Georgia. I was there in Austell for a while. But last summer we had about ten days of nonstop rain and Noonday Creek had swollen and closed highways down. That flood filled my house and destroyed everything I owned."

"Sorry to hear."

"I had battled my ex-wife and alimony and child support, but nothing took away as much as that damn flood. I almost drowned in my own truck. But I had broken free, fought a surging river in the downpour and darkness, and held on to a fallen tree, rode that tree until it hit ground two miles later."

"Sounds unbelievable."

"That was my Katrina. So pardon me if I sound bitter as I drink wine and relive the tragedy. All I owned was what I had on. The only money I had was inside my pockets. That act of God had wrecked my home and my life, had washed away my positive spirits. I'll never tithe again. That had turned out to be another bad investment. So, Dmytryk, that's part of my story. The part I'm recovering from."

"No wife?"

Eddie Coyle shook his head and smiled. "Not at the moment."

"I see."

"I'm on break. Women love you if you are willing to kill for them or die for them. If you're making a killing and bringing in money or somewhere working until you die, they love you to death, bury you, and move on to the next guy who is willing to kill for them or die for them. I'm taking a break from killing myself."

One of the televisions was on a live party in New York.

I said, "So, my wife says you need a driver."

He nodded. "I need another wheelman."

"To be up-front, as you either know or have guessed, I've never done anything like that before."

"Can you drive?"

"At times I drive my wife crazy. Been doing that for six years. So, yeah, I can drive."

"You have a sense of humor."

"At times. But it's esoteric, dark, and seldom appreciated."

"If you stay calm and drive, you can do it. That's what a wheelman does."

"And I take it to mean I don't have to go inside, but I would have a large responsibility."

"Outside of making the withdrawal, you would have the largest responsibility of us all."

I looked at the swank bar I was inside at the moment, at the five-star restaurant, looked up at the wall and took in the extensive collection of wines, then I stared at a lifestyle that had abandoned me, and then I looked at my callused hands.

"I read that the average take on a bank job is about four grand. That's not a lot."

"We do better. Most bank robbers work alone. We work as a team. Most use drugs or alcohol. We're clean. Most have never robbed a bank. We have experience. Most live near the bank they rob. We're not that stupid. Most escape on a bicycle or by foot. We're not that stupid. And making a grand a head is not enough to get me out of bed. We have inside information. We're not amateurs."

"Why not one big job?"

He smiled. "One day."

A moment went by.

I said, "I'm ready to work in the banking industry. I'm as ready as I'm ever going to be."

He downed the last of his wine, then looked at his watch before he stood up. "We're making a decent-sized withdrawal in the next seven to ten days. It won't be enough to make you the next Donald Trump, but if you're conservative, your cut will buy you and Cora some breathing room for a few months."

"My schedule is wide open." I stood, then grabbed my hat and coat. "But I have one condition."

"Which is?"

"The first fifty-two hundred I make, that goes back in your pockets. Cora is my wife. If anybody buys her a coat, even if it's a second-hand coat from the Goodwill, that's for me to do, not any other man. So, that money you spent to keep my wife from catching a cold, which I appreciate, will be considered a loan."

He nodded. "No hard feelings about yesterday or last night."

"Depends."

By then we were at the elevator. As soon as it opened we stepped on, but before the door closed we were interrupted by a swarm of inebriated, happy people who crowded onto the elevator, and that left over a dozen people standing shoulder-to-shoulder in a crowd of loudness and laughter, colognes and perfumes. I opened my pocket watch and found enough light to see that it was seconds before midnight. Hundreds of patrons were blowing party favors and singing "Auld Lang Syne." One woman was sloppy drunk and two men were holding her upright. She was giggling and putting her hands on both men in a way that let me know how her year would start. Outside, down by the bridges and across the waters, fireworks were going off. It was the start of a brand-new year in a bankrupt America.

I felt nothing. It was a new year and that meant absolutely nothing to me.

The descent from the seventy-second floor was both spectacular and nerve-racking. It was a descent that was as metaphorical as it was frightening. The view of Windsor kept my mind in a bad place.

I asked Eddie Coyle, "Did you engage in any form of sexual activity with my wife?"

"It was all business."

"Well, we live in a world where oral sex is the new good-night kiss."

"Everything with Trouble—Cora—everything with Cora was all business."

"Then no hard feelings."

He smiled and I smiled and we held eye contact while we shook hands.

He said, "This has been fun, but I have to get back to Rome now."

"When is the job opportunity?"

"The job is in a week, so I need you to meet me there in three days.

The crew will be there, so you need to come down and get the approval of the crew. Guys are named Rick and Sammy. We have a stage-two driver. I always use a woman for stage two. You'll meet her too."

"Roads should be wide open, so I'll drive down tomorrow."

"It's a long drive, especially in this weather. Snowing up top and raining down bottom."

"I can handle it. It's a little over seven hundred miles. Gives me time to think."

"One more thing."

"I'm listening."

"You wouldn't happen to know a good place to dump a body?"

When I made it home, Cora was sitting up on the bed, wearing her green and pink Life Is Good pajamas, waiting for me. She already knew how the meeting with Eddie Coyle had gone. I saw anxiety and optimism in her eyes. I stood in the doorway, my wet coat dripping water on the carpet. I was a changed man. In the soft lights inside our bedroom, she looked both young and innocent again, nothing like the woman I had seen at that club, nothing like the woman who had been consumed with hostility this morning. She looked like the woman I'd met when I was working on the line.

She whispered tentatively, "Happy New Year."

"Is it?" I'd almost told her I'd seen a man and woman murdered. I said, "Not for everyone."

She took a breath. "So we're in with Eddie Coyle?"

"I'm in with Eddie Coyle. You're done with Eddie Coyle."

"Dmytryk—"

"*Say it.*"

A moment passed before Cora said, "I'm done with Eddie Coyle."

"It's done," I snapped.

The room went quiet.

Cora looked like she was afraid of me. She looked at me like I was a monster.

I took a breath, swallowed, and softened my tone. "How are you holding up?"

"What happened to your suit pants? They're wet and ruined."

"I'm in business with Eddie Coyle. That's what you wanted, so the rocks come with the farm."

"What happened, Dmytryk?"

I said, "Cora, you have what you wanted. Let's leave it alone for now."

"What happened? You look . . . strange . . . what happened tonight?"

I paused for another moment, the images of death inside my head.

I asked, "Have I not been a good husband to you?"

"What?"

"Answer the damn question, Cora."

"Yes. You have your moments when you get frustrated, and you say things—"

"Same for you, Cora. Same for you."

She took a moment. "You've been a good husband. Yes."

I took another breath, struggled to clear my head.

Cora asked, "Are you okay?"

"No."

"What's wrong?"

"I'm sorry for the way I talked to you. I'm sorry for cursing at you. That's not the way a man should talk to his wife. That's not the way two people should communicate, even at times like this."

"I'm sorry for what I said too, Dmytryk. That wasn't me talking. It was the stress."

Gunshots echoed inside my ears. "So you're done at that gentlemen's club."

"I'm done."

"I want to make sure we're on the same page."

"You were right. I never should have worked there. It made things worse, not better."

"We'll get through this. We'll get to the other side of this, Cora."

"I know we will. I've been praying all day."

"How did that work out for you? Did it change anything?"

"I need you to forgive me too."

A long moment passed before I spoke again. "Where is the fur coat Eddie Coyle bought you?"

"Did you hear me?"

"What, Cora? Did I hear what?"

"I need you to forgive me too."

"I do forgive you."

"Do you?"

"If you've told me the truth, then I do forgive you."

When I went to the dresser to take off my cuff links and necktie, I looked in the mirror and saw my father staring back at me. Henrick used to wear classic and timeless three-button suits. He wore steel-toe boots from Monday until Saturday, but on Sunday he shaved and put on a crisp white shirt and dressed like the man he had wanted to be. My father shined when he dressed like a businessman. Classic, leather, handcrafted, lace-up shoes like the ones I had on were his style for our Presbyterian Sundays. My father didn't believe in superstitions, neither did he own the ability to praise what was intangible, but my mother owned those sensibilities, so we all sojourned as a family. Henrick ran the house, but Zibba read the Bible and made the rules. People respected people who went to church, and the churches were crowded. Some people went to socialize and some went mainly for the music, which was why the churches with the best choirs had the largest congregations. More than once my father told me that there were liars in the world and people were afraid to speak their truths. Not many mustered the courage to tell the truth and many never became who they were destined to be because they were too busy trying to emulate someone else.

He told me that there would be trials in life and a man is defined by how he reacts to his trials.

His trial had been inside a boxing ring, where a blow to the side of a man's head ended a life. He had become a boxer because that was his father's wish. So it goes. My father's gloved hand had killed a man and left that man's family without a husband or a father. A man had died for no reason. It was impossible for my father to comprehend a god who would allow a hardworking father to be the instrument of destruction against another innocent man. Despite what my father felt or didn't feel, on Sunday mornings he put on his suit and a crisp white shirt, laced up his wingtips and smiled as he led my mother and me to the family car, and then, if the radio was on, church music led us down our path.

I never asked my father to explain himself. No man should have to explain who he is. But what stuck with me all these years was his Sunday-morning ritual, seeing his face slathered with shaving cream. The minty smell of his shaving cream, the sound of the straight-edge razor against his stubbly chin. Zibba always prepared our suits on Saturday evenings; that was her way of telling us there would be church the next morning. And on Sunday mornings after my father was dressed, he always stood in the mirror, eased on his fedora, and smiled. He smiled at the reflection of the man he always wanted to become. Not a man with deep pockets or smooth hands, but a man whom other men respected.

He'd see me studying him, then his eyes would meet mine, and he would tender a small smile. He would adjust his necktie and look at me, his nose slightly crooked from the years of boxing, and once he was perfectly dressed he would nod twice. I'd nod twice in return. Message transmitted. Message received. Real men wore fedoras.

My wife came and stood behind me, wrapped her arms around me. "What are you thinking?"

"Nothing you need to know, Cora. Nothing you need to know."

"Tell me, Dmytryk."

"My mother was there for my dad. She washed his clothes and cooked his meals and cleaned our house and gave him a son and my father worked and put a roof over our heads and made sure food was on the table and did laundry and washed dishes and helped my mother cook and painted and repaired and fixed what needed to be fixed and my parents were there for each other from the start to the end and no one complained because it was a marriage from the heart and not just a marriage of convenience. They loved each other. Not fantasy love, not the crap that's in dime-store books and in movies, not the fantasy that Hollywood and television sells and no one can live up to, but they had a real love. They understood commitment and teamwork. Even if they didn't love each other that way at the start, they learned what love was about long before the end. We are supposed to fight together. We are supposed to starve together. And in the end we are supposed to come out the winners. That's what a marriage is about. Anybody can be married when things are easy. Anybody can be married when there is plenty of money."

"I'm still here."

"But I have to know you're going to stay here. I'm not going to be here alone."

"I'm your wife, Dmytryk."

"Are you? I mean, are you really? If you are, then I need you to start acting like you're my wife."

I'd seen two people killed and I was afraid. I was afraid of what I had seen and what I had become. It looked like she was getting choked up. It looked like she wanted to scream. Or cry. Either way, it looked like she finally felt my pain. I accepted that Pyrrhic victory, because that was all it was.

She kissed my neck and my face.

She whispered, "Come to bed. Let's start the year right."

I undressed and crawled into the bed; I lay on my back staring at the ceiling, a changed man. Cora came and snuggled up next to me, wrapped her body around mine, gave me her heat. She cuddled up next to me and ran her fingers up and down my skin, then she kissed my neck, my chin, eased her tongue inside my mouth, her hand moving between my legs. She whispered that she loved me. She told me that she would always love me. She said she was sorry for the things that she had said earlier.

I said, "You know I'd live underneath a bridge with you if I had to. I'd take two sticks and make a fire to keep you warm. You're my wife, Cora. You're my wife and I take that commitment seriously."

"I know, Dmytryk."

"But you're not the type of woman who would live underneath a bridge."

She laughed.

Cora pulled off my undershirt, ran her tongue down my chest, then tugged away my boxers. My wife positioned herself and took me inside her mouth and did her best to calm my frustrations. I held her hair, rubbed her face, released bits of anger, and moaned the start of my reluctant surrender.

I looked at her face and saw tears in her eyes. "Cora, what's the matter?"

"I see your pain. I see how deep it is. I see how much you love me, that's all."

"I'm doing what you asked. Right or wrong, I'm doing what I have to do."

She whispered, "You're going to go work with Eddie Coyle."

"That's what you wanted."

"I know. But—"

"It's too late for buts, Cora."

"Dmytryk—"

I shushed her. "It's done. I met him and . . . it's done."

She pulled her lips in. "Dmytryk—"

"Whatever happens, Cora, remember who made this night possible."

I touched her eyes, let her tears stain my fingers, then I licked my fingers, tasted her frustration.

She touched my eyes before she put her fingers in her mouth, tasted my salty frustration.

She whispered, "Baby, come be my husband."

"I've always been your husband. I was your husband before we ever married."

She climbed on top of me and whispered, "Then let me be your wife."

And while she did, all I could see was what the devil had done on the side of I-94.

She whispered, "Dmytryk?"

I closed my eyes so tight my headache spread from temple to temple.

She said, "I don't excite you anymore?"

I stopped her and pushed her away from me, unable to be a husband to her.

She asked, "What's wrong, Dmytryk?"

"Stop."

"Let me make you feel good, baby."

"An orgasm is not the answer. An orgasm is not the goddamn answer."

Silence covered us.

I said, "I never should have . . ."

She whispered, "What? You never should have what?"

"Nothing."

"Married me?"

That was when I told her what I had seen and done with her friend Eddie Coyle. It was too heavy to keep inside. There was no one else I could talk to about what I had seen, no one else I could tell. I wanted her to know the size of the sinkhole she had pulled us into.

Her voice trembled. "He's not my friend, Dmytryk."

"What is he then?"

"A fool with money."

Again I asked her where the fur coat was. She resigned, moved away from me, and put her back to me before she told me that she had hidden it underneath the bed. I pulled on pants and a sweater, pulled on shoes, and took that fur coat and dragged it into the backyard. She didn't fight me. She knew fighting me wasn't an ideal move. I doused the fur coat with low-grade gasoline, then I threw a match on that beast. The flame roared and threw heat in my face.

My wife was standing in the kitchen window, watching me.

She was angry. I didn't care. I felt violent, exiled from the life I deserved. Hostile toward the life I had at the moment, the new life my wife had coerced me into. My wife's hair was down and she looked like a riled vixen. Meeting with Eddie Coyle had changed my life and sealed my fate. Witnessing a murder, being part of a murder, then watching a woman being carried to the slaughter like she was an animal, that had made me nervous and careless.

I stepped to the side of the garage, stood there in the cold, feeling nauseated.

While the fur burned, I went back inside the house that had been my parents' dream home, the house I had taken a second mortgage on to keep us afloat, the house I refused to lose and for which I was willing to rob a bank to keep from sliding into that failure called foreclosure, and I took the hand of my wife, gripped her wrist as panic rose in her eyes, panic that caused her to yell and try to pull away. But there was no pulling away. I was willing to sell my soul to the devil to protect her, and I had sold my soul to a man named Eddie Coyle, and now, as she was still my wife, I took her back to our bed, the same bed we had made love in since the day we married, and I put her on her back, held her down, kissed her with fervor, and I entered her with anger and greed and passion. I entered her with an obsession and a love and jealousy from which I could not escape. I had expected her to fight me, but she welcomed me, wrapped her legs around my body, and put her fingernails deep into my skin while I held her backside and pulled her into me over and over. Tomorrow I might relive the moments spent on the side of I-94 and wake up screaming like a man trapped in nightmare alley, tomorrow I might have my first panic attack, but tonight my wife would comfort me in carnal ways. She moaned like she was falling, set free a spiraling moan that echoed like a damaged angel who had lost her wings and was plunging from the only heaven she knew.

Outside our window, that fur coat burned like it was the gateway to hell.

It felt as if that fire, that flaming demon, was inside of me.

That burning fur threw flames and created shadows on our bedroom wall, shadows that gave form to dark desires during a connection of love that had been tainted.

That coat burned like desire.

But no fire could burn forever. Even the brightest star, one day, would die.

*   *   *

I left the next afternoon and ten days later I was back home. I had seen two people murdered and I had gone in with Eddie Coyle and his friends and robbed a bank, then I'd driven back home and walked in the front door holding roses and chocolates like I was coming home from a corporate business trip. Robbing a bank, when it went as planned, was one of the easiest crimes. Eddie Coyle had been reimbursed and I had ten thousand dollars in nonsequential, unmarked bills inside a black bag. It wasn't a fortune, but it was money, and financial relief was what we needed to keep our world from crumbling. We had spread the ten thousand across the bed and stared at the money with nervous expressions. I convinced myself that my wife was right and what I had done wasn't wrong. The world had robbed us, and we were only responding in kind.

It was amazing the power money had over people. Its seduction was a force to be reckoned with.

The next job had left me with another twenty thousand. We kept to the necessities at first. I put some money into the Buick, brought it back to near-mint condition. We needed a reliable car, and buying a new car would raise flags, especially if we paid cash. Cora and I fell back into our normal routines. We woke up at dawn and searched for jobs during the week, clipped coupons on Friday, had dates on Saturdays, made love on Saturday nights, and held hands and went to church on Sundays. We always went to the first service. Church had always been her thing, not mine. She prayed and cried, but I could only imagine what she prayed for or what her tears meant. Guilt.

Shame. Anger. People around us thought those tears meant that she was closer to the CEO upstairs. But we had signed a contract with one of His former employees.

My wife wanted to go to Vancouver, so we went to Vancouver and stayed at the best hotel we could afford, came home for a week, found our world too gloomy, then we flew down to Nashville and spent another week at the Vanderbilt Hotel. We had shut out the world, had hidden from our problems, taken baths and laughed and made love and ate room service like a king and a queen.

My wife mounted me and while she moved and moaned she looked down on me. Her stare was unreadable. It was like staring in the face of a woman I'd never seen before.

It was like gazing into the eyes of extreme danger.

She whispered in a voice that was as sultry as it was dark, "Dmytryk."

"Yes, Cora?"

"Tell me about robbing banks."

"No. The less you know, the better."

"I'm your wife. I'm your confidante. Tell me."

"That excites you?"

"Yes, it excites me."

"I'll tell you when we're done."

"No, tell me now."

"Now?"

"Yes, baby. Tell me right now."

She rose and fell, moved against me, and I whispered the stories that Rick and Sammy had told me. Rick and Sammy had worked together all over the U.S.

My wife moved and shivered while I held her hips and moaned out my words.

She said, "Baby, I want to do it."

"Do what?"

"A job, baby. I want to pull my weight. I want to do a job."

"You want to be a wheelman?"

"I want to dress up, put on a business suit and shades, designer shades, then carry my attaché case and sashay inside and smile and tell them it's a stickup, tell them to not try anything funny, like they do in the movies you watch. I want to make them respect me and I want to feel the rush while they do."

"You're serious."

"We don't have to wait on Eddie Coyle."

"Cora."

"You need to be your own boss. You've spent your life working for other people. And I've done the same. And see where that has gotten us? Dmytryk, we could be a team . . . we could do everything together. Teach me what Eddie Coyle has taught you and we can be better than his crew."

"That fantasy can get you twenty years in jail."

"But you know how to do it. You can show me how to do it. We can do it together."

"Cora."

"Just think about it."

She leaned forward and kissed me for a while. My hand moved over her skin while we tasted each other. We stopped and she moved up and down until I moaned like I was dying a slow death.

She whispered, "God, I love making love to you."

"I love making love to you too."

"I was born to make love to you."

I moaned.

"Dmytryk."

"Cora."

"What if that . . . that day I said that I was in Detroit with Eddie Coyle, what if he had flown me down here to Nashville? What if I walked into a SunTrust bank in Nashville that afternoon? What if I had on a business dress and dark glasses? And what if I had a gun? What if I demanded money and they complied?"

"Did you?"

She asked, "If I had robbed a bank, would that excite you?"

My words caught in my throat. "Did you?"

"Would that excite you as much as knowing what you do excites me?"

"Cora."

"Yes."

"I'm coming. . . ."

My wife moaned, moved up and down, and I saw white lights, heard fallen angels singing.

Days turned into weeks and stolen money was spent. As the money ran low, the tension rose like water in a sealed room. Tension was fear with a softer name. We had gone downtown and parked, then walked along the Detroit River, the Ren Center behind us and Windsor on the other side.

Cora said, "Have you given any thought to it?"

"To what?"

"Us doing it together, without Eddie Coyle."

"My answer stands. You're not getting into the business."

"You like that, don't you?"

"Like what?"

"Telling me what I can and can't do."

"I'm doing what I stood in front of the minister and promised to do, protect you."

"You're controlling me, Dmytryk."

"Don't become one of them, Cora."

"One of who?"

I shook my head. "One of those women who are so busy trying to be a man that they have forgotten how to be a woman. One of those lost women. You can't have yours and claim mine. You can't have it all, then throw it away when you realize how hard it is on my side of the fence. Stay on your side of the fence, Cora. Be a woman. Be my wife. One day become the mother of our children. Be a woman and I'll be a man. We'll work together as a team. We'll make decisions as a team."

"You're controlling me, Dmytryk."

"If I am, then who or what is controlling me? Stop talking crazy."

"I'm not crazy."

"Maybe I was born forty years too late."

"Maybe you were."

"Maybe."

"All I know is this: I had a mother who had to do everything. My mother wasn't like your mother. You mother could afford to wait for your father to find solutions. My mother had to make things happen.

Your mother stayed at home and played housewife while mine worked three jobs at a time."

Not much was said after that, not until we had made it back home.

I said, "Cora?"

Her lips turned downward. "What, Dmytryk?"

"Maybe you should go back to school. It's time for you to think about going to college, start a new career. It'll give you something to do other than looking at these four walls."

"What good did going to college do you, Dmytryk?"

"That's not the point. You're smart. But you could do better. Then we would've had options. All you know is working the line. If I made it back to grad school, I could do better. We both could do better. That's the type of team we should focus on trying to be. If you had a degree in something, anything, you'd have options."

"Why are you always pushing college on me?"

"Why are you so comfortable being . . . never mind."

"No, say it."

"Let it go."

"Why am I so comfortable being ignorant? Is that what you were going to say?"

"Let's not go down that muddy road."

"When I was working the line and making money hand over fist, my education wasn't a problem."

She went to the wall and looked at my degree.

"Maybe it's you, Dmytryk." She shook her head and frowned. "Maybe you've been my bad luck."

"I guess you've been thinking that for a while."

"My life was fine before you came into my world. I was doing just fine."

"You haven't exactly been a pot of gold underneath a rainbow. If you were as ambitious about things legal as you are about things illegal, my luck would be better too. Yeah, if you see robbing banks as a good thing, then I guess I'm as rich as you are smart, so I guess we're a match made in heaven."

She pulled my framed diplomas off the wall and threw them across the room. She faced me and waited for an equal and opposite reaction. When there was none, she folded her arms, went inside the bedroom, and slammed the door. I walked out of the house before another argument erupted. I walked down Baylis Street. I walked down Normandy Street.

Shaking my head, I looked around. There weren't any penthouses or mansions. This was the zip code of the workingman, the steel-toed workingman who labored hard to send his kids to college. The workingman who worked long hours so the next generation would have a better chance. This was where I was born, had been the zip of my parents for four decades. Again I examined my callused hands, an oxymoron with the degree I had on the wall. There was nothing to be ashamed of. Nothing at all. I'd been part of the backbone of society. Without the workingman, there would be no castles, and there would be no kings.

I went back inside my house and stood in the bedroom door.

My wife was lying across the bed, the most beautiful woman I'd ever seen.

We had become prisoners trapped inside a shrinking jail and willing to do anything to get free.

I said, "One bank. That's our compromise. One bank."

She sat up and gave me a nervous-yet-excited half smile. "When can we do it?"

"We'll have to find a bank that's at least one state and ten to twelve hours from here. We can drive that long without having to stop for anything but gas. We can't chance walking in and seeing someone we went to high school with working as a security guard or as a teller. We'll have to pay cash for everything along the way. And if the weather's bad, we'll have to sleep in the car. That's how it goes. It's not pretty and it's not first-class. Don't forget what happens if it goes wrong, Cora."

"How much do you think we can get?"

"We won't know until we have it."

"When can we leave?"

I took a deep breath. "After we have a plan. We'll need a stolen car on the other end."

"Outside of a wig and a note, how much of a plan do you need to rob a bank?"

"This isn't a game. You need an exit strategy."

"If you can do it, how hard can it be?"

Once again, she challenged me, put a sharp blade inside my ego and turned it slowly. My hands opened and closed. I smiled an angry smile and let that insult go by unanswered. It had gotten to the point that whenever I asked a question, or whenever she yielded an answer, all words seemed like an attack. Six years after I had taken my vows, I realized the type of woman I loved and had married.

She said, "When we leave, let's just keep going and never come back."

"I can't do that. We can't do that."

"Why?"

"We live here."

She fell quiet for a while. "Let's go in the kitchen and talk about finding a bank."

Weeks later, Eddie Coyle called again. There was another job. I wanted to pass on it, but I was already in too deep. I had become a team player, habit from working in corporate America, habit from working in the union, habit from playing sports. Eddie Coyle didn't have to hold that gun over my head or remind me of that night we'd stood on the side of I-94 with the Uniroyal tire at our backs. I needed what he offered because the money was running low and my marriage was once again coming apart at the vows. Trips to Vancouver and Nashville and staying at the Townsend and paying bills and stress shopping had been like a quick trip around the Monopoly board, but there was only one way to collect another bonus for passing Go.

Eddie Coyle.

It felt as if the world had nailed me to a financial cross and he had become my savior.

Every time I left Detroit, every time I walked through the door, it felt like it might be the last time I saw the Motor City. Or Cora. That was why I kissed my wife the way I did, with a combination of love and fear. I knew right from wrong. But I had become swept up in the current and quick profits that came from wrongdoing. Part of me lived on the high, and another part of me reminded me of the inevitable. I'd told Cora that if I was caught, she was to disavow any knowledge and not say anything that would cause her to be incarcerated as well. The same if I was killed along the way.

In my mind I was being a man, protecting the kingdom and the queen, while the queen risked nothing in return.

At times I felt like a king was nothing more than a slave with benefits.

Responsibility was only a euphemism for the burdens of man.

Then there was the job in Pasadena, Texas, the job that changed everything. I packed my duffel bag and kissed my wife good-bye, hugged her and looked in her eyes and told her everything would be okay, then left and came back two weeks later with another fifteen thousand.

When I returned from Pasadena, when I entered my house carrying roses and chocolates, I walked inside a home that reeked of cruelty. It felt as if I had been robbed, but at first glance I couldn't tell what had been stolen. The television was there and the furniture remained, but I rushed from room to room calling out for my wife, terrified that someone had broken in and attacked her, afraid I'd find her body beaten, bloodied, violated, and without life, until the truth grabbed me and shook me. I opened her closets and saw they were all barren. Cora had packed everything she owned and left. I stood in front of an empty closet like a mourner standing in front of a casket. Fear changed to panic and I searched our bedroom, took my dread from room to room, saw all of her belongings had been removed from the home. The carpet had been vacuumed and the bed left made. The house was so clean it looked like a model home. Everything I owned was in its place, as if she had never lived there.

A yellow Post-it was left on the side of the bed, placed on the pillow where she used to sleep. I already knew that it wasn't a billet-doux. The days of Cora writing me love letters had come and gone.

The note told me not to look for her. She wanted her freedom. She wanted a new life.

She'd had enough of being married.

I'd never tell anyone she left a note. She was gone. That was all anyone needed to know.

I'd lost my parents. I had been shoved out of my white-collar career and I had been severed from my blue-collar job. Now I had lost my wife. I wondered how many times a man could die in one lifetime.

I was okay. For a few moments I was okay. For a few moments I felt as if a burden had been lifted. For a few moments I felt free. I went to the bathroom and emptied my bladder, then as I walked back into the living room, I saw what she had left behind. Our wedding photo stared at me from the wall. I pulled it from the wall and sent it flying across the room, wanted it to break into a thousand lies. The fifteen thousand dollars I had brought home, I pulled it from my pockets, threw it all at an unseen foe.

Moments later, I sat at the kitchen table and laughed until I came unglued. I laughed until my laughter changed to screams and howls of frustration. When madness had abated, I cleaned up my home, the home that my parents had lived in and loved in for decades, picked up the glass and put the picture from our wedding back on the mantel above the fireplace, and for the first time in six years, I took out pots and pans and cooked dinner for one.

10

Death. Lies. Debt. Deception.

Those demons danced inside my mind as pain enveloped me.

I coughed, tasted blood, then coughed for a few more moments.

"You're in pain? Good, so now you know how I feel on the inside."

The windshield wipers on my Wildcat worked overtime as I struggled to flee east on I-10. The wipers battled to throw water from the glass the same way I fought to throw memories from the surface of my mind. Another sharp pain hit and for a moment it was hard to keep my car between the white lines. Global warming had sent snow to most of the fifty states, as well as dumped an inch of rain on the frigid desert, and with the drop in temperature there was enough chill for me to continue running the heater on low. Joshua Tree National Park and Eagle Mountain were north, but El Centro and Calexico were south, maybe an hour away. Part of me wanted to drive in that direction, run from my problems before they caught up with me, cross into Mexicali, and find a hideout in Xochimilco or Lázaro Cárdenas.

"All I wanted to do was kill you."

"I saved your life." I coughed again. "I saved your damn life."

Eighteen-wheelers passed me and threw gallons of water across my windshield. When visibility was better, I looked up and expected to see helicopters circling in the dismal sky. Expected to see a cavalry of cars following me like in the final moments of the movie *Thelma and Louise*. They weren't there. Nothing was up there but rain clouds hovering and spitting rain down on my paranoia.

Jackie moved around in the backseat, shifted and moaned.

The pain remained and outside of making me feel loopy, the Vicodin wasn't helping much.

A car passed by and I swear I saw Sammy riding in the backseat. The car changed lanes and exited the freeway, and Sammy looked back at me.

I rubbed my eyes. I'd seen Sammy twice in the last three hours.

Jackie moaned again just as I cruised into downtown Phoenix. Bank headquarters, law firms, and government buildings greeted me as I moved through five lanes of morning traffic, cars filled with men and women chasing a dream that only a few would ever catch. First I heard Jackie's breathing change from smooth to heavy, then I heard her moving around in the backseat. She was waking up. She coughed. Then her hand reached up and she grabbed the back of the passenger seat. She struggled to find her center of gravity and sit upright. What I saw rising in my rearview mirror was like something from a Japanese horror film.

I adjusted my fedora and hoped Jackie couldn't get a good look at my bruised face.

"I don't care about your father's fedora."

I whispered, "I do. You might not care, but I do."

Jackie asked, "Who are you talking to?"

I said, "Go back to sleep."

She sat back and licked around inside her mouth. Static took over the airwaves and I changed the radio and stopped at a religious station. I wasn't listening, just hoped that Jackie would think I was in tune with the preacher and not talk for the next sixteen hundred miles.

I liked her better when she slept.

She shook her head. "Change the station. I hate waking up to the voice of idiots."

"Good morning to you too."

"Change the station."

She cringed, then sat back and looked out the window, watched the world go by at sixty miles per hour. She was hungover. It looked like she was reading the interstate signs, trying to figure out where we were. I changed the station on the radio, landed on a conservative talk show, and let it play.

Jackie cleared her throat. "I'm thirsty and I have to use the bathroom, but not in that order."

"Once we clear Phoenix, I'll find a gas station."

"At a hotel. Not a 7-Eleven and not a truck stop. Those bathrooms are disgusting."

"You'll have to go inside the hotel and rent the room."

She ran her fingers through her hair. "I guess I should be embarrassed."

"How much do you remember?"

She whispered, "Sammy is dead."

I let a moment pass. "What do you remember about last night?"

She paused. "I loaned you most of my money."

"You loaned me some money, yeah."

"I was drunk and loaned you four thousand dollars."

"Yeah."

"Look, I need that money back and I want it back right now."

"Sorry, Jackie. I don't have the money, not anymore."

"What do you mean you don't have my money?"

"It's gone. The money is gone."

"How can it be gone? I just loaned it to you. You have to have it."

"As we agreed, I'll pay you when we finish with Eddie Coyle."

"That money is for my kid, Dmytryk. I'll kill you if you screw me over."

"Well, Jackie, you've already tried to screw me and kill me, but not in that order."

"I'm serious. Make your jokes at my expense, but I'm serious."

"I know you will, Jackie. I know you'll go shopping for old carpet and a new gun."

"Eddie Coyle has used a lot of carpet and I'm not afraid to do the same."

When I crossed into the Phoenix/Chandler area, hotels were lined up on the right side and I exited I-10. Jackie wanted to rent a room at the Holiday Inn Express. I parked out front and stood off to the side while Jackie rented a room. She had straightened herself up the best she could, but she still looked like a shapely hooker who had a very bad evening and worse skin. It hurt me to stand up straight, so I guessed that I looked like an ailing businessman who was the next customer on her sexual merry-go-round. It was early morning in Arizona and a dozen families were down for the free high-cholesterol buffet the hotel offered. Most of the faces were Native Americans. Peaceful families and their children. By the time Jackie had the card-key to her room, I had pulled a self-serve cart up and fought my pain and loaded her bag. I was in too much agony to carry the bag more than ten feet. Driving wasn't a problem, not as long as I was sitting in one position and going in a straight line and not changing lanes too often. That was constant pain that I could handle. Jackie led the way and we checked into a second-floor room that had yellow walls, abstract art, and a Philips Magnavox television.

Jackie said, "I got drunk and passed out and slept in my makeup."

The agony came in waves. I took a step and stumbled.

Jackie came closer and looked me up and down. "What happened to you?"

My body betrayed me and revealed that I was in pain, severe pain, but I tried to not let the extent of my misery show, not to Jackie. She would kill me and dump me on the side of the road if she knew.

She said, "Did you get into a fight?"

I took my fedora off and tossed it on the bed. "Don't worry about it."

"Did you get robbed?"

"I don't have your money, so you can stop asking about it, okay?"

"Somebody took the money I loaned you?"

"Go get cleaned up. You smell. Get cleaned up and get some rest."

She took her carry-on and rushed inside the bathroom. The weather report was on. It was minus 3 degrees in Memphis, minus 33 in Bismarck, and minus 1 in Atlanta with a hundred accidents. Detroit's temperature was at 12 degrees. That was twenty degrees below freezing. No one was at my home. It had been left on its own. Abandoned.

I hoped the pipes at the house hadn't frozen or burst. But a burning in my gut and another shot of pain told me that busted pipes in an old house were the least of my worries. I tossed my keys on the desk, then went to the window and grimaced out at rain and 38-degree weather. There was a row of eighteen-wheelers underneath my window. A La Quinta hotel was next door, beyond the parking lot and the sparkling waters in the swimming pool. Mountains were in the distance, beautiful mountains that outlined the edges of the Sonoran Desert, nature as beautiful as the line of palm trees.

I grabbed my fedora and picked up the keys to the Buick again. My pain-filled strides took me through the lobby, past a line of Native Americans, and out into the brisk air that helped cool the sweat on my skin. I went to the Buick, started it up, and drove around to the back of the hotel. I crawled out and opened the trunk, then stood there for a few moments, looking at traffic passing by on I-10, looking at people leaving the hotel and loading up their family vans and trucks. It felt as if I were underwater. When the parking lot was clear, I summoned my strength and tugged out Sammy's and Rick's bags. It took all of my power, but I growled and pushed them inside a green Dumpster. Rick's bag busted open and a thick green Bible tumbled out. I tried to adjust it, but I made it worse and other things, maps and papers, fell out. The maps were of the streets in some part of Alabama. There were schematics for two, maybe three buildings as well. One large building and several small ones. The other papers were programs. A Bible and church programs. I guess I didn't know Rick. Maybe that was what he was going to tell me. He'd turned religious and wanted out before it was too late. Without looking the programs over, I collected everything and threw it all into the Dumpster. It had been too much. I was not in any condition to labor and my mind wasn't in gear, so I was unable to process the maps I had disposed of. I moved at a pace a baby's crawl could beat. Again I coughed and tasted blood in my saliva. I stood still until I could handle the pain.

At the mouth of the entrance of the hotel, my world began to spin like a top. Still I pressed on. I needed to get back to the room and fall across the bed.

I staggered into the lobby and stood surrounded by convivial brown-skinned Native Americans. A wave of agony battered me, its tide as high as a tsunami, and I fought a battle I couldn't win. My world went dark and I collapsed on the floor as a beautiful woman screamed.

Wrapped in darkness, I was plummeting from the seventy-second floor of the Ren Center, but I was close to consciousness, trapped with my bloodshot eyes halfway open, neither here nor there. Both worlds were out of focus. Jackie's voice surrounded me, her rapid words strong yet inaudible.

The Ren Center and the Detroit River and Windsor faded away and the descent ended.

At first I thought I was inside a hospital or had been arrested and was surrounded by police officers, but I was inside the hotel room, no police officers or FBI in sight. I heard a fight. It wasn't a physical fight, but the slamming of the bathroom door was like a gun going off. Grogginess held on to me, pulled me like the undertow of a mighty river, but I heard Jackie arguing and I fought my way through twelve layers of darkness, headed for her voice. It was a fight to wake up, a battle to get free from whatever was weighing me down, but I snapped to when she raised her voice and said my name, said that I had passed out and now she was freaking out because she couldn't wake me up, said she couldn't leave me in Arizona, said she wanted to but she couldn't. I heard her say that I owed her over five thousand and there were no other options, then she said the name Eddie Coyle over and over, asked why he invited me on the job in the first place. She snapped that she knew Sammy was dead. She said things about Rick and Sammy, said things about Bishop. It all felt like a bad dream.

Then I thought I heard a name that pulled me from the edges of dreamland and startled me back into this murky world. Cora. I thought I heard the name Cora. Jackie was inside the bathroom and her voice echoed. I had been dumped on the queen-size bed, had been left on my back, my white undershirt pulled off and the covers pulled up to my waist. The curtains were drawn, but there was enough light for me to look down and see the dark bruises on my arm and across my abdomen. Jackie's argument died down. It didn't end, but it lowered until her words were nothing more than inaudible mumbles. I heard water running in the bathroom and heard Jackie's voice and looked around. Her luggage was near the door, like she was ready to leave this town. My suit was draped on the back of an armchair, my shoes on the floor.

Jackie hurried out of the bathroom. Her hair was pulled back into a ponytail and she had a plain black baseball cap on her head. Her dress was gone and she had on blue jeans and pink Reeboks and a black sweater. Her jeans hugged her frame, and her complexion—with the makeup—was tolerable.

I said Jackie's name and she jumped like she had been shot.

She caught her breath, saw me sitting up, and said, "You're still alive? That's disappointing."

It took me a moment to find my voice. "You were talking to Eddie Coyle."

"Was. Yeah. He wanted to see where we were."

"Sounded like there was a problem. What's wrong?"

"It's nothing. Nothing is wrong, but it's something I wasn't aware of until now. Sammy and Rick were aware, but I had been left in the dark. Everything is on schedule with the job."

"Cora."

Jackie paused. "What about her?"

"While you were on the phone, it sounded like you said my wife's name."

"You're delirious. You must've been screwing her in your dreams. Or getting screwed by her."

"Well, I know that I heard you say my name."

"What were you doing, eavesdropping?"

I said, "You look nervous."

"My boyfriend was killed robbing a bank, one of his incompetent partners might still be alive and turning snitch, his other incompetent partner took my money and now he's having blackouts, and my skin is breaking out, and I'm tired of the legal system and planning a kidnapping, planning to rob another bank in a few days, I'm planning on getting a new identity, so pardon me if I look preoccupied and nervous."

"Not that kind of nervous. Something else on top of that. Seeing me awake scared you."

"And you look as drugged as a crackhead. You friggin' passed out in the damn lobby."

"Lower your voice. I'm okay now, I'm okay. I had to . . . my body had to adjust . . . that's all."

"Were you on something yesterday morning? Is that what happened? You fell asleep on the job and you cost Sammy his life? Is that what happened, Dmytryk? You've been doing drugs?"

"No, Jackie. And please, stop engaging in this insane revisionist history."

"I thought you had dropped dead, you idiot. Maybe you should skip the job in Atlanta. It would be for the best, the best thing you could do for everybody at this point. Just go back to Detroit."

"Why? Because the Wells Fargo job went to hell?"

"*Look in the mirror.* You're in bad shape. This job with Eddie Coyle, it might not be for the best."

"I owe you four plus interest."

"You owe me five thousand two hundred dollars."

"Well, if I'm not in on the job, only God knows when I'll have the money to pay you. It might be months before Eddie Coyle calls with another job. You know that. That's the way it is, Jackie. If you want to call Eddie Coyle and get me pulled off the job, go ahead. Just remember that you'll be putting the money I owe you on indefinite hold. And if that happens I will pay you what I owe you, but I'm not paying any additional interest."

She nodded and looked like she wanted to say something but didn't.

She said, "I need my money. I need you on that job no matter what."

A moment passed with her looking as if she were filled with insurmountable stress.

I asked, "What happened with Eddie Coyle? Why did my name keep coming up?"

"That's for you and Eddie Coyle to talk about. I'm in this for one friggin' reason and it isn't for the joyride. You've been professional no matter what, so let's keep it that way, no matter what."

I pulled the covers back and looked at the bruises on my left leg, then I pulled the covers back up.

Jackie watched me. "I've already seen it. I saw your body. Somebody beat you up real good."

I nodded. "You undressed me and then we had sex."

"Don't joke with me. Not at a time like this."

"Come get on the bed with me, Jackie. Maybe I can help calm you down."

"You're joking, right? Sammy died yesterday and you're coming on to me?"

"I'm lightheaded and feeling good."

"Don't come on to me. Respect me."

"Here's your chance. I saw the way you looked at me when you were with Sammy."

She walked away shaking her head.

I said, "I guess you're sober."

"Go to hell."

"And I see you didn't shoot the television."

"Go straight to hell."

My wallet, pocket watch, fedora, cuff links, change, and personal effects were on the dresser.

I said, "You went through my pants pockets."

"I sure did. And I went through your car. You don't have the money I loaned you."

"I told you that."

"You have bruises like you've been beaten in a hate crime. When did that happen?"

"No one asked you to undress me."

"It had to happen between when we left the safe house and when I woke up in the car."

"Shut your mouth for a while, Jackie."

"You're in bad shape, but we have to leave. You've been unconscious for over six hours." She took a breath. "Get dressed. I can drive. We can make it as far as Fort Worth before we stop to rest. That's another twelve hours from here. That's as far as I'll go. It's time to get out of Arizona. But I'm going to catch a plane from Dallas to Atlanta. I'm not riding in an old car for two days. Not with you."

"You're suffering from a hangover."

"Was. I'm fine now. And we need to leave this hotel and get out of Phoenix as soon as possible."

Jackie dropped my wingtips at the side of the bed, then picked up my suit pants and threw them to me. After I pulled on my pants and shoes, she tossed me my white shirt. When I had pulled it on, she grabbed my coat and held it upside down. A bottle of pills fell out of the inside pocket. I wanted to stop her from picking up the pills, but I wasn't in any shape to do much more than groan.

"Are you serious?" She read the label on the pills. "You were popping Vicodin and driving?"

"That's not yours. Give me the medicine, Jackie."

"You're medicated? You're driving and you're high as a kite? That's what has you dizzy. You could've friggin' killed me, you moron. Vicodin is the devil's medicine."

"Just give me the damn bottle before I get up—"

"This isn't your wife's name. This is an L.A. prescription. With an L.A. address."

"Hand it over, Jackie."

"Abbey Rose? Who is Abbey Rose? What kind of last name is Brandstätter-Hess?"

I shook my head. "Nobody."

"Were you in contact with someone in L.A.? Did you jeopardize the job in any way?"

"They were gunned down coming out of the damn bank, Jackie."

"If I find out the Wells Fargo job was your fault, Dmytryk, I swear to God, I'll come see you."

I struggled to my feet and she threw the bottle and it hit me on my chin. It took me a moment but I bent over and picked up the bottle. Jackie went and stood in the window, arms folded, the stance of anger and irritation. She turned and headed for the door, grabbed her luggage, then looked back at me.

She said, "Your old car is leaving in fifteen minutes, whether you're inside it or not. The rain is still coming down, but it's going to get worse and there is going to be snow all across the South in the next few days, so we need to get to the other side of Dallas, at least to Fort Worth, before we're trapped in ice. Fifteen minutes. Try me and see if I'm serious."

"Jackie, I might owe you a lot of money, but be careful how you talk to me. Be careful."

She snarled. "Fifteen minutes. Not one second longer."

"If you drive off in my car, you better head to South America."

"You should be dead, not Sammy."

"Find a new song to sing because that one has gotten too much airplay."

"Fort Worth is as far as I'll go with you, you drugged-up, incompetent moron."

"Well, if the courts have taken your kid, I'd guess they found you just as incompetent."

She cursed me. I ignored her.

The door slammed behind her. Before she could walk away her cellular rang again. Jackie stopped where she was, right on the other side of the door, and answered. I thought it was Eddie Coyle calling her again, but her voice changed, switched from an unyielding tone that was both harsh and distended with anger and became the soft and tender tone of a mother who desperately missed her child.

We had that pain in common. She missed her child the way I missed my wife.

I looked across the room and focused on my fedora.

11

Jackie drove fourteen hours and didn't slow down until she made it to Fort Worth. By then it was three in the morning, and Dallas was less than an hour away, but she was exhausted. We saw a row of hotels from the interstate and Jackie exited and took to the edges of the city nicknamed both Cowtown and Where the West Begins. Driving a car that didn't have cruise control took a lot more energy than people realized, but Jackie had pressed on through the darkness while I had done my best to sleep and stay comfortable in the backseat.

Fort Worth was quiet. Being on Vicodin made the world seem like heaven.

While I stood in the arctic wind and grabbed our luggage, she checked into a room at the Hyatt Place at Cityview, a well-lit area off I-20 that was filed with restaurants, hotels, and at least a hundred places to go shopping. The roads were clear at that time of the morning, but the temperature was right at twenty degrees and the wind made it feel like it was below zero, so the city was frozen.

The nerdy man working the front desk told us that a heavy snowstorm was scheduled to hit the Dallas/Fort Worth area in twenty-four to forty-eight hours. The windows in all of the cars in the parking lot were frosted. Ice was forming on most of the bumpers. As soon as we walked inside the room, I found the thermostat and turned the heat up while Jackie turned the television on just in time to catch a recap of the local news. Her timing was either bad or it was perfect. The news reported that bank robberies were on the rise. There were a lot of John Dillingers, but the money they stole would never match the fortunes stolen by Bernie Madoff, Allen Stanford, or Hopkins. The news held our attention when they reported the FBI had arrested a bank robber. She was a local mother of five kids who had robbed at least four banks while wielding a gun and wearing a hoodie.

I said, "The financial crisis pushed somebody's mother over the edge."

"And I'm right behind her."

The next story was about a cross-dressing bank robber in Jennings, Missouri.

Jackie headed for the shower, shaking her head. "What is the world coming to?"

"Lots of competition out there. Lots of competition."

"Kill that noise before I get my gun."

I turned the television off and collapsed across the bed.

A lot of people had been pushed over the edge. Less than a month ago I'd gone to the funeral of Anthony Baldacci, a man I'd worked with when I was living in a white-collar world. He'd been out of work longer than he could bear. He'd tossed a rope over a beam in his basement, made a noose that fitted his neck, and stepped up on a wooden chair. People said that he had killed himself out of selfishness, but I know what it's like to wake up every day to diminishing options, and I understood why he had made that terrible choice. He had lost his job and he had lost his self-worth. He killed himself because of his inability to regain his crown as the financial leader of his family. He'd lost his job and lost his place in the world and put a rope around his neck, kicked away a chair, danced his last dance, and went to meet Jesus.

I'd thought about doing that more than once.

But I'd like to think that I was stronger than my pain.

That's what I thought about as Jackie showered.

I was glad that Cora and I didn't have any kids.

Our obligations would have had a different weight if we had.

Knowing my wife loved me had kept me sane.

Still, I'd walked out of that funeral home sad, angry, and afraid.

We lived in tough times.

Those were the thoughts I had as I closed my eyes and drifted toward a thin, restless sleep. I was in too much pain and too anxious to fall into a deep slumber.

I woke up when Jackie crawled in the bed. I set free a grunt of pain, put my feet on the floor, then I staggered a foot or two before I headed for the sofa in the front part of the suite. Another grunt of pain came from me as I sat down and touched parts of my swollen face.

Jackie asked, "Are you okay?"

"Not really. My face. It's still burning a little."

"Burning?"

"From the car accident. The air bag."

"I guess we're both having skin issues."

"I guess so."

"What did you put on the burn?"

"Nothing yet. We've had bigger problems than burns on my face."

Jackie eased back out of the bed and came over to me. She clicked on the lamp at the end of the sofa and sat next to me. She had on panties and a bra, nothing else.

"Why are you being nice to me?"

"I am concerned about something, Dmytryk."

"It's just me and you. You don't have to keep saying my name."

She said, "Abbey Rose Brandstätter-Hess."

"So what?"

"Who is she? I want to know who she is."

"Let it go, Jackie."

"Maybe I'll ask Bishop to find out."

"Ask and you'll lose the money I owe you. That will cost you every dime."

Jackie smiled. "So, I'm sitting on top of a nerve."

I returned the same falseness.

"You're looking bad, Dmytryk."

"Just when I thought I looked like a movie star."

"With that busted nose, split lip, and chafed skin, you look like the bad guy in a horror film." Jackie paused a moment. "You did pretty good with the gun. Nerves of steel."

She was measuring me. She was trying to put two and two together.

I paused. "That was my first time being in that situation."

"I thought everybody from Detroit had killed at least one person."

"Not everyone. Just the politicians."

"First kill and you didn't throw up. Most people freak out or throw up after their first kill. But I almost forgot. You were with Eddie Coyle when he killed Joe."

"Joe?"

"Joe Holden. The other wheelman. Guy from Nome, Alaska."

"I didn't get an introduction."

"And Rebecca. That was Joe's wife."

"Bishop shot the woman. I never saw her face. But Bishop shot the woman."

"You did good in L.A."

"L.A. is behind us now."

"Maybe. Maybe not."

"It's done. So it's behind us."

"You shot that woman in the black BMW. You pulled the trigger, killed her as she sat in her SUV, and kept it moving. What was her name? Any idea?"

"I didn't ask."

"You didn't ask her name?"

"It wasn't the time to sit down and sip tea and make small talk." I took a breath and maintained eye contact with Jackie. "Everything went wrong back there. Now we're back on track. I don't look forward to having to do anything like that again."

"Gunning somebody down is fun."

"Not for me."

She chuckled. "The man with big balls has no balls."

"I have balls."

"I bet you do. I bet you have real big balls."

"Jackie."

"I'm sorry, that was inappropriate. I'm . . . was used to joking like that with Sammy."

"Understood."

"So, the woman in the black BMW—"

"I killed the woman back in L.A. I killed her and I don't want to talk about it."

Jackie backed down.

"Your face got it real bad." She smiled a little. "Hold on for a second."

She swayed across the room and reached inside her oversize purse, pulled something out, then sashayed back with a small tube of some sort of clear gel.

I asked, "What's that?"

She sat next to me before she opened the container and put two fingers in, then Jackie rubbed her fingers across my cheeks.

She said, "Aloe vera. Should help with the burns."

"Thanks."

"Whatever."

"Yeah. Whatever."

When she was finished, she went back to her side of the room and eased back in the bed.

I reclined on the sofa.

"Dmytryk."

"Yeah."

"The bed is big enough for both of us."

"You sure?"

"Just stay on your side." She moved to the far left side. "You're in enough pain."

I eased off the sofa and went to the right side of the bed. I took off my suit pants and shirt, felt my wounds, and wondered how much Jackie knew. I wondered if she was asking me about being an assassin because she knew what I had done. I pulled off my socks and slid underneath the covers.

Jackie was already in a deep sleep.

Not long after, I went to sleep too.

It had been six months since I was in the same bed with a woman.

My side of the bed was on the right. I moved close to the edge and went to sleep craving my wife. But when I woke up I was in the center of the bed, the way I had grown used to sleeping on my bed at home after Cora had left. I had cuddled next to Jackie, her warm body up against mine. My fingers traced her skin, then she captured my hand. I thought she was about to move my hand away, but she brought my hand up to her breast. I rubbed her nipples and squeezed her breast, then adjusted, found myself wanting to kiss her neck, her shoulders, and I did, I kissed her until she turned and kissed me back. She kissed me like I was her husband and I closed my eyes and kissed her like she was my wife. I rubbed her and kissed her and felt her and she kissed me and rubbed me and felt me.

It became too hot, and I eased away from her.

She whispered, "Dmytryk."

"I'm sorry."

"No. That felt good."

"It felt good to me too."

"Put your arm around me again."

"Are you okay?"

"No. I'm not okay. But what you were doing, that made me forget all the bad things in my life."

I moved back and put my body next to hers. Jackie moved back into me and made herself comfortable. A moment later she turned and faced me, put her hand on my cheek.

She asked, "Your face feel better?"

"It's calmed down. Thanks."

Without warning she kissed me again. It was a soft kiss, but it was direct. Her lips felt good and I closed my eyes. It was the kind of kiss that reminded me that it had been too long since I had been intimate. She pulled me closer and she put my hand where she was the softest. Then she touched me where I was becoming the hardest. Some need inside me came alive and I became voracious, put my hand inside her hair, and pulled her face to mine, kissed her while she massaged me.

"You liked it."

"Liked what?"

"You were standing in the door frame watching Sammy and me make love yesterday morning. You wanted to be where Sammy was. You wanted to be Sammy."

"Believe what you want."

"Don't lie, you pervert. You like the way that feels? When I do that, you like that?"

"I do."

"Help me get through the night. Come here and help me grieve for Sammy." Her voice was heated and lined with a sensual pain. "Come give me what I need and I'll give you what your wife stopped giving you. You can close your eyes and pretend I'm her, if that helps you any. You can call me her name too."

"Don't mention my wife."

"I was just saying that if it helped your fantasy, you could call me Cora if you wanted to."

I paused. "Don't say her name. Not now. Not right now."

Jackie kissed me again, kissed my face, sucked my neck, and massaged me.

I asked, "Where are we going with this?"

"I think you know."

Jackie reached inside her purse and proffered me a condom that had been bought for Sammy's pleasures. Holding a condom that had been meant for another man felt blasphemous. Jackie removed her lacy bra. Then she took off her dark, lacy thong. I started to speak but she kissed me again, her soft tongue snaking deep inside my mouth. She kissed me and held the firmness and frustration that came from six months of sexlessness in her hand. It seemed like forever went by before I stopped kissing her. I didn't know how to stop kissing her. I didn't want to stop kissing her. Not because it was so good, but because I knew what came next. Adultery, the most common sin, was sucking my tongue and pulling away my clothing.

I said, "We'd better stop."

"You have values in a world that has no values. You, my friend, are a serious minority."

"You were with Sammy yesterday."

"You're right. You're right. This is wrong."

"On many levels."

She caught her breath. "One of us should go sleep on the sofa."

"Okay. I will."

"But not right now. Hold me for one more minute."

Jackie's body felt good against mine, regardless of whose mistress she was. She felt too damn good. But I pulled away and sat on the edge of the bed.

I asked, "How did you end up here, Jackie?"

She whispered, "Get back in bed and hold me for a while."

It took a moment, but I did what she asked. I snuggled up close, wrapped around her body. It had been a long time since I had held a woman. Holding her felt wrong, but it also felt good.

She said, "Sometimes I feel so alone in this world. Sometimes I feel so damn alone."

"Same here."

"You asked me how I ended up here." A moment later Jackie said, "I guess if I was like my mother, then my life would've been better."

"What do you mean?"

"Nothing. I don't like telling my business."

"It's up to you. But I won't repeat it, if that's your concern."

"My mother has two MBAs and a Ph.D. She's a professor. My father is equally educated. So, in their eyes, I'm the slacker in the family. I've always been the outcast. I went into the military, maybe to spite them, married a man they hated, again to spite them. They'd never send a dime to help me. They cut me off when I didn't go to college. Then they disinherited me when I married the loser I married. But the big thing for them was college. No college, no trust fund and you're on your own. My birth name was Cholita Gonzalez de Lupo. But I changed it to Jackie Brown after high school, right before I joined the military. I took the name from the movie that had Pam Grier in it. I loved *Jackie Brown*."

"Why not just go back home?"

"I'm dead to them. No contact in the last eight years. Not even a text message or e-mail."

"My wife was the same way with her family."

"Sorry to hear that."

"Such is life."

I pulled away from her heat and sat up, but she took my hand and pulled me back to her.

She said, "Come back and hold me again."

I held her. She rubbed her body up against me. I became excited. I rubbed her skin. She moaned. I kissed her skin and she pulled me closer. She kissed my hand, sucked my fingers. Then I was on top of her, between her legs, grinding on her, the moment almost out of control. I eased inside the heat of a dead man's mistress. She was on fire, but I dominated her, forced her to feel euphoria.

"Wait. Put a condom on."

I stopped, backed away from the temptation of her flexuous body, and took in a panoramic view of her curves and softness, then shook my head and caught my breath. I'd been with one woman the last six years. She had been gone for six months, but my wedding ring made this feel wrong. I had read that it took half the time a relationship lasted for someone to heal. I still had over two years to go.

Robbing a bank was easier than breaking my vows. No matter what Cora had done, no matter where she was, the ring I wore reminded me of my onus, of my promise.

I said, "We really should stop."

"You've already been inside me. The connection has been made. So it's been done."

"In some ways. Yeah. It's been done."

"Bareback. You were inside me bareback. I don't do bareback."

"Sorry. I was . . . I've been married a long time."

She bit her bottom lip. "Did it feel good?"

I rocked. "Amazing."

"Yeah. That felt amazing."

"This wasn't what I intended, Jackie."

"This won't change your debt, so get that out of your head."

"I don't want you to think that."

"I know. I was joking. But since it's done, we might as well finish the wrong that we're doing."

"You're Sammy's girl."

"Sammy is dead."

"I know."

"And your wife left you."

"I know. But I'm still a married man."

"So. Since this unexpected thing has gone this far, either we finish it, or I'll have to be a lady and excuse myself to the bathroom and complete what we started, and you'll be out here doing the same."

"I'd regret this in the morning."

"Me too."

"But?"

"To be honest, Sammy's inside my head."

"He's inside my head too, Jackie. I saw him die."

"I feel him inside my body. I smell him on my skin. I don't want the last man I slept with to be a dead man. I know it sounds bad, or stupid, or desperate. I might be crazy right now, but I want you inside me. I want you inside so I can stop feeling Sammy. I need to feel somebody else or I'll lose my mind."

"Jackie—"

"Stop being a gentleman and just open the condom."

I'd spent countless nights worrying about my wife. Not knowing where she was had been the hardest part. I couldn't get her out of my head. Some nights I needed to feel her so badly that I had to please myself. Countless nights I pretended my hand was her hand, my hand was her mouth, nights I had to spit in my hand and imagine my wet palm was like being inside her, nights I'd spent looking at her photos and grimacing and grunting and battling thoughts that refused to end, thoughts that had plagued my mind sixty-nine times a day. And when I was done, I'd feel so angry.

After I put the condom on, Jackie came to me and we kissed again.

I caught my breath. "How do you want to do this?"

"Effectively and with aforethought and malice."

I smiled a little.

She yielded a one-sided smile and whispered, "Sometimes sex isn't about sex."

"Really?"

"Sometimes it's about something else."

"Like what?"

"Sometimes it's about getting rid of the ghosts."

She gave me soft kisses, butterfly kisses, kisses on the neck and lips, then my tongue met hers and a ravenous dance began. I didn't know if I was kissing love or tasting an evil that had gone dormant. She eased down on her back and pulled me on top of her. The injuries kept me from moving the way I wanted to, but I moved. I was where Sammy had been. I was inside the warmth of his home away from home. A minute or so later, Jackie reached down and took the condom away. She pushed me on my back and mounted me, just like my wife used to. I moved inside her not knowing I was sinking into the warmth and tightness of a brand-new duplicity. It had been a long time, and right or wrong, my dead friend's mistress or not, I was human and had my frailties. It was crazy. It was erotic. It was wrong. And it felt good. I closed my eyes and pretended I was back in my bed in Detroit, pretended I was with Cora, and every pain went away. When the pain left, the wildness came. Jackie was a rough lover, a lover in search of pain. She began having a spastic orgasm. Her hands pulled the covers from the mattress, then she tugged the sheets as she moaned Sammy's name, and my moment was almost destroyed. I gripped a handful of Jackie's hair, pulled her mane into a ponytail and held it like I wanted to yank it out at the roots, pulled her hair like I wanted to break her neck, then I moved against her with disdain. If this was the season of deception, death, and infidelity, so be it. I came and held her until I could breathe again. I was hot. I was sweating. So was she.

She smiled and whispered, "You're pretty good. I thought you'd be a real bad lay."

"Same for you."

"You've made me get there twice already."

"Really?"

"Not many men have been able to do that, so have a drink and pat yourself on the back."

"You're pretty good yourself."

"We have a good fit."

A few minutes later she went and got a towel and cleaned me.

She thought I was done, but I wasn't.

It had been six months sans intimacy, and now the dam had been broken.

She said, "Put a condom on this time."

"Why bother?"

"Just put it on. Fill it up and I'll dump it when we're done."

I put a condom on and took control again, made her forget about Sammy and scream my name.

She forgot about Sammy while I remembered and fantasized about my wife.

When we were done, Jackie removed the condom, went inside the bathroom, and shut the door.

I listened but I didn't hear the toilet flush.

I waited for her to come back, wanted to use her and keep the fantasy going, wanted to use her to escape this reality, but after an hour of waiting for her to come back to me, I had fallen asleep.

12

When I woke up coughing and in pain at sunrise, Jackie's scent had saturated my skin. The sweetness from her perfume wafted from the bathroom into the suite, but she was gone. Three hours had passed since she'd taken the condom and gone inside the bathroom. It felt like a dream. My guess was that she had slept for two hours, then eased out of the bed, packed her bags, and abandoned me. Abandonment seemed to be the story of my life.

She left a note that said she had caught a taxi to the airport so she could get on the first flight into Atlanta. She wasn't going to risk getting snowed in and miss the job Eddie Coyle had waiting.

The note told me to look between the mattresses on the side of the bed closest to the window. When I did, I found her loaded .22. Catching a plane meant that she had to leave it behind.

Jackie was gone and I was glad. The remorse was strong. I'd betrayed Sammy and his ghost was sitting in the room next to me, a knife in its back.

And now I had betrayed my wife.

Jackie's note said that I'd better be on time for the Atlanta job, and above all to be professional. The word *professional* was written in capital letters and underlined three times.

Last night had been a new mistake for her as well, I knew that for sure. Her note made it clear that it had never happened.

I turned on my laptop and went online. First I searched for news on Rick. Minutes later I hit the Web sites for the news stations back in Los Angeles. Our crime was a day old and it was already old news on the West Coast. Still I searched for about an hour. I called my house in Detroit and checked the messages. There were none from Cora. Then I searched for her, hit the usual Web sites. I went to her friends' pages on Facebook and other social networking sites. I checked the faces of the people on the sites. It was as if she had never existed.

Twelve hours passed like six months in solitary confinement.

I covered the rest of Texas and Louisiana, then took my journey through Alabama to get to Georgia. Since Los Angeles, my Buick Wildcat, the car I had inherited from Henrick, had covered over 2,200 miles of driving through rain, Dairy Queens, Super8 motels, and below-freezing temperatures. I'd been traumatized, beaten, and had lived on little sleep and covered 2,276 miles in less than three days. If I hadn't been on Vicodin and been slowed down by Jackie, I could've made it to Atlanta in two days.

I played foreign language CDs until I stopped in Meridian, Mississippi, mostly Italian and French. I needed something to keep my mind occupied and away from the pain. I needed to close my eyes, so I grabbed the blanket out of the backseat and rested in a hotel parking lot for almost two hours.

When I fell asleep, it felt like someone was inside my car with me. It was Sammy.

I could smell him; his Old Spice scent was inside my car, deep inside the leather.

I had seen Sammy in the back of that car in Phoenix. He had been as clear as day.

The local radio station said schools, colleges, and many businesses were closed. Up ahead, one car had flipped over and another had become good friends with the center divider. I eased around the traffic jam and came up on exit 7. Exit 7 was Cascade Road. The bottom of the ramp was stacked up with traffic, another accident there, and it took another ten minutes before I was able to negotiate a right turn. Going right was easier than going left. Traffic wasn't moving in that direction. I headed west and went outside of the city's perimeter, like the instructions said, and drove toward the strip mall that held the Starbucks.

Another wave of pain and fatigue hit me. Eyes burned. Legs cramped.

I was exhausted. My body hadn't had real food in over two thousand miles and I was famished. Eyes on the road, I reached over to the passenger seat and pulled my suit coat over to my lap, then fished inside the pocket and pulled out the bottle of Vicodin. I shook the bottle and the pills rattled like a poisonous snake. It was dangerous to do in never-ending traffic, but I opened the bottle and popped another pill, then washed the drugs down with cold coffee. I held the bottle in my right hand as I drove, then glanced at the name on the front of the prescribed medication from time to time.

My gas level was in the red so I pulled into the BP gas station on Cascade Road.

Businesses and banks stood sentry on the four-lane boulevard. The area looked like it was populated with the middle class and the new rich. The streets were filled with Benz and BMW owners. This was where doctors, lawyers, and dentists made and kept their money in banks.

When I stopped, first I started the pump, then I pulled on my hat and a wool coat, took cautious steps, and went to the side of BP and used a pay phone to call Eddie Coyle. While the cellular rang, I listened to his hillbilly-rock music. It was a song by Kid Rock, one of his idols, the vulgar lyrics exclaiming that no one had ever met anyone who was as bad as the Kid from Detroit. Across the street was a giant billboard for one of the local newscasters. *The Jewell of the South.* I'd seen at least three billboards with her face on it since I hit the Georgia state line.

Eddie Coyle answered. "Who's calling my private line at seven in the morning?"

"It's the Feds. Come out with your hands up."

"Dmytryk?"

"Good morning. I guess I woke you up."

He paused. "Where are you?"

"Just made it to Atlanta."

"You're joking. You made it here in this weather?"

"I guess I got lucky and cruised in with no problem. I just left 285 at exit seven."

"Jackie's here. She said you and she split up in Texas."

"I'd had enough of her."

"She can be a little intense."

I took a deep breath and smelled her on my skin. I asked, "She's with you and your crew?"

"No, but she called when she landed at Hartsfield yesterday. She barely made it in. Airport is shut down now and so are a lot of the roads and most of the big businesses downtown."

"Well, let's get the ball rolling. I'm at the BP on Cascade Road filling up."

"You're across the street from KFC and the driving range."

"I guess." I looked around. "Yeah, I see a sign for Cascade Driving Range from here."

"I need to handle my morning constitution, then shower."

I took out my pocket watch, flipped it open, checked the time, and asked, "How long?"

"Give me a couple of hours."

"Where the hell are you?"

"Rome."

I took a deep breath and my exhaustion doubled. "Well, you knew I'd be here for the job."

"I didn't expect you this soon, not in this weather. I thought you'd be here much later."

"Well, I'm here. I said I'd be here and I'm here."

"Man of your word."

I nodded. "If nothing else."

"Let me get cleaned up."

"Okay, Eddie Coyle. See you in two hours. More or less."

"Dmytryk, before I get there . . . I need to put something on the table."

"Something changed since L.A.?"

"You could say that." He paused. "Sammy and Rick were in on this job."

"I know. Rick, Sammy, and Jackie. But that's changed. I'm the seat filler."

"I'm two men short. That disaster in L.A. left me in a bad spot."

"It left me in a tight spot as well."

He paused again. "When is the last time you heard from Cora?"

"Cora?" Taken aback, I paused. "Why are you asking about Cora?"

"How long has it been since you heard from her?"

"Well, the story hasn't changed. She left Detroit when I was working in Pasadena, Texas. Rick, Sammy, you, and me did that job. I got back and she was gone. That's the best I can tell you. But she's not a snitch, if that's what you're asking. She's a New Yorker."

He paused. "She came down south."

"How do you know?"

"We ran into her."

"We?"

"Bishop and I."

"You and your brother ran into her?"

"A few times."

"Where exactly?"

"She told me that she was living in an apartment out in Oklahoma City after she left Detroit."

"Oklahoma City? She's in Oklahoma?"

"Was. She was working out that way. She got in the business and stayed in the business."

I took a deep breath and shook my head. "Is she incarcerated?"

"No."

"Where is she?"

"We've been in contact. She needed my expertise. She was in on a job at a Bank of America in Utica Square, then she was in on another job, another Bank of America in downtown Tulsa. A few months ago I'd sent Jackie over to help her out. Together they did a Chase Bank on South Lewis."

"So, you've been working with my wife?"

"She called me and asked for assistance and I sent Jackie Brown to help her out."

"So Jackie and Cora are friends?"

"They know each other, but I wouldn't call them friends."

"She did three jobs in Oklahoma?"

"The newspaper had called them the Freeway Bandits because all of the banks were near the interstates. When men rob a bank, it's a blip. When women rob a bank, it's news."

"What else did Cora say when you ran into her?"

"She said that you took her out on a job once. She told me, not in detail, but she mentioned that you did."

"Yeah. In Guthrie. Small bank. Farmers and Merchants. It was sixteen hours from Detroit. We left late one Thursday night, did the job, made it to Detroit in time for church on Sunday morning."

"Decent score?"

"That's not the point."

"In this business, that is always the point. The penalty is too high to take small risks."

"The score was nothing life changing, but the practice was good and the getaway was easy. It helped keep the lights on and food on the table."

"Maybe that was why she went back to that area. After Jackie left, Cora stayed and things went bad in Oklahoma and she needed some help, so she contacted me to help fix her problems."

I waited for him to run out of words before I asked, "What went bad?"

"It's not important. It's been resolved. The bodies are buried. Let's move on."

"You have a number so I can call her?"

"I have her number. But you won't be needing it." Eddie Coyle paused. "Cora is with me."

"What do you mean *with* you?"

"I mean what I said, Dmytryk. She's *with* me."

An instant headache attacked me; a new level of anger made me want to scream, made me want to attack the world, but I kept it all suppressed.

I had learned that from Henrick. A calm man could make more ground than an angry fool.

He said, "I just wanted you to know she's in on this with us."

"My wife is with you."

"I didn't hesitate nor did I stutter."

"For how long?"

"We'll talk. We'll sit down and talk face-to-face, like men, not over the phone."

"She left Detroit and came down here to be with you."

"That's not what happened. She left Detroit and went wherever she went, ended up back in Oklahoma, and now she's here for a while. She's in on this job."

"But she's back here and she's with you."

"We'll talk."

I swallowed, gritted my teeth, felt my heartbeat pounding like drums inside my ears.

Eddie Coyle said, "Cora is riding down to Atlanta with me."

"Hold up. She's in Rome with you now?"

"She is."

"Jackie knew about this?"

"Keep Jackie out of this."

"She's been with me since L.A. She rode in my car from L.A. to Fort Worth."

"I know."

"This is interesting, Eddie Coyle. This is really interesting."

"You want to pass on this job? If you do, I respect that and understand."

"Respect."

"It's your call. I could use you. We don't have enough people, not with Sammy and Rick out of the picture. This is an important job and, our differences aside, it could make a big difference in your life."

I hesitated. "Let's talk. Come down from your throne in Rome and let's have a sit-down."

"We'll be down as soon as we get cleaned up."

It sounded like he was smiling. On the streets behind me, winds blew and traffic crawled. It felt like I was trapped in Atlanta. My insides were cursing and screaming, the exhaustion making this seem like a bad dream, but I tightened my lips and refused to let Eddie Coyle get the best of me.

Eddie Coyle added, "By the way, Rick didn't make it. He expired a few hours ago."

I said, "Does his wife know?"

"She knows and she knows to keep her mouth closed. If we have to visit her, it won't be to bring flowers. So all she has to do is tell them she knew nothing."

"I'm real sorry to hear Rick didn't make it."

"No you're not. None of us are. And he wouldn't be sorry if you had died."

"He was a good guy."

"Depending on the situation and with whom he was dealing, he could be conceived of as such."

"Well, he was a good guy to me. And that was all that mattered."

"Rick's dying is the good news."

"What's the bad news?"

"The bad news is that the security guard died too."

"If we're caught, it's a capital case."

"If you're caught."

"Me and Jackie."

"There would be no way anyone would know Jackie was in on the job, right?"

I gritted my teeth. "You're right. It's all on me."

"Exactly. If that ship sinks, leave her on the life raft."

Another chill hit me before I asked, "Did Rick come out of his coma before he died?"

"No idea. I just know he didn't recover from his lead poisoning."

Again I paused.

In that space of time I saw Rick's face, heard him telling me that he had things to tell me after the job, things that he wasn't at liberty to say in the presence of Sammy and Jackie.

I said, "So, you're serious. Cora is really there with you in Rome."

"I'm not one for jokes, not at this hour of the day."

"Me. You. Cora. And Jackie."

"And Bishop."

I licked my wounded lips. "So it's the five of us."

"If you're still in, and I want you to be, it's the five of us plus one."

I asked, "Who is the felon hiding behind curtain number six?"

"At the moment, that's not relevant."

"The inside man."

"Of course. The inside man is number six."

Coldness embraced my heart. I cleared my throat and asked, "Where am I going?"

"Thumbs Up in East Point."

"Back by the airport."

"You can take I-285 back toward Hartsfield and get off at Camp Creek."

"Afraid not. The interstate is a parking lot and everything is at a standstill."

"You can take the streets. You know where Delowe Drive is?"

"Let me get a pen and paper out of my coat pocket."

Eddie Coyle told me where to go and I scribbled down the directions.

He said, "Dmytryk, this is an important job. I want everything to be civilized."

"As civilized as it can be."

Back inside my car, I took Jackie's gun, made sure it was loaded, and put it in my pocket.

13

Delowe Drive was a narrow street that a man could miss if he blinked. Eddie Coyle just happened to leave that out, so I drove about two miles too far and ended up down by the West End Mall before I back-tracked. Every mile or a so there was an accident or a car that had slid off the road into a building or a pole. In this weather, that added another forty-five minutes to my trip in the bowels of hell.

Once I exited the prestigious Cascade, I saw how the less fortunate lived. It was like being in Detroit. Or North Carolina. It was like being in New Orleans. The poor were scattered all over the country and the rich lived in pocket communities with walls high enough to keep the poor away. Foreclosures were behind those walls too. A lot of Jacks and Jills had fallen hard.

I passed a man standing at a bus stop, a man who looked like Rick, but when I looked in my rearview mirror he was gone. I rubbed my eyes and kept moving forward.

A few seconds later, at another bus stop I passed a man who looked like Sammy.

Again, when I looked in my rearview mirror, that man was gone too.

I swallowed and felt the lightness in my head and inside my body.

Something told me that I was already dead, that I had died back in Los Angeles. But the pain I felt in my heart told me that I was still alive.

When I landed in East Point, my first impression was that I had driven back in time and landed in Mayberry. It was a nice area with a high concentration of banks. I counted at least six banks within two blocks. Across the street from Thumbs Up, what used to be a nice-size church had been turned into a Bank of America. Banks had been planted in every direction I looked. It was a forest of federally insured financial institutions. But a police precinct sat in the heart of all that old Southern money. Response time to a robbery in this area had to be under a minute.

I hoped this wasn't what Eddie Coyle had in mind. It would be L.A. all over again.

Thumbs Up was inside a refurbished building on White Way, had a brick façade and an open dining room. Waiters and waitresses were rushing back and forth. The sleet wasn't coming down in East Point at the moment, but it was cold enough for me to have flashbacks of walking along the Detroit River. I shook those memories away, tried to make them vanish the way a child erased drawings from an Etch A Sketch. The establishment wasn't overflowing, but they had plenty of business; more than enough people were coming and going to make the owner proud.

I hadn't eaten a decent meal since Los Angeles. The food smelled so good my stomach started doing cartwheels. I had to get away from the aroma before I lost my mind and ran inside and started grabbing food from plates, so I swallowed my hunger pains and walked that strip impatiently waiting on Eddie Coyle, strolled down to the MARTA station that was at the corner, walked around the block, everybody I passed saying good morning like I was their first cousin. It looked like this was another area clustered with banks. A Bank of America sat across the street from the diner and at least two more were a thirty-second job from that one. I saw police driving like wasps circling a nest, kept my eyes away from the cops, and pretended I was just another local checking out the mom-and-pop businesses that populated East Point, Georgia.

My cellular vibrated. It was Eddie Coyle. He was five minutes away.

I adjusted my fedora, rubbed my hands, and hurried my anger and anxiety back toward the diner.

The gun was inside my pocket, the .22 that Jackie had given me in Fort Worth.

Christmas music and cheerful employees in Santa Claus hats aggravated me with kindness as I waited inside Thumbs Up. Nausea rose inside of me and I went to the bathroom and locked the door, stood with my head over the toilet, but nothing happened. I coughed, dry heaved, and spat. Then I washed my hands and splashed warm water on my rugged face before I went back and waited off to the side, found room on a bench. From there I stared out at the streets with fear, anger, and impatience. I didn't see them pull up, but I saw them coming from the parking lot across the street.

They must've arrived in East Point while I was in the bathroom battling queasiness. I was feeling miserable but Cora was smiling and laughing. She was wearing a goddamn black fedora. That was insult to injury. She was wearing a fedora, glowing and skipping ice puddles in the bitter cold. Her hair hung from her hat, hair that was the color of honey. She had colored her hair. She was smoking a cigarette. So was Eddie Coyle. I knew that he only smoked Marlboro Blacks. I'd made her stop smoking a year before we married.

Eddie Coyle tossed his smoke, then my wife took a long pull and tossed hers, her final exhalation sending a stream of cancer from her beautiful lips. Fumes rose around her head and face like she was a starlet in a movie from the 1940s. I wiped my face and did my best to look my best, not wanting either of them to see me looking as angry or as battered as I was feeling. Head to toe I felt like crap, but I fought the exhaustion.

Then I blinked a hundred times, swallowed, tried to remove the bitterness from my palate.

Cora looked like she had put on close to thirty pounds and none of it was muscle. Despite that added softness, she fit in with the women in the area and still managed to look like she had stepped off the cover of a magazine that featured stories penned by Raymond Chandler or Dashiell Hammett, maybe a pulp story about a mysterious, buxom woman who carried a gun, a woman who had sex for fun and shot people for the same reason. My elusive wife had gray wool pants that stopped around the middle of her calves. Toreador pants. She also had on a dark turtleneck, black boots that looked like they cost as much as a fur coat from Windsor.

Eddie Coyle knew I was watching.

He strutted next to Cora, hand in hand with her, like they were newlyweds the morning after. He had on dark jeans and boots, and an oversize American flag belt buckle held up his jeans. He had on an old sweatshirt that advertised for McCain and Palin, bold lettering underneath their grinning faces, THE MAVERICK AND THE MILF. *MILF* was twice the size of *maverick*. Eddie Coyle wore that outdated sexist misogynistic political advert in Obama country and walked like he was looking for a street fight. Knowing Eddie Coyle, he was looking for a brawl. Starting a fight was his cup of coffee.

Pain rose up inside me, the epicenter of that flaming ache trying to destroy that thing in my chest that was shaped like a fist wrapped in blood.

It had been 380 days since her legs moved away from each other on my behalf, 380 days since she moaned because of me, 380 sunrises and sunsets since she welcomed me into the warmth that lived between her thighs.

Customers had to pass through two glass doors to come inside Thumbs Up. The first glass door brought people out of the horrible weather and deposited them inside a vestibule just big enough for a newsstand that housed rags like *Creative Loafing, Sunday Paper,* and *Rolling Out.* That was where my wife was when she looked through the second glass door. She saw me and froze. She stared and blinked over and over like she was trying to wake from a nightmare, like she was trying to make a monster disappear. I raised my hand and waved just to let her know that it was me. For a moment she had a dolorous expression, as did I. Maybe she thought this meeting was coincidental, but in the next blink her eyes widened. She realized Eddie Coyle had brought me here intentionally. Her nostrils flared and happiness abandoned her face. My nostrils flared and my face became the snarl of a rabid dog.

Then her lips moved and she said a single word; its first letter was formed by her top teeth pressing firm against her bottom lip, the action necessary to create all words that started with the sixth letter of the alphabet. She wanted to turn around. But Eddie Coyle was behind her, and so were more people who were desperate to get out of the cold. My wife had to go forward. Once again her bottom lip and her top teeth became intimate, once again she tensed her face and uttered a word that started with the letter *F* and ended with the letter *K*. I nodded and whispered the same wonderful expletive, only with two words, one a personal pronoun, the last word the proper name for a female dog.

Her laughter had died. So had her smile. She adjusted her designer glasses, lowered her head.

My wife went the other direction, toward the bathrooms.

Eddie Coyle walked closer to me. The gun was inside my pocket, but the Mexican switchblade had been slipped up the sleeve of my coat. Bullets were reserved for Eddie Coyle, but not yet.

He said, "You're looking pretty bad, Dmytryk. Like you're in a hurt locker."

"Nothing a Z-pack and a good night's sleep won't fix."

I wanted to let the blade drop down and put that blade inside his heartless chest. In the background, police cars kept passing by to get to their precinct. One patrol car was across the street at the Bank of America. I wanted to hurt Eddie Coyle in a bad way and he knew it.

I said, "Based on Cora's reaction, I take it she didn't know I was in on this deal."

"Not even a clue."

"That's not the way to do business, not even for a man like you."

"She didn't need to know who I was bringing in on this one. It's better this way."

"And you said Jackie Brown is the fourth person. What about your brother?"

"And Bishop is the fifth." He nodded. "Sammy and Rick were in on this with me. It was supposed to be a five-man operation, but we're down to three and there's not enough time to recruit anyone else but you. I'll need you to handle both stages of the getaway."

"Five men? So, I have to handle two getaway cars and four are going in?"

"We'll get to that part later."

"Sammy knew you were with my wife?"

"Once again, as I said before, and this is the last time, I can't attest to what any man or any woman knows, only myself."

"You expect me to trust you?"

"Hit the front door if you feel like you can't. I'm the one taking the big risk here. You might be wanted on a capital case and any association with you could be a big risk for me."

"I guess I couldn't trust you with my wife."

"Women and money are two different things. A man can't keep either for long. And while he has either one, he best enjoy it, has to use them for what they're worth, because when it's gone, it's gone."

I should've shot him right then. I should've shot him and left him bleeding on the floor of the café, the way Michigan has been bleeding people for the last five years. He evaluated me and nodded.

The waitress came and led us to the booths on the left side of the U-shaped eatery. We sat down in a booth about midway. I took the side facing the streets, the man's side of the table.

Cora returned; her hands were deep inside her pockets and her steps were slow and cautious. She was shaking her head. She stopped at the edge of the booth and frowned at me, then used her middle finger to push her glasses up on her face before she slid inside the booth next to Eddie Coyle. A thousand wasps stung my heart when she took her seat. Eddie Coyle asked her to let him out and she did, then he motioned for her to sit on the inside. Now she was unable to leave the table or run away without climbing over the top like an animal trying to escape this zoo. She moved to the wall and wouldn't relinquish any more eye contact, no matter how hard I stared at her.

My hand was inside my coat by then, my finger on the trigger.

But when I saw her, when I smelled her, my finger slipped away from the trigger.

I swallowed, cleared my throat, and said, "Cora."

She nodded. "Dmytryk."

I said, "*¿Cómo amaneciste?*"

"*Bien.*"

Eddie Coyle said, "No Mexican talk. This is north of the border so both of you speak American."

I said, "Go to hell."

Cora said, "You're looking bad, Dmytryk. You're looking bruised and pale."

"Thanks for your concern, Cora, but I'll survive."

She softened her voice. "Who beat you up like that?"

"Life."

Cora picked up a menu. Without reservation, I stared at my wife.

I said, "About six months ago, I went to Texas, came home, and you were gone. I thought that maybe you had Alzheimer's and wandered away from home. And now Eddie Coyle has found you and he's sending you home to me, untouched. Is that what has happened?"

Stress lines grew in her face, a face that wore perfect makeup, and she closed her eyes and took a deep breath. She looked like a child who was doing her best to wish me away.

I put on a smile. "Where is your wedding ring?"

"Pawned it in Guthrie, Oklahoma."

"Pawning a ring doesn't pawn a marriage."

Eddie Coyle said, "Look, you haven't heard from her in half a year. The marriage between you and Cora is done. She said it was over long before we met. She just didn't have the guts to tell you."

"Is that what she told you?"

"You understand what's going on here, right, Dmytryk? If there are any hard feelings, put them all on the table so we can have the waitress come along and throw them away with the other trash."

Still I received nothing from Cora. Her leg was bouncing and vibrating the booth. Underneath the table, my gun was aimed at her pretty stomach. I'd make her look at me. I'd make her feel my pain.

I said, "I was with you for six years, and at this moment, no matter how much I respected you, all I can think is that a slut is just a slut, no matter if she wears a wedding ring or not."

Cora growled. "You're a nasty, pathetic, vulgar jerk, you know that?"

"And you're sloppy seconds."

Eddie Coyle said, "Okay, Dmytryk, that's enough of that. This is where I draw the line."

I gritted my teeth and pointed in his face. "*Stay out of this, Eddie Coyle.*"

My wife leaned forward like she wanted to stab me with her fork.

Eddie Coyle smiled like he wanted her to, but he patted her hand like she was a trained animal. She took a sharp breath and sat back. It was invisible, but her leash was there, dangling from her neck.

I said, "So, wife, you were unhappy with me."

She softened her voice and said, "You knew I wasn't happy."

"I knew you weren't happy with our situation. I wasn't happy with our situation. Only a fool would be happy. I'm asking if you were unhappy with me."

"What's the difference? You were my situation, Dmytryk."

I softened my tone in response. "You were unhappy with me."

"Yes. And when you went to sleep, I used to sit in the bathroom and cry half the night."

"And you're happy now."

She sat back and looked like she aged fifty years. I pulled my lips in, the aches inside my body pulling at me as I turned and faced Eddie Coyle. He was a spectator at a circus and he would jump up and applaud if the lioness devoured the ringmaster.

I nodded and faced my wife. "I see the choices you've made, but I haven't heard why."

"I was done. Do you hear me, Dmytryk? I was done. I'd had enough. I quit."

"You quit?"

"Yes, I quit."

"This isn't high school, Cora. And if standing before God meant nothing to you—"

"God means everything to me."

"Walking out is not the way to dissolve a marriage. Whether we're rich or poor, we're married, so we are rich or poor together. *¿Comprendes, mujer?*"

"I couldn't stand one more day with you. And seeing you now, this brings back all of the stress. I feel it in my back. I feel it in my neck. I feel it in my jaw. I feel it in my head. I'm in a vise grip. It feels like I'm back in Detroit. It feels like I'm back inside that house. It feels like I'm back onstage dancing. And I hate the way I feel. I hate the way I feel when I think about you. I hate everything we ever had."

"You hated me."

"I look at you and see failure. Nothing has changed."

"I'm your husband. Your failures are mine and mine are yours."

I looked at Eddie Coyle. He looked like he had a lot to say but was chewing his words.

Cora shot me a quick glance before her eyes returned to Eddie Coyle. Eddie Coyle had done an excellent job of stealing her balance. Seeing her had done the same for me.

I said, "You're pushing the envelope on this one, Eddie Coyle."

Cora shook her head and put her eyes back on her menu. After that, she didn't move.

Eddie Coyle said, "Cora Knight, this is where you can change sides of the table and there will be no argument, no penalty, no attitude. We can still move forward and work as a team."

She took her fedora off, placed it on the table, then took it off the table and placed it on the bench, before she ran her hand over her hair, clenched her teeth, shook her head, did every move slowly.

I said, "Is there a problem, wife?"

"Don't call me *wife* anymore."

Eddie Coyle said, "Well, I guess that since the truth is out in the open, we can work together?"

"The damage is done. Can you do this, Cora?"

She nodded. "It's too late to turn this deal around. Time is running out."

I smiled. "You've robbed me and now you need me to help you commit a crime."

Eddie Coyle said, "This will benefit you, Dmytryk."

"I'm talking to Cora, Eddie Coyle. I'm having a conversation with my wife."

It hurt her, but she nodded. "There isn't a lot of time and you're familiar."

I said, "Since we're working together, we need to make sure we can be . . . cordial. If we can't be *friends*, for lack of a better word, then we can't work together. If we can't be professional, then this marriage will not work. I know how to make a marriage work, no matter how contentious. Respect and trust. We don't have to have respect, but we need trust to get to the other side of this thing."

She said, "You can trust me, Dmytryk."

"Really?"

"When it comes to money, you have nothing to worry about. I never stole a dime from you. When I left, I didn't take anything. I took nothing from you. You can never say I robbed you."

"What about you, Eddie Coyle? Can I trust you?"

He said, "I might have that gun you touched the night we were in Detroit."

"The gun with my fingerprints. Do you still have that?"

"If I do, I've never given you reason for alarm."

"Not yet."

"If I have it, it's for my own protection."

"I guess I'm supposed to say thank you for not setting me up."

"I've never stabbed you in your back."

"Well, that's debatable. My wife is sitting on your side of the table."

Cora jumped in. "Both of you, just stop it. Now, for the scorecards, I'm legally married to you, Dmytryk, but I'm sorry, really sorry, things have changed and I'm . . . at the moment I'm with Eddie Coyle. This meeting was supposed to be for introducing me to Eddie Coyle's team member, and I will do my best to treat the meeting as such. Now, men, put your peckers away and let's move on, let's get the ball rolling on this job and do what we're supposed to do and then . . . Dmytryk can drive back to Detroit. That's what he's married to. Detroit and a crummy house that we should've walked away from two years ago. Give him his cut and send him back to that damn house he cares so much about."

My finger tested the trigger. The first shot would be under the table, right between Eddie Coyle's legs. The shock would slow him down, but the animal instinct would kick in and he would still come after me. I would have to shoot him in the head, shoot him the same way that guard shot Sammy. And after I blew Eddie Coyle's mind, while Cora screamed and panicked and tried to climb over the table the way Jackie Kennedy had tried to climb out of that convertible in Dallas, I'd give my wife a two- or three-bullet divorce. That scene played in my mind over and over, but I wouldn't go to jail. Not for her. Not over Eddie Coyle. I wouldn't rot in jail and I wouldn't let the state put me to death, not for this. One shot underneath this table and it would all come together and fall apart at the same time. I'd have to save a bullet for myself. I'd be on the same train with Sammy and Rick, dead and ready to be laid to rest in a wooden box.

Cora said, "Dmytryk, the way you saw the marriage and the way I saw the marriage is totally different. I ended up on a stage dancing next to women whose bodies were covered with tramp stamps."

"You're blaming our situation on me? The auto industry goes under and it's my goddamn fault? Maybe you should cut that reasoning open and get a better autopsy. You're revising history, Cora."

Her bottom lip trembled. "I danced naked and it disgusted me, but I did it because it kept the lights on. I danced naked and brought the money home to you . . . like you were my pimp."

"So you're the victim. And what was I?"

"You were the man."

"You're insane, Cora. I delivered pizzas. But I never thought of you as being my pepperoni pimp. I picked up students and taught when I could. We were a team."

"But I was naked. That's how I felt."

"Don't be one of those women, Cora."

"One of what women? Which women are you talking about this time, you chauvinistic pig?"

"One of those women who needs to play the victim."

"I danced naked."

"I told you not to dance. You did it behind my back."

"Eddie Coyle never would have let me dance."

"But he would put dollars in your thong while you did. And he would let you rob banks. That's not protecting you. Fifth-graders have better logic."

She paused and rubbed her temples. "You think you're smarter than me."

"I'm at the same table as you. I married you. And I've allowed you to ruin my life. One could say my level of intelligence has diminished as well."

"This is why I don't argue with you. This is why I . . . I just left."

"For Eddie Coyle."

"I didn't leave you for Eddie."

"Oh. Now he's Eddie. To you he's Eddie."

"He was there for me."

"When you're drowning, you don't pay attention to who throws a life preserver to you."

She took a breath and shook her head. "Why did you marry me, Dmytryk?"

"Because I loved you. I loved you."

Nothing was said for a moment. The sounds of knives and forks on plates and hearty conversations filled the room, and our resentment and frustration heated all the love and joy in the room during this Christmas season.

Eddie Coyle said, "Putting this meeting on task, what's your objective, Cora?"

"There is only one objective in America, and I've learned that."

I sat back and nodded. "Then, as you said, let's keep it about the bottom line."

She nodded in return. "If we can stay focused, you boys can help me do this."

I paused. "We can help you?"

Cora nodded. "This is my job, Dmytryk. Eddie Coyle brought you here to work for me."

Eddie Coyle said, "Your job? Believe that crap if you want. I'm the one with the experience. I'm the one who knows what to look for and how to make this work."

Cora spoke in a harsh whisper. "This is my job. You work for me too."

Eddie Coyle adjusted himself and stared her down. "It was my idea from day one."

"I'm using my connections. You talked the talk, but I'm walking the walk. It's my job."

"You know my résumé. So tell me, what the hell do you know about hitting a bank?"

"I know about dye packs, about those electronic tracers that are like GPS trackers. I know which banks carry those tracers and which ones don't, and that if you show a gun the jail time is different than if you show a note. I know not to go in acting crazy and shooting because everything gets out of control. And I know who is going to be working in the bank we need to hit and on what day we need to hit that bank and at what time that hit should be done so we can be in and out of that bank in a minute. I know which banks don't have bulletproof glass yet. I know the minimum amount of money that is supposed to be on hand on the day we do this job, and the exact time the money will be on hand, and I know to tell them to keep away from the silent alarm. I know the bank we're going to hit from top to bottom and wall to wall. I know when patrol cars won't be in the area. I know about needing a fourth person to be our driver and lookout, and that that person needs to be dependable because they are our eyes and ears and we'll know the moment somebody dials nine-one-one. I know about needing two cars to get away, and that the best place to steal those cars is at the mall. I know we have to switch the plates on the stolen cars and dump the first getaway car for a second getaway car, and then dump the second car for a third that has legal plates. I know we have to change getaway cars within three- to five-minute intervals, and that we should be inside the third car within ten minutes. I know which escape routes to take once we leave the bank and not to leave any fingerprints or physical evidence behind. I know to wear disguises that change our features and chins, and to wear shades because they can zoom in on our eyes and the distance from eyeball to eyeball can't be changed with makeup. I know that in order to make any of this happen, the person in charge needs to know the perfect time, bank procedures, staffing, the building setup, cameras, exits, the vault, and I repeat that I know all of that. Now what the hell do you know, Eddie Coyle?"

Her speech had given me pause.

Eddie Coyle sat back, not possessing the skills it took to argue with the woman I had married.

I said, "Sounds like you've been busy since you left Detroit."

"Well, I haven't been waiting on a president to come save me."

"You're working banks all over the Midwest?"

"Where I've been and what I've done since you last saw me in Detroit is none of your concern. All you need to know is what this job is about. I'm not comfortable with that, but this late in the game, I guess I have no choice. I'm tempted to step out on faith and do this on my own."

Eddie Coyle jumped in. "Well, Cora, you may know how to bake that cake, but you don't have the balls to put it in the oven."

"I have the balls."

"Not on this job."

"Ask Dmytryk. The job we did in Oklahoma, I'm the one who walked inside the bank. That's who has the balls. That's who puts it all on the line. I have the balls and I went in alone."

"Just because you went inside the bank doesn't make you the man in charge and it does not make Dmytryk a lackey. Do it yourself. Run inside a bank all by yourself. You step outside and your ride is gone or you're blocked in and you'll pass bricks through your sphincter. And hitting a little bank in Guthrie, Oklahoma, does not make you a superstar in this business."

"Three banks, not including the one I did with Dmytryk."

"My point stands."

She snapped, "Eddie, go juggle yourself."

I took a breath. "So let me get this right, Eddie Coyle. Cora's running this job, and you don't know jack, is that right?"

"I know where the money is located. She knows when the money will be on hand, and in order to get his cut, her inside man is making it a walk in the park. But she can't do it alone. She doesn't have the wherewithal or the guts to walk in this location and walk out with the money. That dog barks, but that dog don't hunt."

I lowered my head, grunted, then raised my head and saw bad luck dressed in policeman blue. Right then eight police officers entered the establishment, the winter air seeming colder in their presence. Rick and the guard had died and it felt like I had been set up, and what I felt showed in my eyes. Eddie Coyle looked back, saw the officers, waved me off, then drank his water. A waiter went to the officers, motioned for them to follow. They were brought in my direction. Four officers were seated two booths behind me. The other four were seated two booths behind Eddie Coyle.

Our waiter finally came. We'd never put our menus down to show we were ready, so they had waited until we did. We ordered. The waiter took the menus and left the tension at our table.

Eddie Coyle regarded me. "Are you in? Or will this job be more than you can bear?"

"Enough talk, Eddie Coyle. Let's be the men we are and seal this deal."

Surrounded by cops, Eddie Coyle put his hand out and we shook on it. Now we were married to the deal. We were married until death did us part, for better or for worse.

Eddie Coyle said, "Now that you're in, I'll tell you something else."

"What else?"

"We're looking at more than twenty each on this one."

"How much more?"

He smiled. "We'll talk about it. Just wanted you to know the real deal."

The sensation of possibly coming into a small fortune didn't last. What I wanted was priceless.

My voice was soft, my words just above a whisper as I motioned at Cora. "Wife."

Her words wore barely a whisper as well. "Don't call me that."

"I could call you a lot of things at this moment, so be glad I'm using the word *wife*."

Cora rubbed her forehead like she was fighting an aneurysm. She chewed her words, her face a mixture of anger, shame, and relief. To see the one you used to love but no longer love is a sobering moment. To see someone you still love who no longer loves you, that is hell.

I said, "Handshake. Let's rewrite the terms of this marriage. We have new vows now."

She regarded my extended hand and cringed. Her tongue moved around a mouth filled with saliva. It looked like she was going to spit on my flesh.

I said, "In this business your handshake is how you sign a professional contract."

She frowned at me before she glanced at Eddie Coyle. She had become his queen.

Eddie Coyle nodded. "Dmytryk is right. He needs to know he can trust you until this is done."

She took a breath, swallowed, adjusted her sleeves, then she extended her hand.

I touched her skin and an electrical shock moved from my fingers to the end of my arm. From there the power split and half went toward my heart, the other half surged lower, made my manhood struggle to betray me. Cora blinked a hundred times, my touch disturbing her as well.

We shook once and she yanked her hand back, hurried and wiped her palm on her pants.

I wiped my damp hands on a napkin. My sweat was thick as blood from an open wound.

She lowered her voice and said, "Eddie Coyle. You just railroaded me."

"I didn't railroad you. I made it so you could stop hiding. I was tired of it and so were you."

"You didn't tell me you were bringing Dmytryk in on this. This had nothing to do with him. Absolutely nothing. So, way to go. You got me on this one. But don't *ever* railroad me again. I don't like being played. I don't appreciate being used."

The waiter brought the food.

Catfish and scrambled eggs and pancakes and sausage and grits and biscuits and omelets and toast and sweet tea and lemonade and orange juice. I was famished, weak, subsisting on very little sleep and too much Vicodin, but I'd lost my appetite. I asked the waiter to put my food inside a Styrofoam box.

Eddie Coyle started eating. My wife frowned at me. Her lips were tight with anger at the things I said.

I smiled a very thin smile. Eddie Coyle did the same and drummed his fingers on the table.

I said, "I don't think that you're giving me the details of the job this morning."

Eddie Coyle said, "Later. Not now. I wanted Cora to meet the other man on my team."

Cora said, "We'll meet again later and lay out the details of the job."

I maintained eye contact with Cora. "I look forward to that meeting."

The waiter came back with my to-go box, and I stood to put on my overcoat, scarf, gloves, and fedora. And now, once again, it was time to get away from the scene of a crime. But so much anger was inside of me and I had to leave before I exploded. Cora looked at me. Our eyes met and I saw a glimpse of the woman I had met when I was working on the line.

I said, "Eddie Coyle?"

"Dmytryk."

"Safe house."

"It's in Dallas."

"Dallas? That's another twelve-hour drive in the wrong direction."

"Not the Dallas where President Kennedy's head was opened up. It's next to Hiram, Georgia. Small city with about six thousand people. Safe house is off Memorial Drive."

"How far is that dream city from here?"

"An hour. In this weather, might be two."

"I need the info."

"I'll text it to you after I eat."

"Big place?"

"Two bedrooms."

"It's five of us here. We're all staying together?"

"Yeah. Same protocol for the team. We're all staying together so we can cover the details."

"All of us."

"All of us."

"I look forward to all of us being together. Until then, *que tenga un buen día*."

"No Mexican talk."

"It's not called Mexican talk. It's called Spanish."

As I limped away, the glass door to the diner opened and Jackie came inside. She wore a gray dress—one that made her look like a CEO—and dark leggings. Her boots came up to her knees and looked both classy and expensive. She had makeup on, but I could see the acne. Stress had exacerbated her ailment and her skin looked worse than it had two days ago. Pimples spread like a row of small mountains, her right cheek being the side with the biggest problem. She was pretty with the pimples but would probably have been beautiful without. Not magazine beautiful, but average-woman beautiful. If she lost thirty pounds and fixed her skin, she'd look like a brand-new woman. But the weight she had fit her frame and gave her the kind of curves that men adored. Sammy's mistress was wearing a red midlength coat. I evaluated that vixen, then passed by her and gave her a simple nod. She paused when I passed her, then I heard her turn around, her square heels clicking as she came behind me and called my name. I kept going. She caught up with me, grabbed my arm, stopped me inside the vestibule.

I turned and faced her, my expression that of an animal ready to bite her throat. "You knew."

"It wasn't my place to say anything. Dmytryk, it wasn't my place."

"So you knew where my wife was all this time."

"She sold herself to the highest bidder."

By then other people were trying to exit while another couple tried to get inside from the cold. As sleet fell against the window, I put my hands in Jackie's hair and pulled her face close to mine. In heels, she was much taller than I was, but I pulled her down to my height.

"You're hurting me, Dmytryk. Stop pulling on me."

I kissed her. I put my tongue inside her mouth and hoped my wife and Eddie Coyle enjoyed the show. When I let go, Jackie was wide-eyed and nervous. She'd used me the way she had used Sammy, and now she carried herself like she was an honest woman.

Jackie frowned. "She's a writer and a writer ain't nothing but a damned reporter."

"Who is?"

"The Vicodin. So, do you want to play stupid, or do you want to play along?"

I smiled at Jackie and held eye contact.

She said, "Abbey Rose has a Web site and a Facebook page. A Facebook page that was updated this morning. Dead people don't update Facebook pages. Abbey Rose. I know all about her. She writes stupid books about mysticism and thaumaturgy."

I nodded.

Jackie asked, "What happened in L.A.?"

"It doesn't matter."

"It does matter. Especially since she drives a black BMW. It's on her Web site."

I held my stern expression.

She said, "We'll talk."

"Sure."

"Before I tell Eddie Coyle and Bishop, before I drop that woman's name in their laps and see how literary they are, make yourself available to talk to me. And bring your wallet."

Jackie went inside, her face down as she shook her head side to side. From here, it looked as if Cora was staring at Jackie and my wife's eyes had become an evil shade of green.

Wrapped in my overcoat, my father's fedora on my head, I vacated Thumbs Up and took to the inclement weather once again. I didn't look back, but I knew they were watching me and talking. I knew Eddie Coyle wore the smile that came from a Pyrrhic victory, and Trouble wore anguish, disappointment, and anger. I had no idea what expression Jackie would wear.

I crossed White Way with sleet assaulting and bouncing off my fedora and my coat. I jumped around a river of rain and slush and made it to the curb as the winds picked up and the coldness began numbing my toes. My aches and pains grabbed at me.

Again I coughed and spat on the frozen sidewalk. My saliva was thick and tinted the ice with spit the hue of my wounded heart. Sartre must've built this wretched world, a rotating purgatory that had blizzards, earthquakes, bitter wives, and no exit.

I stared at the bank in front of me. If I had money, I could move on.

As I drove away and found the slick streets that took me back to Cascade Road, it felt like my insides were coming apart and in turmoil, possibly ruptured. I'd driven that damage across the country without stopping for medical assistance.

Maybe that well-earned death was following me, as inevitable as the next sunrise.

This death had started in L.A. and since then it had teased and refused to let me go free.

14

To break free from Eddie Coyle and Trouble, I needed to make bank withdrawals on my own, and I had to make my move right then. Plotting, I sat in the parking lot at one of Magic Johnson's Starbucks and waited for the traffic to clear up, then I drove Cascade Road and searched for an escape from this situation I'd fallen into. The only thing that could get me out of the nightmare was money.

Rick said, "Be careful, Dmytryk. The roads are slick and these country bumpkins can't drive."

I was back near exit 7, cruising through another forest of banks, trying to pick one to rob.

Rick said, "You can do this, Dmytryk."

"We're right here, Dmytryk," Sammy said. "We have your back. I've had your back for a year."

My friends were inside my head. I took a breath, then chuckled nervously. "Maybe I'm not cut out to be a criminal." Then I looked in the rearview and saw Rick and Sammy, clear as day sitting in the backseat.

It took a long time to battle through two traffic lights and drive to Fairburn Road. I turned left and went inside the strip mall that housed a Walgreens pharmacy. A SunTrust bank was in the middle of the shops. I sat outside and did a two-minute countdown using my pocket watch.

I whispered, "We were like brothers, Rick. Did you know? Did you know Cora was down here?"

"We let each other down, brother."

I glanced at him and saw blood gushing from a gunshot wound in his chest.

"I'm sorry, man," I said, lamenting. "If I could do it over . . . I'm sorry."

Rick groaned and shifted. "You left me, Dmytryk. I could've made it and you left me."

I put my eyes back on the street. "I'm sorry. Everything happened so fast, Rick."

"You left me dying on the damn concrete like I was a stray animal. I looked in your eyes and you looked in mine and I begged. What did you do, brother? You drove away like a damn coward."

I turned to face him and expected to see Rick frowning at me, but no one was there. Then I adjusted the rearview and looked in the backseat. I saw Sammy. Half of his face was missing.

I blinked and when I opened my eyes, Sammy was gone. No one was there.

I said, "How would we do this, boys? Which bank should we chose? None of these, right? Right. Not in this weather. What was that, Rick? Closer to the interstate?"

I listened for Rick's and Sammy's voices. I listened for one of them to tell me that the odds were against me, that the lone bank robber was the fool bank robber and that at best I'd get two or three thousand. Rick and Sammy were supposed to talk some sense into me.

But they were gone. For now, they had abandoned me.

I told myself, "Get it together. Pull it together. You can handle this. You're stronger than them."

I headed back toward Cascade and found a Washington Mutual Bank waiting on the other side of the traffic light. I'd been the getaway man but I knew enough about how to step inside a bank and pull a job. I'd been around criminals like Eddie Coyle, Sammy, Rick, and Jackie long enough to know how to do a job by myself. The weather was my primary concern.

The bank was no more than a mile from the on-ramp to I-285 at exit 7. On a clear day I could make it to exit 7 in less than two minutes. But with these conditions, with the way the streets and interstates had been brought to a halt, the back roads would be the best bet for an easy escape. The back roads could have been iced over. One ice patch could have left me sitting upside down in a ditch.

I was going to take a chance.

There weren't any large businesses or houses on this end. There were strip malls, every other one being a place to get your cholesterol refueled. I parked at the end of the strip mall, saw another bank, a Wachovia. This bank was in a better position, its lot feeding right onto Fairburn Road, that two-lane road flowing east, the same direction I'd come here on I-285.

I exited at Fairburn Road, timed the drive back down to I-285 in this weather and traffic. There were two lights and more than enough traffic heading in that direction. But the traffic had me concerned. I crossed under 285 to see what was on the other side. An empty lot, second-rate gas stations, then another strip mall, this one anchored by Blockbuster and Kroger, a few small shops in between.

Another Bank of America was inside that lot, on the edges of Cascade Road and Cascade Parkway, no more than sixty yards from the interstate on-ramp. This area had more banks than the financial district. I parked across the street at a Marathon gas station and let my windshield wipers wipe away the sleet, my heater ratting as cool air seeped in through any imperfection my Buick possessed.

It would be a hard escape, but it was doable.

Sweat gathered across the back of my neck as I wrote out a note using simple block-style letters, a note that said this was a robbery, no dye packs, no alarms, and there wouldn't be any problems. After that I moved from the Marathon gas station and parked outside the bank, backed in so when I left I'd be able to jump inside and go. I left the car running. I didn't have a getaway man, so I had to leave the motor going. Then I adjusted my clothing, stood tall like I was Cary Grant, walked like I wasn't in pain, entered the bank, and stood in line behind two more people.

The two transactions in front of me took a lifetime. When I made it to the teller she looked me in my face and asked me how she could help me. She had a natural hairstyle that made me think about Abbey Rose. I had traumatized her. But so be it, trauma was part of the business, just like losing a job or a home or watching your wife laugh in the sleet with another man.

I put a smile on my face, hoped my split lip and bruised face had healed enough to make me look like a businessman in a wrinkled suit, a man who had slipped and fallen on an icy sidewalk and had a bad morning. The teller looked like she was a young college student, not quite out of her teens yet.

I slid her the note that let her know I was robbing the bank, a note that told her to stay calm and to quietly put all of her money in a bag. At that same moment, a worker at the drive-through called for her attention. She was distracted and looked upset and didn't take the note. Without reading the instructions, she slid the note back toward me.

She said, "I'm sorry to keep you waiting, sir, but I have to close my window. Please go to the next window. I do apologize."

Then she walked away, went to the drive-through area to assist her coworker. I looked down at my note.

I took my note and put it back inside my left pocket, caught off guard by what had happened, or by what hadn't happened. The next window was occupied, so I had to step back to the front of the line. I regrouped, did what she asked, and when the next teller was free, I went to the next window.

This girl had straight hair parted on the right side.

She said, "Good morning, sir."

I started coughing and raised my arm so I could cough into the bend in my suit coat, and the coughing escalated, became bad enough to make me bend over and put my palms on my knees.

When I stood upright and wiped tears from my eyes, she was looking at me, her eyes wide.

She asked, "Mister, are you all right?"

I waved my hand but my severe coughing returned and refused to end. It took me a good thirty seconds to get it under control. By then every employee and customer was looking in my direction.

She stammered, "You sure you're okay?"

I slipped my hand inside my left pocket and the sides of my fingers clung to the note, wanted to pull it out in a way that left no fingerprints. The young girl wore a cross. There wasn't any barrier between us, only the counter itself. I could reach out and grab her if I wanted. I pulled my hand back out and with my other hand I reached inside my right pocket. The Mexican switchblade was inside that pocket. My fingers moved around that blade and came out holding a wrinkled twenty.

With my fedora tilted down over one eye, I handed the teller the twenty and asked her to give me change, said I wanted all singles. She smiled and then counted out twenty ones, slid them toward me, and told me to have a nice day. I held the money and paused. It wasn't too late. I could hand her the note. I could be out of there in two minutes.

When I glanced to my right, a guard I hadn't seen before was standing by the entrance, his eyes on the teller. He was a middle-aged dark-skinned man, and his body language said he was cold and overworked. He must've been inside the bathroom. Or he had stepped inside one of the managers' offices.

Something clicked on inside my head, an intense realization that returned me to the tragedy in Los Angeles. I imagined that was what had happened at Wells Fargo with Sammy and Rick. The guard had stepped to the side, then seconds after the robbery had been set in motion, he had returned. Sammy had seen the soldier-turned-security-guard first, panicked, then flipped out and drew his gun. I'd bet the security guard had done the same, panicked and made it a showdown.

Sammy and the guard had fired at almost the same moment and both of their shots had found flesh and blood. Then Rick had grabbed the money and Sammy and did his best to flee the bank.

I heard laughter, the jovial laughter that came from two dead men, Rick and Sammy. They were standing by the door with their guns drawn and pointed at people. They looked normal.

All of a sudden I felt nervous, my mind first telling me that I was robbing a bank, then my mind reminding me that the note was still inside my pocket, that no crime had been committed.

The security guard stared at me, as did everyone else. Coughing had put an unwanted spotlight on me. This wasn't a business that could stand up to the heat from spotlights. Then insult came to stand with my injury. The security guard came to me, not to arrest me, but to bring tissues.

Under the eye of every employee and customer, I bumped by Rick and Sammy, exited the bank coughing. When I collapsed inside my Buick Wildcat, I shivered like I had fallen inside a block of ice.

Rick and Sammy were sitting in the backseat. I saw them in the rearview mirror.

My cellular rang. It was Jackie. I didn't answer.

Sammy's head was split wide and blood ran down over his face like sweat. Rick's chest was opened, his insides ragged and exposed, his white shirt turning a deep red.

Rick said, "You'll be with us soon, Dmytryk."

But when I pursed my lips and I turned around in anger, no one was there.

I rubbed my eyes and tried to purge my madness and erase the ghosts of crimes past.

I reached and touched the backseat where they had been, felt moisture and trembled when I looked at my hand. For a moment I saw blood on my fingers. Dark red blood. Then that blood was gone and the moisture staining my fingers and palms was nothing more than my own sweat.

Cars pulled into the lot and parked illegally in front of Blockbuster and the Kroger grocery store. People hurried by, but frozen windows that were fogged over hid my heated misery. My body wanted to ball up into the fetal position, but there wasn't enough room. I leaned forward, my hands gripping the steering wheel with all my might. I was sweating like I was in labor. Anger flowed from my eyes like water from a broken faucet.

My cellular rang again. It was Jackie. Part of me had hoped that it was Cora. I answered.

Jackie said, "What happened in L.A.?"

"What did Eddie Coyle and Cora have to say?"

"Answer me. What happened between the safe house and when I woke up in Phoenix?"

"I have no idea what you mean, but we can talk. But not over the phone."

"The phone's not bugged. I'm alone and driving. And I'm not recording. I don't need to."

"In person. Not on the phone. Face-to-face."

"I'm on Camp Creek heading toward Dallas. Meet me at the safe house now."

"Not the safe house. Find some other location in the same area. Maybe in Hiram."

"Don't give me orders. This runs the way I say it will run, Dmytryk."

"Don't pull my strings like you're in charge."

"You're underwater on this one. Be careful what you do or say."

"Jackie Brown, I will get to Dallas when I get there."

"Where are you?"

"Off I-285, parked outside a bank wondering how much money they have inside the vault."

"I know you're not about to put us at risk by doing a job."

"Then wondering how long it will take to drive to Mexico."

"You're not thinking about skipping out on me, are you?"

"Why would I do that? Because I owe you a few grand and now you're trying to throw a noose around my neck?"

"Maybe six hundred thousand."

"What?"

"This job they have. We're looking at six hundred thousand."

"They said twenty grand each."

"This is a real job, Dmytryk. This is what we've been aiming for."

I paused. "You're lying."

She said, "Didn't Cora and Eddie Coyle give you the updates this morning?"

I took a deep breath. "They haven't told me the details, not yet."

"Only Cora knows the details. And by the way, this being a six-figure job, what you owe me has gone up drastically."

"I hear the greed in your voice. It sounds like sweet music in my ears."

"Don't patronize me. My silence does not come cheap."

"All so you can be a good mother and kidnap your kid."

"Get to Dallas. If you're smart you'll get there before Eddie Coyle and Cora get there."

"When I'm ready. If I'm ready. I'm having second thoughts."

"You owe me and you will pay me."

"You lied to me. That betrayal should cancel out my debt."

"Mess this payday up for me and I'll come to Detroit and I'll bury you, Dmytryk."

"Is that supposed to scare me?"

"It could take a week or months, but I'd find you."

"I wouldn't hide from you, Jackie. I'd meet you halfway and put a hole in your head."

"But before I did any of that, I'd fly back to L.A. and put one lucky writer six feet under the ground. One way or another, Abbey Rose is on borrowed time. Were you sleeping with her? Is that what this is about? I don't know how you ended up in that SUV with her or why you let her go, but I'll go back and do what you should've had the guts to do. If she was your mistress, I don't care. She knows too much."

"Abbey Rose isn't in this, so leave her out. I'll pay you what I owe and not a dime more."

"We'll see about that. We'll see how much Abbey Rose is worth to you."

"Touch Abbey Rose, just say her name one more time . . . if you even *think* her name, you'll see a side of me that will make you run to meet Sammy's open arms."

"You don't scare me."

She hung up the phone.

I did the same, closed it and let it fall into my lap.

I whispered, "Six hundred thousand dollars."

Behind me, Sammy frowned while Rick smiled like a politician.

Rick said, "She's lying, you know that, right?"

Sammy said, "I was barely dead and you were in bed with Jackie."

"She came on to me, Sammy."

"That's no excuse."

"You chickened out in that damn bank, Dmytryk."

"No wonder Cora left you for that smooth-talking Eddie Coyle."

"*Shut up.*" I rubbed my face and groaned.

"You're nothing but a piece of crap of a man in a nice suit."

"I bet Eddie Coyle was hitting that while you were home waiting for her to come back."

Teeth gritted, I turned around and fired two shots where Sammy had been. No one was there. A few deep breaths later I dropped the gun on the passenger seat.

I whispered, "Come back, Sammy. Come back and I'll kill you again."

I stared at the Bank of America for a moment, my windshield wipers on high, battling a mixture of snow and sleet that was coming down. I rubbed my eyes to get some clarity, then I pulled out and drove Cascade Road past I-20 and on toward Fulton Industrial.

Rick and Sammy were living and breathing inside my head.

Jackie had become a vise grip and she had me by the balls.

And Cora had me by the heart.

15

Two days ago in L.A.

After I had stuffed Jackie's drunken body into the backseat of my Buick Wildcat, I returned to the scene of the crime to dispose of the stolen getaway car I'd totaled. It was gone, and by now they had run the plates and knew the car was hot. My DNA was on that airbag. If the car had been there, I was planning to pour gas inside and set the car on fire. I couldn't go to the tow yard without being arrested.

With Jackie unconscious and moaning in the backseat, I'd driven another mile east of that richness and parked across the street from a one-level stucco home. From there, I saw a soft light was on inside the front window. A television was on in what must've been the master bedroom, its screen lighting up a small window on the left side of the house. It was after three in the morning but someone might've been awake. From where I was sitting it looked like she had a Christmas tree up too.

I was in the Crenshaw District, right off Vernon in the heart of the

Leimert Park area. I opened my car door and stepped out into a two-way street that had timeworn foreign cars parallel-parked in both directions. Hands inside my pants pockets, jaw clenched, and shoulders hunched like James Dean in his iconic photograph, I focused my eyes on the modest home where Abbey Rose lived. Cars passed every now and then, but the area was serene.

In the distance, a car alarm sounded. Every step of the way I searched for police cars. My heart beat like I was being chased. Very few homes had lights on. Homes meant families. Homes meant people who worked nine to five, some beyond those hours. The barrio was lined with single-level homes, the streets and yards decorated with palm trees. A block away was the start of a series of two-level stucco apartments that had been built at least fifty years ago, the same time frame for all of the stucco and brick homes. Most of the palm trees were tall enough to feel just as old. Nothing in the area looked any newer than half a century.

There was a five-foot-tall white metal gate that led to Abbey Rose's yellow stucco home. All the houses on the street were close to each other, no more than three trash-can widths from one driveway to the next. I opened her gate in small degrees before I stepped inside and paused. Her wrecked SUV was in her driveway. It had been backed in. That damaged BMW confirmed I was in the right place. I frowned, then I slid my hand inside my pocket and took out what I needed. I took another step toward the front door.

From the front window I had a good view of a dining room table and a small Christmas tree. What I saw sitting on the dining room table pulled me closer. My father's fedora was on that table in plain sight, spotlighted where I could see what I had left behind.

I'd do what I had to do in order to get that hat back.

I took another step forward, a step that activated the porch light. Brightness hit me like the spotlight from a police car. At the same moment, grass rustled behind me and I heard intense breathing.

Someone or something lurked behind me. I turned around in time to realize something was being swung at my head. I ducked, but not fast enough. The solid object grazed the left side of my head against my ear. It wasn't a dead-on blow, but it was enough to make my world erupt. The fire that had been inside my heart created electric colors in my brain, a display of fireworks as the ground rushed up toward my wounded face. If that blow had been dead-on, the only color I would've seen would've been black.

My hands reached out to break my fall, but it was too late.

My first fear was that the police had been waiting on me. Another blow came down on my shoulder and added to my agony. When I moved, three more blows came in rapid succession, two to my left leg and one to my lower back. The animal instincts inside of me took over and I growled, struggled to get up, and prepared to rush and tackle my aggressor. Then another blow assaulted the muscle in my right leg, put pain right above my knee, and that pain spread up and down in rapid waves. I battled the pain and moved, but that agony erupted like a volcano and I met the ground with unbridled force.

My attacker backed away and waited. Angry words were said but all sounds were a distant hum. I kept growling and struggling to roll over and get to my feet. I'd never been in the ring like my father had, but I was my father's son. My mind screamed for my body to get up, but pain held me down. All I could see was the silhouette that was dominating me. The shape of a woman and miles of wild and incensed hair were all I could see.

Abbey Rose lorded over me, an aluminum baseball bat in her hand.

She said, "All day, since you kidnapped me, all I've wanted to do was kill you."

I made it up on my good knee and pressed on, moved through the pain, became Atlas standing up with the world on his back. Before I could struggle to my feet she was standing no more than three yards away from me. She was close enough for me to stumble and tackle her, close enough for me to grab her and slam her on the ground, but I saw why she was so bold. She had dropped the aluminum bat, but she was brandishing a gun. It wasn't a big gun, but it was a gun. That didn't lessen my anger.

I looked up at her, her porch light on behind her head, its light coming through her mountain of hair. There was enough light from the streets to reveal her face as an outline of anger and horror.

A sharp pain took me back down on one knee. I reached inside my jacket and she aimed the gun like she was ready to shoot me in the center of my face. She was afraid, but she held the gun like she'd had training. I took out a golden business envelope that had been folded three times. Lips tight, I slid the package toward her, then raised my hands. Her full name was written across the face of the envelope.

She asked, "What is this?"

"That . . . the things I took from you, the insurance card and your license, everything is in the envelope. Along with five thousand dollars, enough to cover getting your German-made SUV fixed."

"I don't want your money."

"God, you have me hurting bad. I'm in pain."

"You're in pain? After what you did to me, do you think I care? You're in pain? Good, so now you know how I feel on the inside. I've been suffering and crying and trying not to lose my mind all day. The damage you did to my truck is nothing compared to the terror I've felt all day. The damage you did to my truck is nothing compared to what you have done to my soul. I have relived the experience in my mind all day long. Do you understand?"

Abbey Rose aimed the gun at my chest and I put a hand up like my flesh was bulletproof. She came around me and patted me down like she was looking for a weapon but stopped when she felt the outline of my wallet. She took my wallet and opened it up. She took out my driver's license.

She read my name. "I know who you are, I have your address in Detroit, and I know what you did today. I know why you were running. I know why all the police helicopters were over the bank."

I shifted in my pain. "You hid in your yard and you waited for me until three in the morning?"

"I've been jumping at every noise since I came home."

"With a damn baseball bat? What, are you crazy?"

"You came to hurt me. Or worse."

"Do you think I'm dumb enough to walk up to your front door if I was coming to hurt you?"

"You fired a gun at me. You fired a gun at me two times."

"I saved your life. If I didn't pretend to shoot you, the people I work with would've killed you."

"*Did you hear me?* You traumatized me in ways that I can't begin to explain. *I've spent every second since you ran into the back of my SUV . . . every second I have been living in fear.*"

"I just wanted to pay you for your damages and get my father's fedora."

"*I don't care about your father's fedora.*"

Her voice remained low and intense, but it trembled with anger, fear, and the desire for revenge.

She said, "I had no idea what you were going to do to me. I had no idea. Do you have any idea what that is like? I knew I was about to die, but I didn't know how, and I didn't know how long it would take. But what scared me even more were the horrible things I imagined you would do to me."

"I'm not a rapist."

"How would I know that?"

Her anger was palpable. She wanted revenge.

Face bruised, nose bloodied, distressed, and down on my knees, I grimaced at Abbey Rose.

"I'm sorry. Those simple words are all that I can offer. That's all I can say."

"You took me hostage, put a knife to my neck and threatened me, fired a gun at me twice, and all you can do is throw money at my feet and say that you're sorry, as if that could erase what's happened?"

I could see the bottomless pain in Abbey Rose's eyes. The light hit her eyes and what I saw was like looking inside a movie projector. I saw myself getting inside her SUV and knocking her books and coffee cup to the side, pulling out the Mexican switchblade while her heart beat like it wanted to explode inside her chest. I heard her begging me not to give her a horrible death as sirens and helicopters sounded all over the city of fallen angels.

She said, "Move and I'll shoot you."

Abbey Rose had on blue UCLA sweats and runner's tennis shoes.

She backed away and disappeared inside the house, but she was back within seconds. She had my father's fedora in her hand. She tossed it at me and it landed near my feet. She kept her eyes on me, then tucked the bat underneath her armpit and squatted, picked up the envelope and moved into the light, read the front of the package, read her name and the two-word message, then paused before she stuffed it inside her sweats at the small of her back.

Abbey Rose didn't say anything for a long time.

She whispered, "Close your eyes."

"I'm not closing my eyes."

She clenched her jaw and came a step closer. "One way or another you're going to close your eyes. So do it your way, or do it my way, and if you do it my way, you'll never be able to open your eyes again."

She had the gun. She believed that she was in control, that she held my life in her hands.

So with reluctance, I closed my eyes.

The temperature had plummeted and was in the upper forties. Over an hour went by before I heard Abbey Rose move around. By then I was in pain and cold from head to toes. Jackie would wake up soon, drunk and in custody, kicking and screaming.

I whispered, "You still there?"

Her voice trembled. "How does it feel?"

"Cold. Fingers are numb. Everywhere you hit hurts bad."

Another moment passed.

She asked, "Is there a reward for your capture?"

I didn't answer.

"I hope there is. God knows I could use the money. And the publicity. I could be on CNN or even *Oprah* talking about how I trapped a despicable creature in my front yard. I captured a dangerous man all by myself. How does that sound to you, *Dmytryk from Detroit?*"

After that she said nothing. It felt as if thirty more minutes passed.

Abbey Rose snapped, "I've had enough of this. I've had all I can take of you."

"What does that mean?"

"Leave. I want you to leave my property. I want you out of my life."

Fury rose in her voice and I imagined that same fury was in her body language.

And that fury had probably moved from her heart and rested in the hand holding the gun.

It took me a moment to open my eyes and adjust to my surroundings. If she was ready to give me my freedom, I wanted to hurry and seize the moment before her mood changed. But I couldn't get up without falling flat on my face. My legs were in severe pain; every muscle tingled from the cold and lack of circulation. After three hours with nothing supporting my back, standing up was torture. My body ached and my sinuses drained as the cold air hugged me. I didn't have the energy to raise my hand to wipe my face.

She asked, "Why?"

"Why what?"

"Why do you rob banks?"

"Sounds like you're asking for a thirty-second job pitch."

"Why do you do something so . . . disgusting?"

It took me a moment, because for a moment I didn't know where to start. Part of me wanted to remain silent, but the other part of me, the part that needed to talk through the pain, took over. I talked like I was on the stand at my trial, twelve of my peers staring at me through unsympathetic eyes, my words strong and intent, but at the same time filled with dignity and not begging for mercy because I accepted my life for what it had become.

Abbey Rose said, "Your wife."

"What about her?"

"You robbed banks for your wife."

"I did it for us."

"But she asked you to?"

"She saw it as a viable option."

"I don't understand. Why would you do something like that?"

It strained my neck to turn, but I glanced back and saw Abbey Rose had lowered her gun.

"Is your wife with you?"

"No. She left me. I haven't heard from her for the last six months."

Lights were coming on in the houses in the neighborhood. Car after car passed by.

I said, "You're a writer."

"Part-time."

"What else do you do?"

"Why?"

"You know all about me, so I was asking."

"I was a teacher. But after nine years, I lost my job when our wonderful governor cut the budget and sent thousands of educators to the unemployment line."

"I'm sorry to hear that hard times have come to your front door."

"So the money you brought me, I really need it. I just don't know if I can keep it. That wouldn't be right to do. This is probably stolen money. This is dirty money."

"I borrowed four from a loan shark and the rest came out of my pockets."

Abbey Rose stood. Her features remained outlined, but the heat from her eyes illuminated her anguish. It was the second time that night I looked into the eyes of a heartbroken woman. Abbey Rose shook her head like I was the saddest thing she'd ever seen.

I said, "I'm sorry, Abbey Rose. I'm sorry for everything."

Her frown was strong. "I can't believe you actually came to my home."

"With honorable intentions."

She watched me for a moment. "Your bruises—"

"Don't worry about me. Whatever I received, I deserved ten times over."

"You're lucky. I was aiming at your head, but you ducked."

"My father was a boxer. I guess that I inherited some of his natural instinct."

"Either way, you'll need medical attention."

"I don't have insurance, so I'll have to buy a Band-Aid and rough this on my own."

Abbey Rose told me not to move, then she went inside, locked her screen door, and vanished inside her home. A few moments passed before she opened the door and handed me a white bottle. I looked at the bottle, could make out CVS PHARMACY across the top, heard at least twenty pills rattle, but my eyes were too watery to read the smaller lettering on the label.

"What's this?"

"Vicodin."

"This won't be necessary."

"Take them," she said. "And go."

"You haven't called the police?"

"Not yet. I should have, but not yet."

"But you have to."

"You're a criminal."

"It's been a bad day. My friends were shot. One of them was killed."

"He was a criminal and he received what he deserved."

"Maybe. But he was a family man. He had a wife and kids. My other friend was shot too, and he had a family as well. All they were trying to do was take care of their families."

"What about the family of the security guard who was shot?"

"He's a hero too."

"Stop searching for empathy. I have none for people like you, not after what you did."

"I panicked. I was afraid. Things went bad and got out of control."

"How could you do something so heinous? You sound and dress very smart. You're very educated, I can tell that. I want to know what it's like to do what you have done. I saw the news. I saw them interviewing the people who worked at the Wells Fargo. One girl was crying so hard she couldn't talk. You've ruined the lives of over a dozen people."

I coughed and wanted to spit but swallowed. More coughs came before I licked around my mouth and tried to see if I tasted blood. I couldn't tell how much damage she had done.

I dropped the bottle of Vicodin Abbey gave me inside my coat pocket, then fought to my feet and found my balance before I slipped my fedora on my head.

I limped to the gate, looked back, and said, "For what it's worth, I'm sorry."

"Am I safe?"

"What do you mean?"

"Are your friends going to look for me, come back to my home and . . ."

"They have no idea who you are. They don't know your name. You're safe."

"How do I know that you're not lying to me right now?"

"I've sacrificed everything to protect you. I lied to the people I work with. If it falls apart, it's me they'll kill. They don't know. And they have no way of finding out. You're free. No matter what happens to me this morning, you're free. I'm the wanted man."

She shook her head and took a step away from me.

She snapped, "*Ahora, te vas de mi casa y de mi vida.*"

Her Spanish was firm and crisp, her pronunciation good enough to stop me where I stood. Her Spanish was better than my wife's Spanish, maybe better than mine.

Each word sounded like agony as I responded "*Te escucho, y te comprendo todo . . . todo lo que dijiste.*"

I fought with my injuries, hurried and limped to my Buick, then leaned against the car and grimaced. Jackie was just as I had left her. She sat up for a moment and looked around, then collapsed again. I took a hundred breaths and saw the sky becoming light enough to reveal the army of mountains that stood around Los Angeles. It took forever for me to open the door and crawl inside. It took another forever to pull out my keys and slide them inside the ignition. Then I made a U-turn and drove away, sped toward Vernon, and turned left, mixed with early-morning traffic that was battling toward I-110, and from there I would hide among thousands and find the I-10, the sun rising over the palm trees, the body that housed my soul dying a slow death.

16

Dallas, Georgia. It was a red, white, and blue land inside America's zip code 30132.

Jackie was waiting. When I called her, she said that she was right off Merchants Drive and parked on Main Street close to Curl's Pharmacy, a strip that had free parking from post to post and was lined with Christmas decorations and old election campaign posters for the local Republican. The heart of Main Street was simple, a city block long and lined with the Dallas Theater, Beauty Nook, Main Street Sandwich Shop, and sprinkled with one- and two-story buildings. A few of those historic edifices were antique shops that carried this area's history back into the Civil War. What concerned me had been planted where Main Street turned into North Confederate; at that intersection was the building that housed the local police department.

Jackie was inside Sal's Pizzeria. She was sitting at a table and eating chicken soup when I walked inside. She was alone reading the front page of the *Dallas New Era*. A *Paulding-Neighbor* was next to her, unopened. For some reason I had expected Eddie Coyle to be there too. I'd expected a setup. I sat down and Jackie reached to her left side and pulled a book out of a Barnes & Noble bag. She slid the book across the table.

I picked it up. It was a heavy book, almost six hundred pages long. I flipped the book over and stared down at a beautiful picture of Abbey Rose's face.

I slid the book back to Jackie. She put it back on her left side.

She said, "Wanted to make sure we were on the same page."

"You're a manipulative woman."

"I go after what I need and I get it. Same as you, Dmytryk. Same as you."

"But you don't care what the collateral damage might be. I do. I care about the damage."

"You'll get over it and you can survive this, provided I don't tell Eddie Coyle or his brother. Eddie Coyle is a murderer and a sociopath and an opportunist and his personality flaws make him good at what he does. That's why women love him. He's an evil bastard and evil bastards are irresistible."

"To someone who is weak and lost and suffers from diminished self-esteem, yeah, he would be."

Another mild coughing fit attacked me. When I was done, the pain in my back grabbed at me.

Jackie asked, "Do you want to go to the emergency room?"

"I'll be fine, Jackie."

"Despite any other deals we make, make sure you pay me back my money."

"What do you know about the pending withdrawal?"

"They've been tight-lipped about it. Rick knew the details. Sammy didn't know everything. With Rick and Sammy gone, Eddie Coyle pulled you in. That's the best I can tell you right now."

"Why don't you know?"

"Because I don't care. I just want to do it, get the money, and do what I have to do."

A moment passed. She'd said Sammy's name and her face became flushed.

She whispered, "Sammy told me he loved me."

A pretty waitress named Mo came to the table, brought us glasses of water, and asked me what I would like from the menu. I ordered the same thing Jackie had, chicken soup. She looked at my split lip and bruised face. Some surprise registered in her eyes, but she didn't ask any questions.

When Mo walked away, I looked down at my left hand, stared at my wedding ring for a moment before I raised my head and frowned at Jackie. She didn't say anything, just held the arrogant demeanor of a desperate woman who thought that she had the upper hand.

Jackie said, "Now you know about your loyal wife and your buddy Eddie Coyle."

I nodded. My eyes were on the ghosts standing in the middle of the street. "Let Los Angeles be the topic of this sub-rosa meeting, not Cora and Eddie Coyle."

Jackie sipped her soup.

I asked, "What's your bottom line?"

"I want my money repaid. Plus another ten thousand to keep Abbey Rose between us."

I smiled my father's "you've gone too far" smile. He gave that smile to men and never hesitated to extend that same smile to a woman like Jackie.

"Me, you, Cora, and Eddie Coyle."

"And Bishop."

"And Bishop." A moment passed. "Jackie, you played me."

"No more than Sammy and Rick played you. We all have roles and I'm playing mine."

"You're blackmailing me, is that what this is?"

"Dmytryk."

"What?"

She took a deep breath. "Sammy used to give me this formula. Zinc, fructose, potassium, vitamin C, protein, and free amino acids. It clears up my skin."

"That's good to know."

"And now I need a fresh supply."

"You're joking, right?"

"Sammy understood all of my problems and he didn't judge or try and ridicule me."

"Zinc and protein. That's what you wanted from me in Texas."

"At first."

"You were in the bathroom for an hour."

"I did what I had to do. At first. I'll admit that. That was all I wanted. But . . . you're different. I was thinking, if the guy I had a child with were someone like you, then I wouldn't have the problems I have now. Your wife, she took you for granted, Dmytryk."

"You played me big-time."

"I felt for you and wanted to console you the best way I could."

"With sex."

"It was better than sending a text message."

"What is up with you and this soft attitude, Jackie? This isn't you. You're an alcoholic who sleeps with married men, has sex with the bedroom door wide open for everyone to see, kills people for fun, and shoots innocent televisions to make a point."

"If that's all you see when you look at me, then I wish you were dead, Dmytryk. You're nothing to me and you'll never be anything more than a nerd in an insurance man's shoes."

"Now, that's the frantic, inconsiderate, self-centered Jackie I know."

"I'm a good woman. Sammy was going to leave his wife and be with me."

"I wouldn't take bets on that one."

"He was. Sammy was a man of his word. Everything that Sammy did for me, every promise Sammy ever made, you messed that up for me and now you owe me."

My attention remained outside. For a moment I saw Rick and Sammy.

Jackie gave me a one-sided smile. "You have to make good on Sammy's promises."

"I'm not kidnapping your kid."

She paused. Frowned. Then she smiled again and said, "Cora knows we slept together. She didn't look too happy about it."

"Why did you tell her?"

"Because I don't like her. I've never liked her. Eddie Coyle doesn't need her in his crew."

"Because she's prettier than you. She's prettier and has the kind of skin you wish you had."

240

Jackie threw her frigid water in my face. I picked up my glass and returned the gesture. Water crashed against her face and she howled and choked. I picked up a napkin and wiped my face, then I smiled.

Jackie picked up a fork. I picked up a knife.

The waitress had seen the double assault and hurried our way with her mouth open wide.

Jackie snapped, "Mind your own business and go away."

The two customers in the room looked at us, then turned their eyes away as the mumbles began.

I wanted to put my knife in Jackie's throat. I wanted to feed her some lead.

Jackie put her fork down. I put my knife to the side.

She said, "You've changed."

I coughed a bit and tasted my own blood before I answered her. "Have I?"

"You're acting like you're one of us now. All it took was for someone to beat you to Death's doorstep and for Cora to break your heart. But I think what Cora has done to you is the greatest injury."

"Say her name again and I'll break your neck."

"Cora. Cora Knight. Cora, Cora, Cora. You don't like it? Cora, Cora, Cora."

"Grow up," I said as I picked up my spoon and began eating my chicken soup.

Pain coursed throughout my body. I wanted another Vicodin. I wanted two more. I told myself to ride it out. The side effects of the medicine were getting the best of me. Jackie picked up napkins and wiped water from her face, trying to dab her dress and stop the water from soaking in. In this weather, stepping outside in wet clothing could be instant pneumonia.

I said, "No wonder they took your kid."

She pulled her lips in, swallowed, then sat there in silence. She was in her own kind of pain, an inner pain that made her irrational. Her suffering made her reckless, taking risks that could have everyone in jail or dead at the scene of a crime. Sleeping with Sammy had been a calculated risk, a means to an end. And now she needed me to put on a dead man's shoes.

She whispered, "When this is done, Dmytryk, will you help me get my kid?"

"Are you deaf or just stupid?"

"Please? My kid is in Chattanooga. That's two hours from here. Go with me, help me out. Just be the driver. You won't be seen. I'll cancel the debt. You can keep the four grand and I'll throw you five more. How does that sound? It won't take more than an hour. I just need you to drive us back toward Mexico."

The tables had turned. When she was done I shook my head as my final answer.

I looked out the window and said, "Yeah, Sammy knew how to pick his women."

"Is that tone and look supposed to scare me? Save that look for Cora. My bad. She's with Eddie Coyle. That's where she's bouncing up and down. That's the pole she's swinging from these days."

"You're slipping off into the deep end of the pool."

"You want me to apologize? I mean on my knees, mouth wide open, apologize."

"You're filthy."

"Did you enjoy our time in Texas? Did that mean anything, or did you just use me?"

There was no light inside Jackie, only darkness. She was disgusting and lewd. And the carnal dirtiness of a woman always appealed to men, no matter how clean they were. Maybe because no matter how many showers we took, no matter how long we bathed, we were all made of dirt and would forever be creatures of dirt. Jackie had a filthy, arrogant, and dark demeanor that angered me. And her darkness appealed to the resentment inside me, the part that had taken control. Jackie was a powder keg of trouble. But then again, to a thinking man, all women were.

Jackie asked, "Well, in that case, are we going to have sex again, or was Texas one shot?"

That was when I saw the Paulding County sheriff stop out front.

I told Jackie that law enforcement had pulled up outside and double-parked.

Jackie wiped water from her face and whispered, "FBI or local?"

"Local."

"How many cars?"

"One car."

"How many officers?"

"Two."

"We can take them if we have to, Dmytryk. I'll never let a small-town cop take me in."

"Sit still. Sit still and act like a lady. I know that's difficult for you, but do it."

Two young officers brought the cold inside. They looked at us in a way that told us they were there on business. They didn't greet us, just went directly to the waitress, then came to us and asked us what was the problem. The waitress had called and reported the disturbance. I smiled, said that everything was fine. Nothing to worry about.

Jackie said, "It's called foreplay. You've heard of foreplay, haven't you, or don't they do that in Dall-ass, Georgia? You should see what we do at ice cream parlors or in the whip cream section of Kroger. Whip cream on breasts like these, can you imagine that, officer? Well, we used water, but maybe we should've ordered some honey. Imagine that, officer, me butt naked, on this table with honey smeared over all God gave me. Now, that would have been a reason for the waitress to call all the men in town."

The officers turned red, swallowed, looked at each other, then asked us to leave their city. Their stares said that it was that or we'd take a short walk to the police station on the next corner.

The men who guarded this Republican and Christian haven knew what I knew. Jackie was cynical. Jackie was evil, and evil had to be run out of town before that disease spread.

We stood up to leave, the gun inside my coat pocket weighing more than five years in jail, and as we left Jackie told them all to have a merry Christmas, only she added a curt and powerful word that started with the letter *F* and ended with the eleventh letter of the alphabet, that singular word to give a deeper and more personal meaning to that clichéd and overbearing yuletide expression.

17

Eddie Coyle's murderous brother was inside the safe house when I arrived. Eddie Coyle wasn't there. Neither was Cora. Bishop was dressed in jeans and boots by Harley-Davidson, his heavy coat open wide as he smoked a Marlboro and maintained a firm grip on a loaded .38. He was keeping guard.

He said, "Dmytryk."

Then he smiled. It was a grin that spoke of Eddie Coyle and Cora's intimacy.

His smile got to me and I felt the blood boiling underneath my skin.

I pushed away my pains and stood tall. I took off my fedora and my overcoat, loosened my tie, pulled off my suit coat, checked the time on my pocket watch, then said, "What do you have for me?"

He motioned with his head. "Kitchen table. Everything we need to know is right there."

I dropped my hat and coats on the black sofa.

With the exception of a six-foot-tall Christmas tree that had flashing red, yellow, blue, and green lights, the apartment was unadorned. It had dreary beige walls, dull beige carpet, and furniture that looked like it had all come from the returns area in IKEA. The only thing that stood out was the fifty-inch television in the living area. It was on CNN. Copies of *The Trussville Tribune* and *The Birmingham News* had been dropped on the floor.

Diagrams were on the kitchen table, and at least half a dozen architectural layouts. It was the same diagram that had been inside of Rick's luggage. One of the programs he'd carried was to the edifice for this job. It must've been his part of the job, the area he'd had to memorize to pull his weight on this gig. That let me know that Rick had visited the building at some point and had surveyed the halls to verify the diagrams were on point.

I said, "The vault is in the basement?"

Bishop nodded. "We'll have to handle two, maybe three security guards and make our way to the basement. That's what me, my brother, Jackie, and Cora will do while you have us ready to roll out. The location for the stage-two vehicle is already set. It's on Chalkville Road. We drive about a mile and a half, dump the primary, load up the secondary within ten seconds, and you get us back to the safe house. We split the money. We say good-bye. It's a simple plan."

"I'm still looking at the location of the vault. Long hallway. Stairs. This diagram is telling me that there aren't any windows in this hallway. This bank used to be a fallout shelter."

"It's not a bank."

I looked at the diagrams again. "This is a part of a property that belongs to a church."

Bishop said, "Six Flags over Jesus. That what we call it. Six Flags over Jesus."

I read the details on the map. The megachurch was off an interstate that connected to I-20, only it wasn't the section of the interstate that ran through Atlanta. The area I was looking at was over two hours away. We were robbing a church in Alabama.

I said, "I thought this was a bank job."

"Now you know it's not."

"So this isn't going down on Friday."

He shook his head. "It's going down on Sunday."

"Robbing on the Sabbath."

He nodded. "Amen, brother. Amen."

I stared at the drawings.

Bishop said, "By Tuesday, I'll be in Ocho Rios sipping on drinks."

Entry and exit points were all circled in light blue ink. The immense architecture had a gigantic parking lot, plenty of open space, numerous doors, and a lot of security cameras.

Bishop said, "Most of the cameras aren't in use. They trust the people and they've never had a problem. The cameras are up for insurance purposes, but that's about it. The ones that are working, they'll be pointed up at the sky; Cora's contact will make sure that happens."

There were a lot of hallways, but based on what I saw, two entrances were used the most. The principal entrance was in front and the secondary entrance was in the back. The best entry and escape routes were highlighted in yellow. The secondary or backup exits were highlighted in green. Jackie walked in while I inspected the route that had been highlighted as our getaway. The book she had bought at Barnes & Noble, she put it down on the table, photograph-side up.

I read the location on the map and said, "Trussville?"

Jackie said, "It's right outside of Birmingham."

I looked at her and her expression told me that she had known all along.

She said, "It wasn't my job to give you any information."

"That's very military of you."

"It's about trust, and I can keep secrets, Dmytryk. Everybody knows that I can keep secrets."

Jackie went to the counter and found a fresh bottle of vodka waiting on her. She poured herself two fingers' worth in a glass, then she did the same for Bishop.

I headed inside the bathroom and a panic attack came as soon as I closed the door. It came at me hard, just like it had in Los Angeles, only it was more intense, its waves higher and pounding me with almost too much force to bear. I threw water on my face, then looked at myself in the mirror.

I saw my father's angered face. I saw the anger he held when things were getting to him.

Banks were federally insured. What we stole the government put back. We traumatized the bank employees, but the tellers and security guards had also been trained for what we brought. Each bank knew that being robbed was as inevitable as sunrise.

This job was a church.

I wasn't the most religious man in the world, but I understood morality and degrees of wrongness. This was who my wife had become. This was who *I* had become.

We were monsters now.

The front door opened again and I heard Eddie Coyle's voice.

I heard Cora Knight talking to either Eddie Coyle or Bishop.

When I heard the woman who was still my wife, the world stopped rotating.

She was on the other side of that door and I could smell her, feel her, taste her.

Every vile word she had said at Thumbs Up echoed inside of my head.

Every angered word battered me.

I raced out of the bathroom and hurried toward the front room. Cora saw me running straight toward Eddie Coyle with my hardened hands in fists. I was an executive, a laborer, a man, but before all of that I was a fighter's son. Henrick's blood was in my veins.

If Eddie Coyle had any doubts, they were removed when my right hook connected with his chin and took him down to the floor. Before I could get to him again, his hulking brother had made it to me.

18

Cora screamed.

Jackie sipped her vodka and laughed.

Bishop grabbed me.

The blow put Eddie Coyle flat on his back and scrambling to get to his feet.

Jackie sashayed toward Eddie Coyle. Cora ran toward me, made strong eye contact, and then backed away when she saw in my eyes that she would be next. She began pleading with Bishop, telling him not to take this to another level and mess up the job. They needed me.

They needed me. Her focus was on the bottom line. I'd expected her to run and protect Eddie Coyle, or run back to me, but she remained in the neutral zone, became political and redirected the hostile energy in the direction that would benefit her the most. She said to focus on the job. I'd expected Bishop to come at me in retaliation. They were blood, and Bishop was protective of his brother.

We didn't trade blows, but he wrestled with me, tried to get a good grip on me, maybe hold me so his brother could beat me. My adrenaline was high and my strength had doubled. It was enough to surprise Bishop and take the wrestling match from the kitchen to the living room and we fell into the Christmas tree, made it topple, then we fought and fell on top of it before we rolled to the carpet. The way I was hurting, the damage Abbey Rose had done to my body made that battle short and it didn't end in my favor.

Bishop pushed me near the sofa and I grabbed my coat but dropped it when he grabbed me again, yanked me up, and pushed me up against a wall. He drew his fist back in threat but then he realized I had a gun pointed at his gut. It was Jackie's gun. When he had pushed me on the sofa, I had grabbed my coat and pulled the gun from its pocket. With the injuries I had, I couldn't beat Eddie Coyle and Bishop in a fight. One-on-one I'd take on Bishop and lose, although I'd do my best to make a good showing in the first round. But I didn't expect to win this battle. That blow to Eddie Coyle's chin had been my swan song.

Bishop took his hands off me and backed away. I lowered the gun, grunted when a wave of severe pain coursed through my body, every ache singing Abbey Rose's name.

Eddie Coyle made it up on one knee and had the look of my death in his eyes. Jackie reached for him but he pushed her away and made it back to his feet on his own, his mouth bloodied.

Jackie wasn't laughing anymore.

Cora looked terrified.

My expression was rabid. Christmas tree crap was all over my clothing. My shirttail had been pulled out of my pants, and my shirt was ripped, missing more than a few buttons. Not to mention that I had spots of sweat underneath my armpits. The tree had scratched my face like a passionate lover during a night of wild sex. Bishop's face had received the same fate.

Cora yelled, "Dmytryk."

She said my name the way she had said my name during the first four years of our marriage, spoke my name with fervor and passion, said my name as a wife who loved her husband. All eyes were on me. Each expression was different. I saw fear and anger and respect.

Jackie put her vodka down on the counter and sashayed toward me with her palms extended, desperation and anger in her eyes as she said, "Don't blow this, Dmytryk. Think about what you're doing. One hundred thousand dollars. Is that two-timing cow worth that much? One hundred thousand dollars. Don't be selfish. You're part of this team, so be a team player. You know my situation. This money can help set me straight. This money can get me what I need for my kid. Now, give me that damn gun."

I tossed the gun to Jackie. She caught it and checked to see if it was still loaded.

Jackie said, "You're lucky, Bishop. That man is a killer. He popped someone twice in L.A. Isn't that right, Dmytryk? Tell everybody how you killed somebody in broad daylight and walked away like you were Jesse James."

Bishop was fuming. He moved like he was coming after me again, and I was ready to throw at least two blows before he took me off my feet, but Eddie Coyle yelled his name and stopped him.

Eddie Coyle came over to me, his face twisted in anger. And guilt. A lot of guilt was in his eyes. I moved past him and grabbed my suit coat and my wool topcoat. When I pulled both coats on, Jackie asked me if I was leaving. She ran to me and grabbed my right arm and begged me to stay. Then her expression threatened me. I moved her out of my way. Jackie held on to my arm like she was my wife, like I was her husband and I was walking out on her.

Cora looked at me too. I couldn't tell if she wanted to run to me or take that gun and shoot me. Her life was no longer tethered to mine, though I remained a planet caught in her gravity. She hated every memory of me. She despised everything I represented. What existed between us was dark energy.

Jackie said, "Abbey Rose, Dmytryk. Abbey Rose."

I went to the door and looked back at Eddie Coyle. He went to the kitchen, rinsed the blood out of this mouth, and put on his coat and gloves before he followed me out into the freezing air.

We walked the complex, moved through the cold with our breaths fogging in front of our faces.

Eddie Coyle said, "I could kill you for that."

"I could've killed you five minutes ago. Every time you take a breath, remember that."

He didn't argue with me. This time he was the one with the gun inside his coat pocket. I knew that. If he was going to shoot me and kill me, I didn't want to die in front of Cora. She wasn't the last person I wanted to see. And I didn't want to die in a room filled with people I didn't respect. I'd have rather died outside in the cold.

I took a deep breath and said, "So this is what you and Cora have been planning."

"All of us. Not Just Cora and myself. Rick, Sammy, Jackie, my brother, all of us."

"Six months. Cora's been on your team. She's worked with you and

Rick and Sammy and your brother for six months. You'd pretty much laid me off, pushed me to the side like you were another CEO."

"We did a few jobs. We needed the money to make it happen. A lot of people had to be paid off."

"You robbed banks to finance this church job."

"The last few jobs we did, yeah. Sammy and Rick had done the same, worked and contributed toward financing this payday. We're going to church. That's where this ride is headed. Now you know."

I asked, "Do you have Cora's back?"

"What do you mean?"

"Are you looking out for her best interests or just your own?"

"What's your concern?"

"I don't like her. But I love her. So I'm making sure she gets to the other side of this."

"That's noble of you."

"It's a birth defect."

"She's with me now, Dmytryk. I can protect her if she needs to be protected."

"I know how you operate. Are you planning to harm her when this is done?"

"I told you how I feel about her."

"She's still my wife. Don't touch her in front of me. Don't smile at her in front of me. That's the way it's going to be, Eddie Coyle. I'm here to work this thing for you, like I promised, but I'm going to make sure Cora gets to the other side of this job."

Eddie Coyle pulled his gun out of his pocket. He looked at it, his wounded ego thinking.

He said, "You're loyal."

"I'm a fool. But I know there have been bigger fools in this world."

"Despite that little hiccup you had with Jackie in Texas, you're loyal to Cora."

"I was with Jackie one night. I've known Cora for eight years."

Eddie Coyle rubbed his jaw. "Jackie announced that you'd spent some time getting personal. She said that when this is done, you might be going to South America with her."

I didn't answer. Part of me wanted to believe that he had green-lighted Jackie taking me to bed before Sammy's body had cooled off. If I was going to be in on this deal, he needed a wedge between Cora and me, and Jackie was that wedge. But part of me knew that no man had that power over Jackie.

"Eddie Coyle?"

"Yeah."

"If you're going to shoot me, then shoot me. Otherwise put the gun away."

Eddie Coyle put his gun back inside his pocket. "Don't attack me again, Dmytryk."

Unfazed by his thinly veiled threat, I said, "You've been planning this withdrawal since I met you."

"I'd considered other avenues, but my mind always came back to this one."

Eddie Coyle said that once upon a time he thought about robbing a strip club, but too many of the patrons had guns either on their person or in the trunks of their cars, and security was nothing but gorillas on steroids carrying loaded guns. He wanted to go where there was plenty of money and the likelihood of there being zero guns.

I said, "So you decided to rob Jesus or Moses or Jehovah or whoever their CEO is."

"You have the wrong perspective. I'm talking about making a withdrawal from a big business. A place for the capitalistic to congregate for the price of ten percent of their income as cover charge."

"Get to the end of the sermon. Hurry up so the choir can start singing."

"And we're not the first to rob a church. They have been getting hacked for years."

I didn't say anything. My hand had begun to ache from the blow. I was disappointed that my blow had only knocked him to the ground and didn't knock him into the netherworld, or at least leave him sprawled out and unconscious. My father had thrown a blow and killed a man in the ring. I wanted to hit Eddie Coyle and watch his head explode, like Sammy's had.

Eddie Coyle rubbed his face, spat out blood. "At the risk of sounding redundant and a tad bit paranoid, you're not backing out, are you?"

"Will you stop asking me that? I shook hands with you . . . and Cora."

"You sucker-punched me."

"Well, what did you expect a sucker to do?"

Eddie Coyle spat blood.

I said, "So everything has been worked out?"

"Sammy and Rick and Cora and Jackie and me had it all worked out a month ago."

"And Cora. She said this is her job. How did she manage to make this connection?"

"When she was dancing in Detroit, she met the right people. One of the associate ministers frequented that club whenever he was in town for a gospel event. He was also on the treasury committee. He had a thing for my . . . for Cora. He had a thing for her and he talked a lot. Told her about how much money there was for the taking."

"Security? Megachurches have security better than the White House."

"All worked out. He's given us the info on all security, in uniform and in plainclothes. We have their pictures and we know where they are posted. Cora pulled it all together."

Nothing was said for a moment. I closed my eyes and again I could see Sammy's head being blown apart as Rick struggled to carry him across the parking lot at Wells Fargo. I played it over and over inside my head and asked myself what I could've done. Sammy was dead and Rick had done the same. Sammy and Rick were out there with us. I felt their presence. I saw their shadows.

We walked. The frigid air was numbing my feet. I had the wrong kind of shoes on for this ice.

I asked Eddie Coyle, "You've calculated the risk on this job?"

He nodded. "Six months of preparation. Six months of greasing palms."

"But it all boils down to two minutes."

Eddie Coyle nodded. "Then you get us out of there."

A moment passed. My hand ached from hitting Eddie Coyle in his hard head.

Eddie Coyle said, "What happened with Rick and Sammy?"

"I already told you."

"Did somebody get stupid? Did somebody get nervous?"

"The men who can answer that are both dead."

"No way you could've saved them?"

"Eddie Coyle."

"What?"

I took a breath. "We should send their wives part of this take."

"You can send part of yours. I have my own bills and nothing to feel bad about."

My hands were as numb as my feet. I licked my lips and they felt frozen.

As we made it to the door of the apartment, we heard screaming and shouting.

Cora and Jackie were in an argument.

We stepped back inside the apartment and they moved away from each other. Walked away and fell silent as if nothing had happened. Eddie Coyle asked what the problem was. Cora remained silent, evaluating the awkward moment, and I think I saw some fear abate, fear that she had been made a widow during that short window of time. Jackie said that nothing was wrong, nothing that she couldn't handle, then she sipped on her vodka and came over to me. She put her hand up to my face and smiled. Her touch looked romantic, but I knew she was playing her cards and playing Cora at the same time.

Bishop walked in the door ten seconds later. "Are we ordering pizzas or what?"

I stepped to the dining room table and Eddie Coyle followed, pointed at the diagrams, and told me the plans they had made. I wasn't interested in the details, but I had to listen. I only wanted to know what I was supposed to do to get us all home. I wanted to get back to Detroit and push reset on my life. Cora came over and stood next to me. She filled in the parts that Eddie didn't reveal. She wanted to show she was in charge. Jackie came over and stood next to me, her arm touching mine. Bishop stayed in the background.

I pointed at an area circled in money green and said, "They have a vault inside the basement of the annex. What do you know about it?"

Cora pointed to the vault's location. Our fingers touched.

Electricity was shared, then she pulled away.

She looked disturbed as she said, "It's just like a bank vault. It's a walk-in and it's on a time lock. There aren't any panic buttons. It can only be opened once a weekday, but three times on Sunday, after each service. Only three people are authorized to get inside Fort Knox."

Cora's sweet scent was too much for me to bear and I walked away, went into the bedroom. I looked out into the living area. Jackie picked up the book that had been written by Abbey Rose, held it so the photo on the back could be seen by all, then she followed me, moving her hips side to side and smiling like she was up to no good. I turned away. Jackie closed the bedroom door and I turned to face her. She tossed the book on the bed, then came up to me and put her hands on my chest. She wanted me to sex her right then, wanted me to take her with my wife standing in the next room.

Jackie said, "I figured it out."

"What did you figure out?"

"The four thousand. You used it to pay Abbey Rose to keep her mouth shut."

"You're a smart woman. Wow, you're so smart it's scary."

"I'll kill Abbey Rose. I don't care if you bribed her. She's a threat to my freedom."

"She's innocent. Leave her out of this. Deal with me."

"You know what?"

"What?"

"We should have sex right now. Let them hear. Let Cora hear me and you having fun."

"Back off, Jackie."

She laughed an impudent laugh, her stance distinctively smart and stylish, everything about her bold and vigorous and lively as she ran her mouth like a popinjay who thought she ruled my world.

I walked away, went back into the living room. Jackie followed me, holding her drink and smiling as she put Abbey Rose's book down on the coffee table, picture up, left it there for everyone to see.

Jackie said, "Eddie Coyle, I think you should give the bedroom to me and Dmytryk."

Jealousy emanated from Cora, jealousy and hatred.

Cora threw on her overcoat and announced that she was going for a long walk.

Eddie Coyle said, "You're not allowed to leave this apartment, not alone. You know the rules."

Cora vented her frustration. "I'm going alone. This has become too much. First you railroad me and bring in Dmytryk behind my back, knowing I wasn't ready, and now Jackie shows what kind of *prostituta* she is. I can't handle this crap right now. I need some fresh air, Eddie."

Jackie said, "Tigress Woods having a bad day?"

"Call me that again and I will beat you back to your apartment in Denver, Colorado."

"Tigress Woods, Tigress Woods, Tigress Woods. Bring it, Tigress Woods."

"You better straighten her out, Eddie. Straighten her out before I drive a stake through her heart."

Jackie laughed. "You can dish out adultery but you can't take it. Who would've known?"

"Alfredo. Johnny. Sammy. Now Dmytryk. What is it with you and married men, Jackie?"

"What is it with women who marry good guys like Dmytryk and treat them like crap?"

"What is it with you and married men?"

"It's me, baby. I do something to men; my smile, one kiss, and sanity flees holding hands with rationality. All they know is that they want me, and that becomes their singular obsession. But I'm too smart for any man. A smart woman knows that leasing is better than buying. I screwed your husband, so get over it."

"Eddie, tell her to not talk to me anymore. If she wants to stay on this job she—"

"What's the matter, Cora? You can dish it out but you can't take it?"

"I hope your pathetic kid grows up and is just like you, you nasty . . . jacked-up skin, fat and ugly—how many men have you used just so you could get their come to smear all over your jacked-up skin?"

Jackie headed toward Cora. I grabbed Jackie's arm and she tried to jerk away. Cora came toward Jackie but Eddie Coyle grabbed her left arm. She jerked away. Eddie Coyle stood up and his brother pulled him back down to his seat. He looked at his brother. His brother shook his head and rubbed his eyes like he was tempted to shoot everyone in the room. Cora changed her course, her expression saying that too much was at stake. She headed for the door, opened it, then shut it hard when she stormed out into the cold. Eddie Coyle looked at me. Cora was a wild horse that he couldn't handle.

I said, "Get used to that, Eddie Coyle."

Eddie Coyle looked at me and frowned. I smiled and released a short but vicious chortle.

I said, "Nothing personal, buddy. Just stating the facts."

Before he could respond, I turned away like the woman I had married meant nothing to me.

I wasn't the kind of a man who would chase a woman. I'd love a woman, but I would never make her stay where she didn't want to be. Still, I was human. We had an eight-year history. I knew Cora better than Eddie Coyle ever would. Part of me wanted to follow her. That was the protective part of me that I could never seem to defeat.

Bishop turned on a radio and Mariah Carey let the world know all she wanted for Christmas. He went to the phone in the kitchen, called information, and asked for Domino's Pizza.

I went back to the cluttered dining room table and studied the information they had accumulated. With Sammy's poltergeist standing on one side of me as Rick's specter stood on the other, I felt the Vicodin moving through my veins, slow and sensual, its scent on my every exhalation, a lover that was nose to nose, its side effects embracing and nurturing me as I reviewed the schematics and diagrams for the streets and pathways leading to the annex section of the megachurch. I took out the bottle and took another one of Abbey Rose's feel-good pills. I was lightheaded again. I felt nothing for the atrocious crime they had planned for the last six months.

Money. This was about money. Money was the root of many marriages. Not love.

I had been living in the past. The days of my gallant father had come and gone. And women like my mother were all but extinct. I now accepted what I understood and I had to continue moving forward, ease toward what could be my demise. I swallowed bitterness and focused on what I needed.

Cora came back inside, looking like she was freezing. She and Jackie exchanged fiery glances, dares, but no words were spoken. Cora looked at me for a moment and I saw the memories in her eyes.

In the calmest, kindest voice I could manage I said, *"Nuestro matrimonio se acabó."*

"Lo sé y lo siento."

Eddie Coyle barked, "English. Talk in English. I've let that Mexican talk go on long enough."

With a fresh glass of vodka in hand, Jackie smiled at me, grinned like Sammy had never existed. She glanced at the novel that she had left displayed on the coffee table, then regarded me and winked. She took a slow sashay toward the bedroom and paused at the door, stood there in the frame, posing, shifting her hips side to side, as if she were in heat, inviting me and aggravating Cora all at once.

Cora peeled off her coat and went straight to the bathroom with her head held down.

Abbey Rose would die because of a mistake I'd made in Los Angeles. The walls continued to close in, the concrete pressing against four sides of my head.

Cora exited the bathroom with pursed lips. Her Dominican eyes avoided my glare as she moved back toward the plans and the protection of Eddie Coyle.

I watched my estranged wife stand side by side with Eddie Coyle, and Jackie looked at me and smiled. I headed back to the bedroom. Jackie held her new favorite novel and followed.

She put the novel on the end table, then she closed the bedroom door.

Jackie said, "Cora has feelings for you."

"Not the right kind."

"How do you know?"

"Because she's on the other side of that door and you're in here."

Jackie pulled her dress up, reached a hand underneath, and pulled away her thong, pulled it down and pulled one leg through, let it dangle from her left leg.

I shrugged. "Sometimes sex isn't about sex. Sometimes it's about something else."

"I said that to you."

Outside I heard the television. And I heard laughter.

I heard Cora's laughter.

Jackie said, "Well?"

I unbuckled my pants, unbuckled my belt, and let my suit pants fall.

Abbey Rose watched us. Jackie was on the bed, her rear in the air, having a spastic orgasm. I gave her resentment; I gave it to her like I wanted to destroy everyone. Her hands pulled the covers from the mattress, just like she had done with Sammy, then she tugged the sheets as she broke down and moaned Sammy's name. I didn't know if she thought Sammy was inside, if she saw him in this room, or if she was begging for Sammy to save her. I opened my eyes, looked across the room at the picture of Abbey Rose, saw her judging me. Jackie caught her breath and told me not to stop being rough with her. But I stopped and rolled away from her. This wasn't the kind of intimacy I wanted. But she wanted something from me.

Not long after, she collapsed on the bed, sweat draining down her neck.

I rolled away from her, listened to the voices on the other side of the door.

She kicked her legs and whispered, "Did you make it to the finish line?"

"No. I didn't."

"I needed you to."

"But you and Sammy did."

"I said his name, huh?"

I thought she would apologize, but she didn't. She chuckled and I rolled to the side and stood up. My suit pants were bunched around my shoes. I pulled them up, my pocket watch adding weight to my right pocket while my loose change jingled inside my left. I'd taken my shirt off, but I hadn't removed my white T-shirt. Jackie's blouse was opened and wrinkled, and her bra had been loosened but not removed. Her dress was pulled up to her waist.

I stared down at Abbey Rose's face. Jackie rolled over and rested on her stomach and kicked her feet over and over, just like she had done in L.A. I'd done to her what I felt like the world was doing to me. But I didn't own the sensation of victory.

She grinned and asked, "Want to try again?"

"Not right now."

"If it feels better, we could do it without a condom. You could give it to me that way."

I smiled at Jackie.

She tugged her skirt down in a way that said the candy store was closed and the owner was taking a break. Jackie went into the bathroom and closed the door. A minute later she returned.

Jackie sat down on the bed. I sat next to her with my back against the headboard.

She said, "Sammy told me he loved me. Right before the last job, he told me he loved me. He told me he would give me whatever I needed and wanted to stay with me and forget the world. This is getting to me. Before Sammy, I hadn't had a good night's sleep in a year."

She touched her face.

She whispered, "Come to South America with me, Dmytryk. I promise I won't be like this. I'll be good to you. I'll be better to you than Cora ever was. You, my kid, and me can be a family. And I can give you another kid. I can give you two if you like. You don't have to love me, but you're the kind of man I wish my evil husband had been, and I know that I can love you. Hell, I'll even lose a couple of pounds if you want me to. I'll forget about Sammy. It'll be me and you and my kid. We can be a family."

For a moment, I imagined me and Jackie and her kid living in South America. I imagined freedom and happiness. Then I heard Cora's voice on the other side of that door.

Jackie said, "You're not going to try and cross the finish line?"

Silence was my answer. My mind was on my past, the robbery, the car accident, perseverating those regrettable moments over and over.

I went back to Abbey Rose's book, picked it up, and stared at her photo. Then I put the book down and looked at Jackie. She had turned over and was still bouncing her legs like she was a teenage girl. Everything about Jackie irritated me. But she was all I had.

Jackie asked, "Do you think Sammy really loved me?"

"Of course Sammy loved you. Just like my wife loved me."

I stepped out of the bedroom and went back toward the kitchen. Eddie Coyle was sitting on the sofa and his brother was doing the same, the movie *Reservoir Dogs* on the DVD player. Cora was in the kitchen looking at the plans. She was tense. She had heard Jackie singing her hallelujahs. Jackie's scent was on my flesh, the truth about our marriage was on my pants, and Cora inhaled and shuddered. I stood next to her, stood close to her, the same poses we'd had when we stood before a minister over six years ago.

In a bitter tone she said, "When this job is done, we should file papers for divorce."

I wanted to scream and tell her that I had come from a family that had values. Where I came from, divorce was what Other People did. I now had to accept that I was one of the Other People.

I said, "As long as you pay for it. I'm not spending a dime to get rid of you, not legally."

"What does that mean?"

"It means you know my address. You know where to send the papers."

I went to the sofa and sat down between Eddie Coyle and Bishop, sat back and watched bloodshed and violence and betrayal. When the movie ended, Bishop put on another DVD, *Two Hands* with Heath Ledger. Cora was sitting at the dining room table. Eddie Coyle picked up his worn bible called *The Myth of Male Power* and began rereading his favorite scriptures. Cora glanced my way, her gaze long and empty, but I'd known her for years, so I recognized that expression that for others would be unreadable. She felt betrayed. By Eddie Coyle. By Jackie. By me. I wanted to tell her welcome to the club. The club that was only loyal to money.

I went into the kitchen and poured a glass of water. On the way out I paused by Cora. When she looked up at me I said, "We get this done, we'll never have to see each other again."

She nodded.

I went back to the bedroom.

Jackie was waiting. She was standing next to the bed holding that novel.

She put it down when I entered the room.

I closed the door and opened my duffel bag. I took out a red necktie and two pairs of black socks. I pushed Jackie down on the bed and used my tie to cover her eyes. Then I used my socks to tie her wrists. I gagged her too. When I was done I told her to open her legs.

I was ready to cross the finish line.

19

From the safe house in Dallas, Georgia, to our next destination, we covered one hundred and thirty miles in less than two hours. Eddie Coyle and my soon-to-be ex-wife rode in a white Chevy Suburban with Bishop at the wheel. It was Bishop's vehicle, what he drove when the weather was unfavorable for driving a Harley. Jackie Brown rode with me and we followed them up two-lane interstates that were decorated with snow and melting ice. Jackie was on her cellular phone for the first thirty minutes, her voice soft and motherly, lots of laughing as she had a long conversation with her kid. She was a different person when she talked to her kid. She was likable. She was wrong and hypocritical, but she was loyal. I wished that Cora had been that way with me, as I had been with her.

The call ended and Jackie fell silent, looked incurably sad and heartbroken, then closed her eyes and went to the land of Nod. Maybe she was thinking about her kid and all of her problems, or maybe the vodka and staying up all night were finally catching up with her. We all had a past. We all had a present. We all wanted a better future.

Country music played on the radio and I fell into a lull and let my mind drift. My mind was on the job, but my mind was on Cora too; I thought about who we were eight years ago.

The way Cora and I met was simple. It wasn't forced. It just was a man meeting a woman. I'd seen her working the line. We'd passed each other dozens of times, but we'd never shared a word. She was the woman that most of the men had wanted to become biblical with, but she never dated any of the men she worked with at the plant.

Then on a freezing, gray winter day in Detroit, a day that was too much like today, she had run through the blizzard and caught up with me as I made it to my car, her breath fogging from her face as she looked me up and down and she said, "Your name is Dmytryk, right?"

I cringed with the cold and said, "Yeah. I'm Dmytryk. What's the problem?"

"Saw your name written down. Wasn't sure how to pronounce it."

I nodded. "You have an accent. You're from the East Coast."

"Born in Brooklyn." She shifted from foot to foot. "Been in Detroit most of my life."

We stood in the winter's chill and she shook my gloved hand. When she let go, she had left a small piece of paper resting in my palm. A slip of paper that had ten digits scribbled in red ink. It was the number to her cellular.

She said, "Up to you. Call or not."

I read the name that had been written over the phone number. "You're Cora Mature."

"I'm Cora Mature."

We stood in the cold, the kind of coldness a man or a woman became accustomed to when they lived in the Midwest. We didn't say a word as the snow fell like angels throwing feathers. Cora was beautiful. She had looked so young, innocent, and trustworthy. In that moment she had reminded me of my mother.

I said, "We could meet for drinks after shift on Friday."

"I get my hair done Friday evenings. Saturday is better."

"Saturday is fine. We can go to Grosse Pointe and stop by Dirty Dog for jazz."

"Lunch would be better."

"We can do lunch. We can go over to Windsor. How does sushi at Oishii sound?"

She smiled. "Call and ask me out on a date. Make it official."

"*Nos hablamos y nos vemos este sábado.*"

"You speak Spanish?"

"Yeah."

She smiled. "*¿Cuál es su apellido?*"

"My surname is Knight. It's spelled with a K. Dmytryk Knight."

"What nationality are you?"

"I was born in this city and on this soil and that makes me American."

"Well, I'm from Brooklyn and I'm part Dominican. That makes me Domini-merican."

"I know." I laughed. "Everyone knows. You used to be in the military."

"You know that much about me?"

"Men talk about pretty women, and you are a pretty woman."

"What did the men say about this pretty woman?"

"You're hardworking and serious and it's hard to get you to say hello."

"What else do they say?"

"I can't say. I'm a gentleman."

She smiled. "Good answer."

"It's an honest answer."

She held on to her smile awhile, then she said, "Another question?"

"Sure."

"*¿Tienes novia?*"

"No, I don't have a girlfriend. *Soy soltero.*"

"You're sure that you're single?"

"I'm sure. *¿Y tú? ¿Tienes algún novio o esposo?*"

"No. No boyfriend or husband. *Soy soltera.*"

"Good to hear."

She jogged away, winter coat over blue Dickies jeans and black steel-toes. She wrapped her red scarf around her neck and adjusted her hat before she looked back, waved, and smiled again. That smile was the beginning of my end.

I had taken my cell phone out and dialed her number before she made it to her car.

I said, "Hello, this is Dmytryk. May I speak with Cora?"

"This is Cora."

"I hope this is a good time to call. I would like to ask you out on a date."

"For which day?"

"Saturday evening."

"Let me check my schedule to see if I'm free."

We laughed. I remembered that first laugh like it was yesterday.

We had cut from I-20 to I-459 North and invaded an area where the population was almost one hundred percent white and the median family income was close to seventy thousand a year. That information had been in the notes that Eddie Coyle shared at the safe house in Dallas. Trussville rubbed elbows with Gardendale, Fultondale, Tarrant, Moody, Irondale, Pinson.

Many of the passengers in cars and trucks were in yuletide spirits; some wore Santa Claus hats.

The area was filled with businesses and churches, but the megachurch stood out on Highway 11. Jackie told me that it was ten times the size of the First Baptist that was two miles away. First Baptist was brick. The main building at Six Flags over Jesus was glass and marble, as ostentatious and magnificent as the Crystal Cathedral, a Hollywood church that had been built in Garden Grove, California. Everything in Trussville had been dwarfed by the elongated shadows thrown over the land by the edifice Eddie Coyle had called Six Flags over Jesus.

As we passed by, I stared in amazement.

We went to the safe house that was right off Main Street. It was a two-level, redbrick town home tucked inside Trussville Springs at Riverwalk Hamlet, a subdivision that had one two-lane entry. The only way in or out was across railroad tracks. Eddie Coyle took us to Cahaba Bend and Spring Street, where four town homes stood adjacent.

All were unoccupied. It was a new community and not many of the houses and town homes had been completed. And it didn't look like any of the ones on this short block had been sold. I looked around. It was secluded and big enough for two hundred residences, but I doubt if two dozen were finished. It looked like the work had stopped when the river of money stopped flowing and the economy came to a halt. I'd seen half-built and abandoned communities like this all over the country. Everywhere we had gone to rob a bank it was the same story. It reminded me of the ghost towns back home.

We picked up a copy of *The North/East News* that had been left at the back door, then went inside and dumped our bags at the base of the stairs. The unit Eddie Coyle had managed to appropriate for a day was the model home, so it was furnished top to bottom. Everything evoked a memory and this property reminded me of the one we had lost back in the suburbs of Detroit. Cora stepped in and looked around, then sighed and looked vulnerable. I was sure it reminded Cora of the same life, of those four years when things had been good.

As soon as the door closed we convened in the kitchen and went over the plans and diagrams again. Just like we had done in Dallas, we put the maps and schematics on the tables and walls. It looked like it was less than a minute's drive from the main church to the annex with the vault. Outside of the members of the treasury, three people worked the transfer, and one of them was the inside man, so there would be only two armed men to deal with.

Eddie Coyle said, "Two to put down and one to leave injured."

Cora nodded. "That's the plan."

We talked through the entire scenario, but I focused on my part of the crime. I was going to enter the property off Highway 11, blend in with any traffic going into the church, then drive the team to the back side of the megachurch, move the team to the area that had several annexes. When they were done, I was going be ready for them to load up and not be seen as we exited. I would get us to the stage-two vehicle, get us loaded, and bring us back here.

I asked, "You're sure the money will be there?"

Cora nodded and took over, made an impatient face, and explained that in the big churches there were treasury teams. She had learned that going to our church. This mission had been in motion long enough for her to know that the target church always collected the money inside the church, then the treasury team always left the main building and counted the money inside the annex.

I asked, "Always?"

Eddie Coyle said, "That's what the inside man says."

Cora took a deep breath and added that the treasury team counted the tax-free monies two, maybe three more times before putting it inside the vault. No one else would be inside the building but the treasury team and their security. That gave us a large window of time. But the inside man was making it possible to get the money before it ever made it inside the vault.

Eddie Coyle said, "I can't wait to look at that money."

Jackie smiled. "I want to see what a half million looks like."

Cora swallowed her excitement. "This will pay off. This is six months of my life."

Bishop rubbed his palms and grinned. "I bet that money will be stacked up on a table like in the opening of that movie *Across 110th Street*. A mountain of money will be on the table and the electronic counters will be there spitting that money out like they're in a bank."

Cora said, "More money will be inside the vault. Enough to make this a big score."

Everyone gave high fives in anticipation of success.

I said, "So after the treasury team exits the church, we're going to meet them inside the annex. This annex, the one on the back side of the property, away from the streets and all eyes."

Cora snapped, "Is this vague, Dmytryk? It's just like robbing a bank. And there is no 'we' going inside. No 'we' that you are a part of. You stay in the van. We will go in when they are the most vulnerable. And you sit and wait. When they think they're safe and are in the middle of their routine, the part of the team that you're not on will take care of what needs to be taken care of. Get it? That make sense? Nothing bad has ever happened here, and they're not expecting us."

I took a calming breath and shook off her rage. "While I wait in the van, you and the crew are going to storm inside to make the withdrawal. There is a long hallway. There are stairs. You're going inside an area you've never seen before. I'm worried about the timing."

Cora snapped, "He's on the friggin' treasury team. That's covered."

Eddie Coyle said, "Relax. Cora's friend will tell us the exact moment. It will all go down behind closed doors. We'll walk in wearing ski masks and they'll know we mean business."

"Masks and guns. That's not your usual MO."

Bishop said, "You rob a bank, the Feds look for you."

Eddie Coyle added, "You rob a church and the world will hunt you down."

I took a breath. "Sounds like the prelude to another North Hollywood shootout."

Cora shook her head. "But it won't be North Hollywood. This is not a bank."

Eddie Coyle said, "If Larry Phillips Jr. and Emil Matasareanu had done what we're doing they would've both been rich and walking on top of the ground."

I said, "Just to be sure, since you've been holding out on information, you're not going to storm inside the sanctuary like it's a bank holdup in a bad movie, are you?"

Eddie Coyle laughed. "They won't even know we're there. The annex will only have a few people. We're not going to rush inside the main church and have ten thousand witnesses."

I took a deep breath and exhaled, my insides tightening up.

Eddie Coyle said, "That makes you feel better, I take it."

"Would it matter?"

Minutes later, Bishop left with Cora. They loaded up inside a ten-year-old van that Eddie Coyle and Cora had waiting for us inside the detached garage. They were back within twenty minutes. Bishop carried in a large box. Inside that box were a dozen pairs of plastic ties that would be used as handcuffs and black bags that were thick and the size of a human head. There were more than was needed. There were a dozen balaclavas and five Ruger P94s. They had nine-millimeter guns, weapons that held fifteen bullets in total, ready to be used on this job. Eddie Coyle had secured the same tools that had been used to pull off the biggest bank job in Britain. Eddie Coyle handed everyone a gun, including me. It was light, but as heavy as death. Cora held a gun in her hand. She looked excited. Anxious. Everything but afraid.

Eddie Coyle came to me. "Jackie said you did good with the gun you had back in L.A."

"I did what I had to do."

"You finally had to put one down."

"Like I said, I did what I had to do."

"Well, here's an upgrade. I'll cover the basics, but if it hits the fan just point and shoot."

"No problem."

There wasn't any food in the town home and everyone was hungry. We ended up near I-59 at a Cracker Barrel, an agrestic Southern eatery that had wooden rocking chairs and checkerboards set up out front. There were deer heads and rifles and plastic fish and cast-iron skillets and fishing rods and washboards on the walls.

Eddie Coyle sat across from me. Jackie sat next to me, and Cora sat next to Eddie Coyle. Jackie and Cora were seated across from each other, face-to-face. Bishop sat at the head of the table. Eddie Coyle was the leader and we were the disciples. That was the way it felt. Knowing what we were about to do had put my mind in a different mood. Robbing a bank hadn't bothered me, not like this. It was wrong, I was aware, hypocritical at times, and I made no excuses, but robbing the government was justified. They had stolen from us directly.

Jackie said, "We should've driven to Five Points South to the Pancake House. They have the best turkey sausage in Alabama. Cora, remember when we went there after that job we did at Region? We ate and then went shopping at the Pinnacle. And we met those nice gentlemen."

Eddie Coyle said, "Shut up, Jackie. Shut up and feed your piehole before I feed it for you."

Jackie threw a half-eaten biscuit at Eddie Coyle, hit him in the center of his forehead.

Bishop laughed hard. I did too. Then Eddie Coyle laughed. His lip was swollen and my face was bruised. And we laughed. Cora didn't say anything. Her expression said that she wouldn't say another word to Jackie until Chick-fil-A was open on Easter Sunday. After that, Eddie Coyle, Bishop, and I chatted like brothers. Jackie sat next to me with her hand resting on my leg, claiming me as her own.

I said, "Bishop, tell me that story about that robbery up in Memphis, Tennessee."

"Which one are you talking about?"

"The funny one you always used to tell Rick and Sammy, the one about those idiots who tried to rob First Tennessee and ended up in that newspaper for criminals."

Bishop laughed harder. "You mean the one about the idiots who tried to rob First Tennessee over by the University of Memphis? Those idiots tried to run in the bank with their weapons drawn, then got stuck inside the revolving doors. They tried to shoot their way out, but the glass is bulletproof, so they ended up shooting each other, then begging for medical assistance."

Everyone laughed except Cora. She wasn't there anymore, not mentally, not emotionally. She was angry. She was nervous. She wanted to run but she had to stay.

Jackie's hand rested on the table. I reached over and held her hand as we laughed.

Abbey Rose's novel rested on the table between us, that reminder in plain sight.

Cora asked Eddie Coyle for one of his Marlboro Blacks. She excused herself, went outside and smoked, then came back inside and walked around the gift shop until we were done.

I understood where we stood. And I knew this was the final fork in the road. And I knew why. It wasn't because of Eddie Coyle. In the big picture, Eddie Coyle was nothing but a flea on the shoulder of God. With Cora, I had clung to the first four years of our marriage. Cora only remembered the last two. I remembered the joy from the first time we made love. She remembered the pain from the last. As they said, there were at least three sides to every story. Ours had been the economy. Love. And the truth.

The truth was something neither of us would understand. It was beyond our grasps.

The last few hours felt as if I had been on an unpaved road that was as long as three trips to Los Angeles and back. My soul had processed the five stages of grief in a matter of hours and my heart was exhausted.

Eddie Coyle said, "Let's go over this one more time before the next time."

We talked through the job one more time. And when we finished, I excused myself and went to the men's room. After I closed the door and made sure it was empty, I put my fedora on the counter, then reached inside my suit pocket, moved my father's pocket watch to the side, and felt the bullet that had killed Rick. I moved it to the side and took out the bottle of Vicodin. I popped another pill and stood in front of the mirror, shaking and holding off a panic attack.

When I came out of the men's room, I ran into Cora. She was going inside the ladies' room. She was startled to see me, just as startled as when she had seen me back at Thumbs Up. We were alone, face-to-face, no Eddie Coyle watching over her. Cora and I stared at each other for a moment that lasted beyond eternity, an awful eternity that put razor blades inside my stomach. It looked as if she was struggling to breathe, both of our stares hot like the sun on each other's winter-dried skin. It looked like she was going to come to me, hug me, kiss me, and cry.

Then, with an abruptness fueled by inner demons, failures, and disappointments, we moved on.

When we finished breaking bread, Cora directed and Eddie Coyle drove us to the Courtyard by Marriott, a hotel that was situated below the Colonial Pinnacle, a seventy-five-acre one-hundred-million-dollar shopping center built on a rocky hillside standing high above Promenade at Tutwiler Farm, all rising over I-459 South. If it had been a sunny day, the view would have been spectacular. Six Flags over Jesus was down below, built across the street from Eastminster, as large as a coliseum with five levels of parking, sparkling and looking out of place in Trussville. A section of annexes was down below. Five of them looked as new as the church. The sixth annex stood out as being old and was probably there when the institution purchased the land. Once the job was done and the loot was divided, I-459 would be our escape route.

Eddie Coyle met with the inside man, the disgruntled sheep that Cora had befriended when she had worked at that gentlemen's club in Detroit. His face was nothing to look at, which explained why he went to dark clubs that allowed women to have conversations in exchange for money. He was built like a gorilla with short, strong arms and a ridiculous receding hairline on a high forehead. Cora went to deal with him while Eddie Coyle and his brother stayed ten feet away and played the bodyguard role. The churchman had come to make sure it was still a go.

He told them who was scheduled to work on Sunday, and there had been no changes.

That done, we drove up to the top of the hill. Eddie Coyle, Bishop, and I went inside Jos. A. Bank and bought new suits, ties, and shoes. Jackie went shopping at Ann Taylor. Cora bundled up in her heavy wool coat and fedora and headed toward New York & Company and did the same. They wanted to dress the way the locals dressed.

Then we headed down Highway 11 and rode by the megachurch one more time. The annex was in the back and I wanted to do a drive through the church grounds and make sure nothing had changed that would stop us from exiting as planned. I needed to see the entrance and exit route firsthand. Later on I would need to see the stage-two vehicle and make sure it was running. I would need to drive it for a few minutes just to make sure there would be no mechanical surprises. It was part of what we did. We checked all the entrances and exits. The church was beautiful and looked as out of place there as I felt in my own life. That edifice of glass and marble was where the citizens of Birmingham and her surrounding cities went to stand side by side in prayer.

Silence held us all as we sat in the van and concentrated, focused on the mission ahead of us.

Back at the safe house, we congregated in the kitchen. Eddie Coyle called another meeting and we talked over the plans again, each player saying out loud his or her role in this operation, each stating his or her obligation from top to bottom. We were like actors who were tired of running our lines. Eddie Coyle seemed like a calm director, but he was nervous.

My hands opened and closed and palms sprouted sweat as we solidified everything.

Cora was going inside. Her contact was going to disable the cameras and open the door for her. She was going to be dressed in a wool pantsuit, like a new age churchwoman who'd stepped off the cover of *Vogue,* dressed the way she used to dress on Sunday mornings when we used to go to church, only she would have a Bible in her hand and a loaded gun inside her purse. Jackie was going inside too. That had been the plan all along, before Sammy and Rick had died, before Jackie had bedded me. Two beautiful women in church clothing, wearing church hats and heavy coats, walking inside with PTL smiles and displaying all of the stereotypical vulnerabilities and distractions a woman had to offer. Any guard or deacon they saw along the way would relax, and if needed, those same men would open doors to let the Bible-carrying women inside the annex. That was what men did. That was the vulnerability of man, his desire to protect and nurture and love what and whom he hoped would love him in return.

283

Bishop and Eddie Coyle would march in behind the women and take over.

I was responsible for two getaway cars, stage one and stage two.

I reminisced about my days as a white-collar worker. I thought about the days I had worked on the line. I remembered my life before Cora. I remembered Henrick and Zibba and water came to my eyes. Then I forced myself to focus and think of Eddie Coyle and his friends.

On a dark Sunday, I would go to church and end my Great Recession. And I would pull the plug on my marriage at the same time. It had been on life support and now it was time to kill the power. Everything must change. Hallelujah, and may we all hold hands and burn in hell.

20

Two minutes had gone by.

During those elongated minutes I hadn't taken a breath. The engine of the van was running and the windows were fogging over. As a blanket of gray clouds blocked the sun, I'd parked in the rear of the Six Flags over Jesus. There was nothing back there except five other inactive annexes and a steep hill that led to the Marriott Courtyard on Roosevelt Road. We couldn't be seen from the hilltop or the streets. I checked the time and looked toward the metal door with blooming impatience.

Snow was falling and there was ice on the roads, and I hoped the flow of traffic remained favorable on Highway 11. Less than three minutes ago when we had pulled into the parking lot, there had been a long line of cars heading both back toward Chalkville Road and in the opposite direction that led toward the interstates 59 and 459.

They had entered the building as planned. They would have taken care of any extra problems, any extraneous people they encountered, left them all wearing plastic-tie handcuffs with balaclavas pulled over their heads. That completed, Eddie Coyle and his brother would have rushed down the concrete stairs into the basement and stormed inside the secret room that held the vault. As they stood over a table filled with money and checks, the treasury team would have been thrown off guard. Nobody expects the Spanish Inquisition. Seeing guns and men and women in hoods would've said it all. While Eddie Coyle and Bishop held their guns, Jackie and Cora would have taken whoever was working to opposite sides of the room, then put plastic ties on their wrists and ankles before covering their heads with material that plunged them into darkness. Instructions would have been given to stay silent. Then Eddie Coyle and Cora, the masterminds of this job, maybe they would've stood side by side with Jackie and collected the money. Bishop would've stayed in lookout position, his gun ready to shoot anyone who moved, the same for anyone who walked inside the basement door.

Enough time had passed. Then I remembered the vault and the details of the diagrams. My mind was on the money from the three services, but I had forgotten about the vault and whatever was stored inside. Based on what Cora's turncoat had told her, Eddie Coyle and friends would be shoulder-to-shoulder, staring at five hundred thousand dollars. There could be more. Either way, the culmination of six months of bank robbing and planning was before them.

I adjusted my fedora and looked at my pocket watch again. No sirens pierced the Sunday morning air. We needed an extra man, someone who was posted around the corner. But this was the plan. All remained calm. All remained gray. I hoped that Eddie Coyle, Jackie, and Cora were frantically throwing money inside of bags.

I wanted my one-hundred-thousand-dollar bailout package.

I was done with Detroit. I had decided last night. I could leave there, leave this behind me and go to Aruba. I could get my life back together. I could finish up grad school in Mexico City. I'd have several job offers in a matter of months.

My eyes went to the metal door on the side of the building, where the team had entered.

A police scanner was on, one earphone inside my left ear. There were a thousand problems in Birmingham, but there was nothing going on in Trussville. The parking lot out front was busy, but only five cars were back there. The winter storm was to our advantage. If it had been a spring or summer day, the rear lots might have been crowded. No one wanted to park back there and walk three hundred yards to receive his or her blessings.

Another minute went by.

As I opened and closed Sammy's switchblade, as I looked at the dash and stared at the bullet that had gone through Rick's body and sent him to his death, as I felt the weight from a loaded nine-millimeter inside my suit pocket, fear didn't have its claws in me anymore.

I wasn't supposed to leave the car. That was my number-one rule, to stay with the car.

My eyes went to the door in search of the people I was responsible for, but no one came to the door.

There weren't any sirens, none that I could hear.

There wasn't anything being broadcast on the scanner. There were car accidents and stalled cars, but there was no call for police or militia to grab their guns and head to this area.

Four minutes went by.

287

Then five.

Then six.

This was different. It would be different if this was a bank robbery and four minutes had gone by. Four minutes inside a bank would turn the exterior of the institution into another *Dog Day Afternoon*. I left the engine in the van running and opened the door, pulled on my fedora, and stepped outside into the falling snow. Something felt wrong. I had to go find out what. I made a handful of rapid steps toward the door on the side of the annex, and then the door opened halfway. I stopped where I was, waiting to see who was going to emerge.

The metal door closed hard.

That frightened me.

I looked back at the van, then my eyes went to the five-level parking structure. Cars were moving, but none were coming this way. I faced the annex and took another step toward the closed door, the weight of the nine-millimeter weighing down the left side of my wool coat. The metal door opened again, but no one rushed from the edifice, no one came outside.

Snow dampened my fedora and clothing as the chill tried to numb my bare hands.

Seven minutes had gone by.

As the snowfall thickened, I saw Jackie, her frame tall and full. Her hair was wavy and her dress had polka dots, a dress that was meant for another era but hugged her frame in ways that made a man believe in both God and the Devil. Her church hat was blown away and her hair lost a battle with an unexpected gust of wind that slapped her mane across her eyes and temporarily blinded her. I anticipated seeing Eddie Coyle and his friends emerging behind Jackie, each of them moving at breakneck pace and carrying similar, if not equal, loads.

My heart became a hammer trying to beat itself free while I searched in vain.

Jackie was lugging a green duffel bag, one that had the emblem and name of the megachurch stitched on its side in black and gold, a bag that had the weight of hundreds of thousands of dollars. The bag slipped from her hands and its weight almost pulled Jackie to the ground, but as snow fell she gritted her teeth and with unbridled determination she gripped the straps on the bag and dragged it across the dirty and wet ground, the bag married to one hand as her other hand held her gun.

She was alone. And she was bleeding, blood dripping down her right arm, spilling over her drawn weapon, and creating pink spots in the snow. All that was missing was a jazz score from the Chico Hamilton Quartet.

When her eyes met mine, I saw four things: betrayal, lust, greed, and murder.

Jackie dragged the bag halfway, then stopped and caught her breath before she moved her hair from her face and said, "Dmytryk. I have the money. We have the money, baby."

I put my hand inside my pocket and touched the nine-millimeter.

She came toward me wearing a stressed, pained smile that highlighted her imperfect skin. Her ruthless walk and unrestricted exoticness could disarm the average fool. She had disarmed Sammy. And in some way she had disarmed me. I admit that. She looked like a sufferer, a woman who had been done wrong by life and many men.

I looked at the door again, but no one came out. I didn't see Eddie Coyle and the rest of his disciples.

I snapped, "What happened?"

"We have the money. Look at the bag. This is what we came for."

My breath fogged as my words rushed from my mouth. "Where is Eddie Coyle?"

"Dmytryk . . . I've been shot. . . . I need you to get me out of here."

"Where is Bishop?"

"Get back inside the van. Do what they pay you to do and get me out of here."

"Where is my wife, Jackie?"

"I'm your wife. I was your wife last night. And I'll be your wife again tonight."

"Where is Cora?"

"I'm your wife and you're my Sammy and we're going to get my kid and go on our honeymoon. Stop talking and do your job and help me with this bag and get us in that van and get us out of Alabama before the cops come. Put the money in the van, baby, and let's go."

We could've left right then.

But behind Jackie, I saw them. Not Eddie Coyle or Bishop or Cora. I saw Rick and Sammy. They ran out of the same metal door Jackie had just exited, Rick firing a gun. Sammy was wounded as Rick carried him and the bags of money. Sammy's head opened up again. And so did Rick's chest. This time the bullet that had killed Rick kept going until it hit my chest.

I jerked but felt no pain. Half of Sammy's head was gone. The bag of money inside Rick's hand exploded and money flew to the skies. Suddenly the weight of the world and all the stress felt as if it hung from me like shackles doing their best to pull me to my knees.

Jackie said, "Cora left you for Eddie Coyle. She left you for this money. You can leave them all. You can beat them and send them postcards and tell them to go straight to hell."

My wife was inside that building and I had every right to leave her, trade abandonment for abandonment. But this moment wasn't about Cora. And it wasn't about me. This moment was about two men who had been left for dead in Los Angeles. It was about Rick and Sammy and everything that had gone bad at Wells Fargo. I had panicked then, but today I wouldn't repeat the same. Jackie came toward me, dressed in black and white and filled with anger.

She grimaced and dragged the bag toward me like she was an evil Santa Claus. Her blood dripped and melted into the snow, the pinkness changing to white.

Her gun remained pointed at me as she issued her demands.

I said, "You're right. Let's get out of here before the police come. It's you and me, Jackie. It's me and you to the end."

"And my kid."

"Your kid will be my kid now. I'll have the family I always wanted."

"Damn. I can't speak Spanish. My kid can't speak Spanish."

"I'll teach you."

"I need you, Dmytryk. I need you to help us."

"I'll teach both of you."

A long moment passed between us and then Jackie lowered her gun.

I went to Jackie and helped her carry the money toward the van. She was hurting but didn't let the money go. I opened the door to the van and pulled her close to me. We had the money. I told her that she was right, we'd leave Eddie Coyle and Cora and we'd run away together, just like she and Sammy had planned to do. I told her that I would love her as I had loved Cora.

Jackie said, "I'll never leave you, Dmytryk."

"I believe you."

"I'll never do like Cora did and leave you."

"I know."

"I'm loyal."

"I love you, Jackie."

"No you don't."

"But I will. In time, I will."

I held Jackie and we kissed.

I was in pain.

She was in pain.

And we kissed the kiss of victory.

And as we kissed, a gun exploded between us. We both looked shocked. We gripped each other tight. I pulled the trigger again and my gun exploded again and ripped a second hole that led from my heavy coat into her polka-dot dress. I held Jackie. We remained cheek to cheek. I held Jackie tighter and looked in her eyes. I held her as her blood drained from her wounds and spilled down my clothing like warm urine, held her as her blood hit the frigid air and turned cold, held her as that cold blood drained to my wingtip shoes.

She said something, but to my ears her words sounded like she was gargling peanut butter. That gargling was her last breath. It was the sound of her soul leaving her body behind.

Nausea rose up inside of me.

I was the sucker. But this was the road that I was on. And, right or wrong, I was going to walk it to its end.

Gripping a warm nine-millimeter inside my cold right hand, I moved from the gray skies and clumps of falling snow and stepped inside the annex. The metal door closed behind me and my eyes adjusted to the whiteness of my new surroundings. The silence sounded like death. The brilliance was shocking and blinded me. It felt like I was plummeting through cotton clouds toward an abyss of sunlight. I had to reach out for the wall in order to break my fall. My hand left a bloody print that smeared as I moved across the pure, white wall.

It was the Hallway of Commandments. Every ten feet, one of the Ten Commandments was framed on the wall, all of the frames identical, golden and six feet tall.

Blood had been on the bottom of the duffel bag Jackie had dragged from the basement, and a bright and wet redness stained the carpet. I followed the trail of blood and money in reverse like a path of the unrighteous, the redness becoming thicker as I made my way toward the concrete stairs. I walked up on a dead body. The blood and the vacant look in his eyes told me he was gone. He had been killed either by Eddie Coyle on their way in or by Jackie on her way out. My bet was on the latter. Eddie Coyle would've killed him somewhere near

Birmingham and left him wrapped in carpet and dumped near the Odenville exit.

Something told me everyone was as dead as Sammy and Rick.

My head was filled with questions. Every ragged breath I took smelled foul, the air thickened by the stench of panic and confusion. The trepidation was stronger than the angst inside a house of horrors.

Two people were on the ground, a man and a woman, both dressed in Sunday clothing, both secured with plastic ties, both down on their sides, positioned feet away from each other, with their heads covered and their faces in the direction of the nearest wall, both alive and trembling in silence.

They had been the first to run into Eddie Coyle and friends, but all they would probably remember seeing was guns and four monsters in masks. I hurried down the concrete stairs and stepped through another metal door that had been left wide open when Jackie had exited dragging a fool's fortune.

In the bowels of the building, light changed to darkness and every step on the concrete floor felt like glue on the soles of my shoes. Each movement told me that I was walking through the stickiness of blood.

A gunshot rang out and a bullet exploded in the wall near me. Someone in the room screamed. The firing continued until the shooter emptied their clip. Not until it was silent again did I hear terrified cries.

It sounded like a baby whimpering. It was a woman. She stopped praying and shrieked. Then she went quiet and her breathing became heavy; she was terrified and trying not to make a sound.

I swallowed and yelled, "*No soy policía. ¡Soy yo! ¿Donde están?*"

As soon as my panicked voice rang out in rapid Spanish, Eddie Coyle's wounded and angry timbre called out from the other side of the room, at least thirty feet away. "Help. We have to get out of here. We need your help. Get the lights. Turn the damn lights on."

Cora had been attacked first. While everyone paused to stare at the money, enraptured by its radiance, Jackie raised her gun and brought it down on Cora, striking her from behind with a blow that was intended to crack her head wide open and maybe kill her instantly. Jackie saved her bullets, not knowing how many people she might have to shoot or how many shots it would take to get from the basement to the stage-one getaway van. Her world spinning from white to black, Cora went down hard. She hit the concrete, banging her head, but she fought to stay in this world. She was from Brooklyn. She was a fighter. She'd come from a single-parent home, from a mother who made hard choices and did what had to be done to provide for her children. She had no idea what was going on, only knew that this wasn't part of the scheme. Eddie Coyle and Bishop, it only took them less than a second to redirect their weapons.

Cora was on the ground, and Eddie Coyle and friends stood over the fortune, staring at Jackie with disbelief.

Jackie had her gun pulled on Eddie Coyle, and Bishop had directed the business end of his nine-millimeter at Jackie. And my wife, the one who had pulled most of this together, she held her bloodied head and fought to get up, only to fall back down. Then she collapsed on her back and looked up at the fluorescent lighting. With vision that was blurry at best, as her heart stampeded inside her chest, she made out what was going on. She saw guns drawn. She saw death. She saw the dead-end road where she had led us all. The girl who was born up in Brooklyn, the teenager who had been reared in Detroit, the woman who had gone into the navy, the autoworker who had given her blood, sweat, and tears to the auto industry, the woman who had married me, the woman who had fallen apart during hard times, the woman who had challenged my manhood, she looked up and instead of lifting her gun and becoming a killer, she recoiled in horror, pulled herself into the fetal position, and became nothing more than a terrified child.

Eddie Coyle had faced Jackie and said, "What's going on?"

She nodded. "You know."

"I'm not a man who makes assumptions. Just so we're on the same page, enlighten me."

"Put your guns down. Put your guns down and move away from the money. Get inside the vault."

"Get inside the vault?" Eddie Coyle chuckled. "You've blown a damn fuse."

Bishop laughed like this moment was absurd.

Eddie Coyle said, "Calm down, partner. Take a step back, rewind, and think about what you're doing here. We've worked a long time on this. We're almost done. What, you want a bigger cut? Fine, I'll give you ten percent of mine. How does that sound? Consider it a bonus. Now, let's wrap this up."

"Stop talking and get inside the vault."

"Put the gun down and let's get what we came for so we can get to the van and leave."

Jackie shook her head, "I have a higher calling. I'm going to get what I came for."

"Is this what you and your new bed partner have planned?"

"I don't need him. He'll get left behind with the rest of you."

"What does that mean?"

"He will never make it out of Trussville. Not with this money."

Eddie Coyle said, "You're not robbing us, so get that idea out of your head."

And there was Cora, dressed like a churchwoman, her head bloodied and clothing ripped, blinded by her own blood, eyes closed tight, and as frightened as a child who'd seen the bogeyman.

Jackie snapped, "I want your guns and I want all of you to get inside the safe."

Bishop snapped, "So you can shoot us? Are you flying over the cuckoo's nest?"

Eddie Coyle said, "If you know what's good for you, if you want this to end in a way that can still be beneficial to you and your kid, you'll put your gun down now."

"Or what?"

"You knew what when you made that stupid move."

Jackie said, "I'll put you down."

Eddie Coyle gritted his teeth. "No you won't."

"I'm just like you *and you know that.*"

"Think about what you're doing."

"I've gone too far already. It's a done deal."

"No one has gone too far, not yet."

"And I know what you'll do to me when we leave here."

"You don't know that."

"I know you better than I know myself."

Eddie Coyle said, "We're two minutes behind schedule."

"You know what this is about for me."

"Your kid. We've heard that sob story a thousand and one times."

"I'll kill you and your brother if I have to."

"Obviously you haven't thought this through to the final curtain. If this is your plan, if this is your damn plan, you should've waited until after all of us had left with the money. You should've made sure we'd gotten away. See? You're not thinking. Your plan is flawed."

"Stop talking and put your guns down."

Bishop said, "That's not going to happen and you know that's not going to happen."

They stood in a triangle with a mountain of prosperity glowing between them.

Jackie fired at Bishop and Eddie Coyle fired upon Jackie. Bishop fired last, his shot meant for the center of Jackie's heart. The hostages screamed into their gags and prayed and called out for miracles, one kicking and shouting muffled neologisms, nonsensical words that were like speaking in tongues. The noise inside the basement had to be harsh, like being trapped inside a shooting range.

Explosion after explosion after explosion echoed in the death room, while not too far away, on the other side of Trussville, a peaceful congregation at First Baptist was singing the Lord's Prayer. Bishop had taken shots to the gut, left leg, and shoulder; Eddie Coyle had been hit twice, but Eddie Coyle shot Jackie in her left shoulder. Bishop went for the kill shot but missed, and Eddie Coyle's mistake was not going for a kill shot. I didn't know if that was because Jackie was a woman, or because she had been dependable for so long, or if Eddie

Coyle thought she would snap to her senses. Maybe he wanted to scare her back to sanity. But in the end, he would need her to have two good legs and able to walk out of the annex on her own, even if he had to grab her neck and frog-march her to the van. That had been Eddie Coyle's second mistake in this business, thinking that Jackie wouldn't pull the trigger on her gun.

The broker of greed attacked desperation and desperation responded with equal fury.

I clicked the lights on and again a saintly brilliance attacked my eyes. When everything became clearer, I saw spots of blood and rivers of redness, and I saw more money that had been spilled when Jackie fled. The blood that soiled the front of my suit, my coat, the blood that saturated my clothing, the blood that had run down to my shoes, it was turning cold. But the blood that soaked into my clothing was insignificant compared to what I saw when my eyes refocused. It was a financial battlefield. I saw the aftermath of greed and insanity. Bullets from four nine-millimeters had been discharged and those projectiles had damaged every wall. The concrete structure that had been designed to be a fallout shelter was solid enough to trap all sounds. The two-feet-thick concrete and steel walls stole every gunshot and moan and scream to God and Jesus.

The vault was across the room, its heavy door shiny and silver and still ajar. Four more men and women were bound with plastic ties and gagged and had been left in different parts of the basement. Eddie Coyle's clean-shaven face revealed that he was in pain. His dark suit no longer looked brand-new. His skin was drenched in sweat. He held himself up with his left hand, wounded and bleeding, his gun in his right hand and aimed at me. His black mask had been removed. The sweat from his forehead streamed like a river. His lips trembled and his trigger finger was nervous and ready to fire his weapon, his expression intense and filled with hate and paranoia. He was ready to have another shootout.

He shouted, "Put your gun down."

"You're going to shoot me?"

He screamed and spit flew from his mouth. "Put it away or I will blow a hole in your head."

He was walking the road that led to insanity. I remained collected.

At first I tried to stick my nine-millimeter inside the waist of my pants. Then I changed my mind and slid the instrument of death across the floor to him. What Eddie Coyle did to me didn't matter.

Eddie Coyle's shoulders slumped as he lowered his weapon. He put his foot on my gun and glowered around the room, scoured from wall to wall and snapped, "She shot up the place and took the goddamn money."

"She's gone."

"Where did she go?"

"It looks like you have bigger problems."

"What are you doing?"

"I'm doing my job. I'm just doing my job."

Cora was down on the floor, blood draining from her head and into her eyes, blinding her and seeping across her lips, moving inside her mouth, the taste of her blood paralyzing her, the reality of her wound leaving her too disoriented to react, too terrified to stand up.

She called for me. She called for me in rapid Spanish. She called for me to save her.

I said, "Dead, alive, or injured, we all came together and we're all leaving together."

Eddie Coyle said, "If the police come, then we'll all go to jail together."

"I know. We'll sing the prison blues at Sing Sing. Two shows a night, three on Saturday."

"You should've left."

"But I didn't."

Cora's gun was no longer in her hand. She was the one who had lost it and began firing until her clip was emptied; she had fired across the room blindly, fired like she was doing her best to gun down Jackie, then dropped her weapon and screamed in frustration, cursed before folding in horror.

I went to her and grabbed her by her arm, then pulled her to her feet.

I asked, "Can you stand up?"

"I think so."

"Get on your feet, walk toward the door, and try to crawl up the stairs if you have to."

"I can't see anything. I can't see."

Bishop was badly wounded. He was unconscious. I couldn't tell if he was breathing. One of Cora's frenzied shots in the dark might have finished what Jackie had started.

I told Eddie Coyle, "We're going to have to carry your brother."

"She shot me in my shoulder and my elbow. I only have one good arm."

"Then use it. Suck it up, be a man, and use your good arm."

Cora didn't make it as far as the door before she went down on her knees.

My body ached all over, but I gritted my teeth and lifted Cora. I swooped my troubles up in my arms and carried her up a flight of stairs. She held her face to my neck, her lips on my skin, whispering to me all the way, saying things that came from her heart, apologizing for everything. I carried her through snow and ice, and as my back ached, I put her inside the idling van with Jackie's remains.

I ignored my agony and ran back to the basement.

Eddie Coyle was standing over his brother with tears in his eyes.

He said, "He's gone. My brother's dead."

"You sure?"

"He took one to the heart. My brother's dead."

"Suck it up, Eddie Coyle. Suck it up and let's get him out of here."

We dragged Bishop to the bottom of the stairs, then caught our breaths and picked him up. It was like picking up a refrigerator filled with frozen steaks. We carried Bishop's dead weight up the concrete stairs, then grabbed his feet and dragged his bloodied frame down the carpeted hallway as far as we could. I struggled and summoned all of my strength and pulled his dead body upright so we could carry him by his shoulders with his feet dragging. His Johnston & Murphy shoes came off and left him in his black socks. We grabbed his suit coat and tugged and turned him until we had him facedown in the backseat of the stolen van with Jackie.

Eddie Coyle cringed with pain and panted, "Jackie's here. She's not gone."

"She's gone. She's dancing with Sammy."

"Throw her body out. Throw her dead body out of the damn van. Tie a rope around her neck and ride out to Gadsden Highway and drag her double-crossing—"

"Shut up, Eddie Coyle."

"Kick her out."

"She came with us. She's leaving with us."

Eddie Coyle spat on her warm corpse and then he snapped, "*She got what she deserved.*"

"Get inside the van, Eddie Coyle. Shut up and get in the van."

"We have the money. She didn't get away with the money."

"We haven't gotten away with it either. We're still in Trussville. I need my gun back."

Eddie Coyle made painful sounds and he pulled the gun from his waistband and handed it to me.

Cora looked terrified, wringing her hands. She wasn't prepared for an outcome like this. Eddie Coyle and what was left of his crew were all in pain and bleeding. Jackie's body was on the floor, looking up at the roof of the van, eyes wide open, that final look of pain and surprise etched in her face. Cora was in pain, but she kicked Jackie's body over and over. She kicked Jackie like she was trying to kick her to the other side of hell. It looked like she had been kicking Jackie for a while. Eddie Coyle stared at the face of his deceased brother.

Then Cora's eyes met mine. I knew her. She was afraid. I was afraid too. Every muscle and bone in my body ached and I was afraid.

I expected to see Jackie standing on the side of the van, bleeding and looking at me with hate in her eyes, but I didn't see her. I didn't see Jackie or Rick or Sammy.

Yet I felt them all. I felt all of their deaths, heavy in my muscles. The recoil from when I had pulled the trigger on that gun, it stayed with me.

Hands shaking, nausea rising, I took a deep breath, wiped sweat from my brow, leaving a streak of blood across my face. I adjusted my fedora, pulled it down low on my bruised face, and drove us away, eased us from the rear of the annexes and past the five-level parking structure. People were still exiting the parking structure. The mega-church was far enough away from the annex. No one had heard the shootout. I drove past smiling families as they left wrapped in coats, umbrellas held up high. A choir was singing "God Bless Us, Every One."

I mixed with the traffic leaving the sacred grounds. I made a left turn, took Highway 11, and headed back toward Chalkville Road. Moans of misery and resentment filled the cab and I cruised back toward the safe house. There was no need to head for the stage-two vehicle that had been left at Highway 11 and Chalkville Road, not when half of my cargo was dead and the other half bloodied. We looked liked we had been fighting the war in Afghanistan. The side windows fogged over and made my cargo obscure. Winds blew and the gray skies spat globs of wet snow on us as the glass-and-marble Six Flags over Jesus damned us all, its steeple long and tall, like a middle finger.

The windshield wipers moved back and forth, screeching and slapping snow out of our way.

No one had been left behind. That was what mattered to me.

Right or wrong, I had done as I had promised. This time no one was abandoned along the way.

21

Sirens punctured the air in Trussville.

We had been inside the safe house for twenty minutes and from the back upstairs window I could see law enforcement and paramedics speeding down Highway 11 toward Six Flags over Jesus.

Forty-five minutes had gone by since I had rescued my team from the annex.

Tension remained high. Eddie Coyle and Cora were on edge. So was I.

Eddie Coyle called out from the bathroom, "You're my hero, Dmytryk. I mean that. You're my goddamn hero."

"No need to thank me."

"I have to. It's from the bottom of my heart. Now I know that you didn't let Sammy and Rick down. My brother is dead and you got his body out of there. You're one of a kind, Dmytryk. You're a much better, a much stronger man than I had given you credit for. And you can throw a goddamn punch. We're going to need you to get us out of here. The plan for taking separate cars, that isn't going to fly, not with these injuries. Get me back to Rome and I can get everything taken care of."

"Jackie and Bishop?"

"We'll leave them here. I'll send over a cleaner."

Wounded but still determined, Eddie Coyle limped in from the bathroom and sat at the dining room table. The shoulder shot had gone clean through, but his wounds were wrapped. Same for the shot that had hit his left elbow. His body was in shock, and his white shirt was soaked with sweat and his own life's fluids. I had gone back to the van and dragged the bag of money into the living room and dropped it there, its bottom leaving a rugged trail of redness from tile to carpet. Head bloodied and wrapped in towels, Cora went and stood over the money.

I told her, "Don't go to sleep. No matter how bad you might want to, don't go to sleep."

"I'm dizzy and nauseated. There is a ringing inside my ears that won't stop. My head aches and I feel like I want to throw up, but I can't. It feels like I'm talking with a mouth filled with cotton."

"Your speech is slightly slurred."

"And I feel tired. I feel so tired. All I want to do is lie down and close my eyes."

"You have a concussion. If you go to sleep, it could turn into the big sleep."

"You saved me."

"I did my job."

My heart filled with relief and animosity, I looked in her red-rimmed eyes.

She was remembering the first four years of our marriage.

I was remembering the final two.

Hands shaking, I walked away. I went to the bathroom upstairs and looked out the window. I'd expected to see a hundred police cars heading this way. I heard sirens but this unfinished and unsold subdivision remained empty. It was like hiding in a ghost town. The echo of sirens continued to sound on the other side of the railroad tracks that separated us from the parks and the populated sections in this part of Trussville. I imagined that the news had hit Birmingham and all the connected cities and a dozen news crews were heading in the same direction. The sleeping town was awake and they were doggedly hunting for the thieves who had been inside the temple.

The nine-millimeter was heavy on my person. I took it out of the waist of my pants and placed it on the counter before I reached inside my suit pocket and took out the bottle of Vicodin.

I popped one.

I whispered, "You're safe, Abbey Rose. I kept my promise. You're safe. *Espero que tenga una buena vida.* I'm sorry for the wrong I did to you. I'll always regret that."

Then I popped a second Vicodin. I was tempted to down the entire bottle and call it a day. I was tired. I was tired of everything. For a few seconds, I wanted to put a rope around my neck, stand on a chair, and get this weight off of my shoulders. That feeling passed.

I heard the water running in the next bedroom. Cora was inside the master bathroom.

I went to the window and saw them outside. Rick was the closest, standing in the street, the snow falling through his ethereal body as Sammy and Jackie danced the tango a few feet behind him.

I pulled off my bloodied suit coat. My white shirt was pink and red more than white.

I looked at the gun that had killed Jackie. I put it back inside my waistband and went back downstairs. Moments later Cora came back down the stairs. Battered, bruised, or filled with bullet holes, we were all covered in layers of blood and this grand plan had turned out to be nothing more than another performance in the Theater of the Absurd.

Jackie's suitcase was in the living room, ready to leave, ready to go get her kid. Bishop's luggage was in the living room also, it too waiting for Godot, and waiting in vain. I stepped away and went to the kitchen, looked at the gas stove, then looked at the beautiful, colorful candles that decorated this model home. A home that was now tracked with blood.

Saving Eddie Coyle was business. That was what I had been recruited to do.

Eddie Coyle said, "I'm not mad at you, Dmytryk. Jackie was, but I'm not."

"What's to be mad about, Eddie Coyle?"

He motioned toward the dining room table. That was where Jackie had left her coveted novel.

Eddie Coyle said, "Jackie told me. She told me about that writer, Abbey Rose. She called me when she was at the airport in Dallas. You let a witness get away. But I'm not mad at you. Jackie assumed you paid Abbey Rose four thousand to be quiet."

"I did what I had to do."

"But you didn't do what you were supposed to do. No witnesses."

"She'll stay quiet."

"They never keep quiet. They always want more money. And the L.A. job, don't forget that the security guard died. Maybe in five years she'll get a conscience and call the Feds. Or maybe she'll write a book and name names. People will do anything for a buck. You made a bad decision back there, Dmytryk. Only one way to fix that. You saved me and pulled my brother's body out of that basement. I'll take care of Abbey Rose for you. In the morning I'll get in contact with this Russian guy they call the Man in the White Shoes. He's an assassin. I'll transfer the funds and he'll take care of our Abbey Rose problem."

I didn't say anything for a moment.

I said, "We have one other matter, Eddie Coyle."

"What is that, Dmytryk?"

"That night we were at the Uniroyal tire. The gun I touched."

"Long gone. I'm not one to sit on a murder weapon."

"Thanks."

"You're not a killer, Dmytryk. I won't hold that against you. In my book you're a legend, Dmytryk Knight. You're a knight in shining armor."

I nodded.

Eddie Coyle said, "Bishop's wife and girlfriends are going to take this one very hard."

"Are you okay, Eddie Coyle?"

"He was my brother. I'm not okay, but give me a minute to pull it together."

While Eddie Coyle grieved over his brother and stared at the stolen money, I took the gun from my waist and shot that miserable bastard in the back of his head. The nine-millimeter exploded and jerked in my hand, sent a wave of orgasmic energy coursing through my body, the same as it had done when I had stopped Jackie from double-crossing Eddie Coyle.

Blood and brain matter sprayed.

Eddie Coyle's body jerked, then he went limp and collapsed hard and facedown on the wooden table. His weight shifted and he tumbled to the floor and landed on the side of his head. A mountain of money rested at his side. Enough money to pay off my mortgage, enough money to pay for grad school, enough money to go home and ride out unemployment and the rest of the madness that was going on from sea to shining sea. Eddie Coyle's body twitched twice, then the lights went out. He'd stabbed me in my back and I had shot him in the back of his head. This wasn't a coward's way of doing business. This was fairness. This was an eye for an eye.

I was a lot of things, but Eddie Coyle had forgotten that I was a man from Detroit.

My father was from Detroit. My father had killed a man with his bare hands.

That meant that living with regret was in my blood. I was stronger than he realized.

As soon as the gun had gone off, Cora shivered in horror and staggered away from me, her mouth wide open, but no scream came out. She looked at Eddie Coyle and then her eyes came to me. She wanted to wake up from a bad dream. This was a version of me that she had never seen before. I was no longer a blue-collar man. I was a man who could be driven to rob and kill. What I had done was as unexpected as her walking out on our six-year marriage.

This was murder. Crimes and hatred ended in that gritty and dark cul-de-sac.

My eyes went across the room, looked at the photo on the novel Jackie had left behind.

Killing Eddie Coyle was necessary. And it was personal.

There was no need for threats or warnings.

There was no need for a conversation.

Eddie Coyle didn't warn me that he was taking up with my wife. There had been no conversation, no consideration for what I might feel.

We'd shaken hands and made a deal, and I kept my end of that deal.

I had rescued Eddie Coyle and his friends. Until the end, I had kept my vows.

And now I gave in to a dark part of me and sought my own vengeance.

I felt no relief. I felt no guilt.

I would've felt more emotion if I had kicked a stray dog.

I faced my wife and said, "You're shaking, Cora."

Her breathing was frantic and she took a step in retreat. But there was nowhere to run. I was the truth and there was nowhere she could run.

I asked, "What's wrong? *Are you cold?*"

She didn't answer me.

I snapped, "*Are you cold?* Is it as cold here as it was in Windsor?"

She took another step away from me.

I asked, "Or do you need a five-thousand-dollar fur coat to keep you warm?"

Cora tripped over furniture and fell trying to get away. I turned to my wife and raised the gun. The fear in her face and the animosity in mine screamed that we were heading for a two-bullet divorce.

22

With dead bodies decorating the town home and the detached garage, I went to the bloodied bag that held the weight of a half million dollars. It felt like bailout money.

I stood over that money for a moment before I picked it up.

The weight of that money in my hand felt like power.

On a cold day, I felt its heat.

On a dreary day, I saw its brilliance.

As I walked out of the back door and limped across the small courtyard to the detached garage, gigantic snowflakes continued to fall. The bag was heavy and I was weak.

I stood in the snow with that money in my hand, then focused on a spot about fifty yards away.

My fedora caught as much snow as my wool overcoat.

Ten minutes later I was easing out of the empty community, moving across narrow streets that led across the railroad tracks. From there I rejoined the rest of the world. I turned left and drove down

Highway 11, back toward Six Flags over Jesus. Snow continued to fall from gray skies, skies that were getting darker as the day ended. My headlights were on and my windshield wipers worked overtime.

Behind me, from the area that I had just left, there was a mighty explosion that sent shockwaves through Trussville. It felt like an earthquake. A short but powerful earthquake.

As flames reached up and licked dark skies, I took I-65 and headed north.

After I passed through Nashville, I threw my smoking gun away.

23

Weeks later.

After the start of a new year, it was another brisk day in the Motor City. I loosened my scarf and took my gloves off, then adjusted my fedora and looked around. The day wasn't as beautiful as it would become in the springtime, not as favorable as it would be after the bitter winter had gone away. A gray blanket covered the sky. The temperature was above freezing and that was enough to allow ice and snow to melt before winter's frigid breath hit the city again. It was months before the heat of another horrid summer would arrive, weeks before hawthorns would start flowering and roses would bloom, but to me the day was beautiful. Maybe because there wasn't anything better than springtime in Detroit and my heart looked forward to a new season.

Detroit.

Most people didn't know that *Detroit* was a French word that was actually pronounced *day-twah*. The city of my birth was founded by a Frenchman whose last name was Cadillac.

I thought about that history as I sat on the grass at Evergreen Cemetery. My parents' tombstones were in front of me, grave markers that stood side by side, as they had in life. Today I cleaned their gravesites and put fresh flowers on each marker. Then I sat there for a while, silent, not hearing any noise that came from Woodward Avenue and the surrounding community.

It was just me and my parents. My mother sat to my left and my father to my right.

The wind soughed and a chill raked across my wool coat as we talked about nothing in particular. After about thirty minutes, I told Henrick and Zibba what I had wanted to say all along. The words didn't come easily, but the truth rarely did.

I said, "I might have to leave Detroit. It was a different place when you were here. People here are praying to deaf ears. I think some of that culture of corruption got into Cora. It got into me too. If a job comes through in another state, I'll have to leave. There aren't any jobs in Michigan anymore, and Detroit's become the redheaded stepchild of the U.S. Nobody loves you when you're down and out. Nobody loves you when you're broke. It's all about prosperity. All about money. The places we used to go on weekends are gone. They're ghost towns and they want to bulldoze other neighborhoods. It's pretty grim. It's like New Orleans up here. Anyway, the house is on the market, but I won't leave without saying good-bye. I'd never leave without saying good-bye. And I'll come back to visit you."

I paused.

I said, "I did some things. Some really bad things. I know you taught me better. Dad, I can see you frowning, but I'll make you smile again. Same for you, Mom. I lost my way for a while. But I'm back now. Mom, Dad, I just need to ask both of you to forgive me."

Not long after I stopped rambling, I took out my pocket watch and saw the time.

I kissed both tombstones and then I left. First I rode past the town home I used to own on the nicer side of town. From there I left the suburbs and drove aimlessly, past Wayne State University, the public library, Cadillac Place, St. Joseph Catholic Church, the luxury property on the riverfront and the Ren Center, the DPM roaring over my head as I stared across the Detroit River at Windsor, Canada. I cruised down Baylis Street, then drove down Normandy Street. This kingdom remained lined with trees, with homes for sale, and with enough foreclosures to remind us of the reality of the country. But everyone was still there. They were strong people. They were good people.

I parked my Wildcat underneath a tree that was in front of my home, turned the engine off, and sat inside my car for about fifteen minutes. The windows were down and it was a beautiful day. I sat there staring at the FOR SALE sign out front, sat there until I started to feel the evening chill.

When I went inside the house, every room smelled of lavender and every nook and cranny was clean. The house was always clean. Cora was inside the kitchen, dressed in a blue dress and high heels. She was cooking dinner. She'd just started. The dress looked good on her; I told her that. She smiled a nervous smile. The extra weight was gone from her frame. Her hair had been cut short, restyled into a pixie cut. It was trendy, but it didn't look good on her. Still I smiled.

She asked me, "How far would you go for the person you loved?"

"What do you mean?"

"Would you lose yourself to keep the person you loved?"

"You know my answer. Would you?"

"For you I would."

After I removed my coat and fedora, we shared a lingering stare, one that spoke of her undying love for me. I went to the garage and pulled out the rake and I started raking up the fallen leaves, leaves that had been there for weeks, one of my many neglected chores in this home of divided labor.

Adam had eaten an apple. Samson had lost his hair. A man being a fool was nothing new.

Back in Trussville, Cora had run from me in fear, and in the end I had lowered the gun and walked away.

A while later, I'd gone inside a bathroom and washed as much blood off my hands as I could. Then I tended to my wounds, wrapped my shoulder and my left arm. Racked with pain, I had shaven, and when I was done I took out a fresh white shirt and a different suit. While Eddie Coyle lay dead on the dining room floor, while Bishop and Jackie began rotting in a stolen van hidden inside the garage, I put on a change of clothing and collected my things. When I was done, I walked back to the garage and sat inside my Buick. The pain I felt in my shoulder and left leg at that moment was overwhelming. I started my engine and prepared to leave. I was going to leave Cora. I was leaving the money behind. I wasn't taking a dollar. But Cora had run out to the car and climbed inside. She had left the money behind too. She begged me to take her back.

She said, "You're right, Dmytryk. Baby, you're right."

Her presence had startled me.

She said, "We're supposed to fight together. We're supposed to starve together. And in the end we are going to come out the winners. That's what a marriage is about. Anybody can be married when things are easy. Anybody can be married when there's plenty of money. Get me away from here. Get me away, baby. I'd live underneath a bridge with you if I had to. I just want to be your wife again."

I'd stared at Cora's face. She was crying. She was afraid. She needed me.

Weighed down with pain and guilt, it took me a moment to accept her back into my world.

I nodded.

I said, "Let me fix this."

"You know how?"

"Stay here."

I'd gone back inside the town home and walked past the scent of new deaths. I closed all of the windows and turned all the gas burners on the stove on high, let that rotting sulfur smell begin to fill the town home. Candles were all over the model home. I lit two tall ones and left one in the living room and the other in the dining room. Then I picked up the bag of money and stepped over the dead bodies and limped out the back door. I dropped the bag of stolen money fifty yards away from the town homes, far enough for the currency to not be damaged. That was what I had hoped. The money wasn't federally insured. If it was destroyed, the government wouldn't replenish the well.

The newspapers said that the town home exploded with a blast so vicious it totaled the three connecting units and sent debris over fifty yards, across the railroad tracks and out onto Highway 11. The buildings were demolished, but the money was recovered, for the most part, unscathed.

From Birmingham toward Nashville, from Louisville to Dayton, then back into Detroit, that journey was seven hundred and forty miles. I told Cora that she had eleven hours to give me a reason not to leave her on the side of the road, seven hundred and forty miles to change from being a woman named Trouble back into the woman I had married.

She whispered, "Trouble is gone, Dmytryk. It's just me."

"Cora."

"It's Cora. It's the woman you married."

Right before Nashville I asked Cora if she had any money. She had close to eight thousand dollars. She told me that it was money from the other bank jobs. I told her to take three hundred out. She did. Then I told her to throw the rest out of the window. She did. We had enough money to eat at McDonald's and get us back home.

That was all we needed.

Cora sat next to me the entire ride back. She came home with me to Detroit.

But still. The guilt.

My left arm was sore, but I was able to move it without too much pain.

And the pain in my left leg had subsided and I could walk without limping.

As I raked up a few leaves and picked up dead branches that had fallen from trees, I heard the neighbor's kids playing in the yard next door. The temperature began to drop at sunset. I paused and wondered what would have happened if Cora had exited the annex first, if she had come running to me smiling, needing me the way I had needed her, holding a half million dollars, telling me she had done it all for me, yelling that every wrong she had done had been for us. She would've jumped inside the van and Eddie Coyle, Jackie, and Bishop would've raced out behind her, chasing the money with a fury I'd never seen before. Maybe I would've realized that we could leave Jackie, Bishop, and Eddie Coyle behind. It would have been a split-second decision. As Eddie Coyle, Bishop, and Jackie reached the van, as their nine-millimeters rang out in chorus, I would've peeled away, cut through falling snow, and left them stranded in front of the annex. I'd regretted leaving Rick behind, even though he was mortally wounded. But Eddie Coyle, his brother, and Jackie would have deserved their fate.

Other times I wondered what it would have been like to leave Cora, Eddie Coyle, and Bishop in the bottom of that annex and flee with Jackie. I wondered what it would have been like to be with her and her kid, living the high life in South America as a family. We could've built that dream house right outside of Tegucigalpa for fifty thousand and had over four hundred thousand to spare. I could've been living inside a glorious mansion. I could've been her Sammy and she could've been my Cora. I could've been teaching Spanish to her and her kid and getting acclimated to living in Honduras. We could've been making love every night.

Jackie's voice came to me. "*I'll never leave you, Dmytryk.*"

I looked around the yard and expected to see Jackie. When she wasn't there I looked for Rick and Sammy. I looked for Eddie Coyle and I looked for Bishop. No one was there.

When I was done bagging all the leaves and branches, I dragged the bags out front before I went to the garage and pulled out a ladder. Christmas lighting decorated the front of the house. I removed the lighting, put it inside a plastic container, carried that container to the garage, then went inside and showered. I put on cologne, dark suit pants, and a blue shirt. By then Cora had finished dinner. She had cooked venison tenderloin, pan seared and served with creamy mascarpone polenta and a blueberry thyme port wine reduction. It had been paired with a pinot noir. She had come home from one of her part-time jobs, showered, put on a nice dress, and cooked my favorite meal.

She was doing her best to fix what had been broken. I was doing my best to meet her halfway.

She asked, "Is this okay?"

"It's fantastic."

"I can't cook as well as you cook."

"You're a great cook, Cora. How's work going?"

"Same old. How is work going for you?"

"I picked up two more students. One for Italian and one for French."

"That's great. Autoworkers?"

"Two former executives." I nodded. "Hopefully they will pay on time."

She hesitated, then looked around the room before she looked at me. "I'm sorry."

"Let's move forward. The past is the past is the past."

"I love you, Dmytryk."

I nodded and whispered, "You're in my blood."

She whispered, "You're my blood. Dmytryk, you're my blood."

"I know."

"Those things that I said—all of those horrible things that I said that morning in East Point . . ."

"Let's eat, Cora. Let's eat this beautiful dinner you made."

Tears fell from her eyes as she ate. My eyes watered as I did the same. I reached across the table with my right hand, palm turned upward. Cora reached across the table and put her hand inside mine.

My name is Dmytryk Knight. My wife's name is Cora Knight. Right or wrong, she's my wife.

She said, "Jackie."

"What about her?"

Her hand went up to the healed scar on her forehead. "What she did in Trussville. When she went crazy. When she took her gun and shot me. When she tried to steal all of the money."

"It was wrong."

"But I was thinking the same thing. When I was with Jackie and Bishop and Eddie Coyle, I was thinking the same thing. It was so much money. I'd never had anything growing up. I thought of all the things that I didn't have and all of the things that I could've bought. I thought about us, Dmytryk. I thought about us. We'd had it so hard for so long. I wanted to take it all from them. You've always loved me. Eddie Coyle had betrayed me to get the money. Jackie had betrayed my friendship and my trust, then she tried to kill me. Everyone I had trusted for six months betrayed me."

"Let's not talk about betrayal. And if you do, look in the mirror, not out the window."

She backed down from that conversation, then said, "That was a lot of money."

"It was."

"You ever think about that money?"

"Every day, Cora. I think about that money every day. Every day I wish I had that money."

"If that had been money from a bank and not from a church, would you have kept any of it?"

"I guess we'll never know."

She paused, then whispered, "Forgive me?"

I sipped my wine. "A little more each day."

"When will we sleep in the same bed? When will you take me to bed?"

Though Cora and I had returned home together, I hadn't been able to bring myself to be with her as man and wife. Not until the smell of other men was scrubbed from her body, not until she dyed her hair back to its natural color and cleaned her insides out, and not until we were both checked for diseases. Only then could we consummate the marriage once again, jump over these hurdles and get back what we lost, maybe renew our vows and have a second honeymoon whenever the money was in our favor. It would be in our favor once again.

She had led me down the path of wrong.

Now I needed to adjust my compass and lead her the other way.

I finished a glass of wine, thought of my promise, then poured another. "Tonight."

"Yes?"

"Let's sleep in the same bed tonight."

"We haven't been in the same bed for . . . a long time."

"Let's see how that feels. Let's see if it feels right."

She smiled. "I want to make love to you, Dmytryk."

I smiled.

She whispered, "Did you love her?"

My response was, "Did you love him?"

No answers were given.

She whispered, "What do we do now?"

"We start over. We keep our heads high and make ends meet like everyone else."

"Things will get better."

I smiled. "Things will get better."

"Would you do it all over again?"

"Which part?"

"Would you marry me again?"

I smiled, but I didn't answer.

I said, "Let me do the dishes."

"I'll do them."

"No, you cooked. I'll do the dishes."

"You just did all of the yard work."

"We can do the dishes together."

"I'd like that."

In the background, the television was on. Twenty-four hours a day, the people who had jobs at CNN reminded me that the problem was debt. Like everyone else, I was going to ride this roller coaster until the ride was over. I wasn't running. I wasn't hiding. I was doing what Henrick would have done. At least that was what I liked to think. I was working hard and making do with what I had. I was an educated man and some company with a decent sign-on bonus, a 401(k), and health insurance would open up its corporate doors for me soon.

Cora said, "You leave some nights. I hear you when you walk out the door. I hear the car start."

"I know."

"You leave and don't come home for two days."

"But I come home."

She paused and her lip trembled. "Where do you go?"

I didn't answer.

She swallowed and asked, "Are you seeing someone?"

Another pause rested between us. Many pauses had rested between us since she returned.

"I love you, Cora. Despite everything, I love you. But I don't love you as a fool loves."

The wine moved through my veins. I filled another glass, drank it until the glass was empty, then I went to Cora and took her hand. I led her to the kitchen counter and turned her around. My lips touched Cora's neck and the memories of when we had first met returned. We kissed and all was forgiven. She forgave me for my stubbornness and I forgave her for her indiscretion. All bitterness was gone and all I could taste was love. The kiss was filled with passion, and Cora shivered and moaned.

"Don't stop, Dmytryk."

I lifted her dress and pulled away her panties, pulled them hard until they tore away from her body. I undid my belt buckle and allowed my pants to fall to my ankles.

And while I kissed my wife, the doorbell rang three times.

I stopped and pulled my pants up, then went to the window and looked outside. A dark sedan was parked in front of my home.

I looked back toward the kitchen and Cora was smiling. She adjusted her dress, picked up her ripped panties, hid them inside a kitchen drawer, then winked at me before she turned around and started washing the dishes.

I called out, "Just a minute."

I put on a suit coat in order to hide my erection. I went to the front door and opened it enough to look outside. I clicked on the porch light and saw two men dressed in black suits.

One of the men said, "Dmytryk Knight?"

"Yes. I'm Dmytryk Knight."

Both men raised their badges and announced that they were with the FBI.

In a tone that had no room for compromise, they asked if they could come inside.

I had robbed banks. I had pulled the trigger and shot Eddie Coyle in the back of the head.

And now the FBI was standing outside my front door.

I looked back toward the kitchen and Cora was gone.

Then, palms sweating, I opened the front door and let the armed Feds inside my home.

One of them asked, "Is anyone else here with you?"

I shook my head. "No. I'm alone. I live alone."

24

The moment I saw the FBI on my front porch, in my mind I relived what had happened back in Trussville. I thought about the tragedy. I saw the truth.

The woman whom I had married had remained ferocious, determined, and persuasive.

Cora wasn't a weak woman, and she wouldn't be turned into a docile housewife.

We were together inside that town home in Trussville. While sirens blared outside on Highway 11, with the police and sheriffs in Trussville searching for Eddie Coyle and friends, that town home had become our prison. No matter what the reason, I had stood behind Eddie Coyle and pulled the trigger on that nine-millimeter. Cora had watched me put a hole in the back of his head. She had witnessed his head exploding the same way I had seen Sammy's head come apart. Cora had watched me murder Eddie Coyle in cold blood. She didn't know why I had done it. She assumed it was because they were lovers.

Maybe that was part of the reason. And she ran from me, stumbled over furniture, and fell down. I had raised the gun seeking vengeance, but I couldn't kill her. I was where I was because of her. I had done what I had done because of her. I wouldn't kill her. I couldn't kill her. She knew that.

It was impossible to kill Cora without killing part of myself.

As snow fell outside, I extended my hand and helped her up from the floor. Cora took my hand and I pulled her to her feet. She stood in silence for a long moment, her head wrapped in bloody gauze, inhaling the reality of Eddie Coyle's death.

She whispered, "You killed him."

I had become a CEO who was executing his business with a calmness that was terrifying. For a brief moment, she was scared of me. I had changed. She wanted to bolt out into the darkness and snow, but she knew that she wouldn't get far. If she ran out the front door, she had no transportation, and with her dizziness she'd be lucky to make it to the railroad tracks.

She repeated, "You killed him."

A surge of power ran through me. I didn't care.

"You killed Jackie. Bishop is dead. Eddie Coyle is dead."

Her eyes came to mine.

She whispered, "The money is all ours."

Standing over the dead body of her lover, that wasn't what I had expected from Cora.

I said, "I didn't shoot Eddie Coyle for the money."

"It's ours now, Dmytryk."

"The money stays."

"The money stays? What does that mean?"

"The money stays here."

"Leave the money?"

"We get our things and get out of here, but the money stays."

"If we leave this money, then everything that I have done, everything I worked and sacrificed for, will be meaningless. I'd be right back where we started."

"We'll never be back where we started."

"Are you afraid?"

I shook my head. "I'm not afraid."

"You're afraid. You're still the coward you were six months ago."

"Not me, Cora. You. You're still the coward that walked out on me. You want everything easy."

"I planned this for six months, and now you think I'm going to walk away? Now it's down to the two of us, Dmytryk. It's back to where it all started. You and me. It's back to the way you wanted it. Only now we have the resources to live a better life. We can start over."

"The money stays. Just you and me. We leave. We start over."

"Broke? We start over broke?"

"We struggle like everyone else. We struggle and we overcome and we make this one of the greatest stories of survival and love that . . . we make it a great love story . . . that's what we do."

"You've killed and robbed like everyone else, and now you want to take the high road?"

"The money stays."

"If the money stays, how long do you think we'll last? Until we get to Nashville? We wouldn't last until Nashville, Dmytryk. We wouldn't last three hours. I left Detroit because of friggin' money issues and I'm not going to go back there as broke as I was when I left. I didn't grow up like you, Dmytryk. I grew up broke. My father died broke and my mother struggled until she died. I'm not going to live that life. Maybe if there was some guarantee that this would end, but it's only getting worse. There is no end in sight."

"The money stays."

"And if I did make it back to Detroit, if I left with you, if I made love to you every night, if we went back to that same routine, if I cooked for while you cut the yard, at some point, I'd hate myself for being so weak for you, I'd hate how much you love me, and I would poison you. I'd think about this moment, and I'd kill you and bury you with your other secret. The one that you and Eddie Coyle left by the Uniroyal tire. Dmytryk, it's us and the money or there is no us."

"I'm in this because of you."

"You made your own choices, Dmytryk."

"You're right. I have. I've robbed banks. I've watched men get shot and die. Sammy and Rick are dead. I've kidnapped. I killed Jackie. I killed Eddie Coyle. Don't you see where this road is leading? Even if we were apart for the last six months, we've danced this dance together. We've been in this together from the start. You pushed me into this business and now I'm pulling you out. I'm not asking you to walk away. I'm telling you that this is done."

"You're jealous of Eddie Coyle."

"Not anymore."

"You will always hate Eddie Coyle. You wish you were a man like Eddie Coyle."

"Is that what you think? Really? Eddie Coyle was living from bank job to bank job the way a man lives from paycheck to paycheck. How much longer before you would have left him? He tucked you away in a small town decorated with Confederate flags. But you're not a small-town girl. You're Brooklyn. You're Detroit. How long was that going to last?"

"The job would've been done. So I would've been done with him."

"Just like our marriage."

"Eddie Coyle would've been finished with me too."

"So he was good until you had your big score."

Cora said, "Clear your head. We don't have to split the money six ways. It's just us. Let's take the money with us. Let's talk about this somewhere else. But let's take the money."

"The money stays."

"Fine. I'll take what's mine and you can leave your share. Better yet, you leave your one hundred thousand inside the bag and I'll take everyone else's cut and we can part ways."

"The money stays here in Trussville."

"Then everything I've done will be meaningless. I have sacrificed everything. I sacrificed my love for you. I have sacrificed my marriage to you. I left you. That was the hardest thing I've ever done. I had to do it when you were gone. I had to do it and not look back. I had to fight wanting to call you every day and every night. I had to leave a man I loved and take up with a man who meant nothing to me. And I'm not going to pretend that it will ever be the same. I've been with Eddie. You were with Jackie. Six months apart. We're new people now. I have risked everything, and it can't be for nothing."

"*I've risked everything.* I'm standing inside this room with blood on my clothes and on my hands, my body battered, bruised, because I risked everything and I did it for you."

"What do you want from me, Dmytryk?"

"I want the woman I married. *I want my wife.*"

"*She doesn't exist anymore.* That woman does not exist anymore."

She was right.

What I'd been praying for the last six months no longer existed. My honest lifestyle wasn't good enough for her. She had become a criminal, and that was who she was now.

I nodded. "What are we going to do now?"

Cora said, "There is only one way out of this."

She held her wounded head and stepped to the table and picked up Eddie Coyle's nine-millimeter. Eddie Coyle's gun had been reloaded. Cora was determined to win this fight.

I said, "Don't do it, Cora."

She stepped on the other side of the money, and for a moment, she paused. In the end she took a deep breath, licked her lips, and aimed the death end of her gun at my heart. She aimed at me with the intent to kill me. Her bottom lip trembled. Her eyes watered.

My gun was raised and pointing at her, only my finger wasn't on the trigger.

My insides were ablaze, a spreading wildfire. I asked, "Did you love me?"

"I love you, Dmytryk Knight. But I can't go back to poverty."

"We can fix this."

She shook her head. "Without the money, nothing changes."

She was delusional and suffering from a concussion and I was heartbroken and high on prescription drugs. With a bag of money and a dead body between us, Cora held her stance.

She said, "Why would I go back to Detroit and bust my ass working at Starbucks or Walmart or at Home Depot? Why would I go back to seeing the bills come in faster than the money? Why would I go back to degrading myself and dancing? Why wouldn't I take this money and go have a better life? We could live seven years with no problems. We could live three times that long if we take this money and go to the Dominican Republic."

I didn't say anything. I took in the scent of Eddie Coyle's death with each inhalation. I took in the scent of Sammy and Rick's deaths. I took in the scent of Jackie and Bishop's.

She lowered her gun and looked at Eddie Coyle, the money, and then she looked back at me. I had lowered my gun too.

She said, "You've always loved me the way I wanted to be loved. You loved me so much it scared me at times."

"I know that."

"I can go back, I want to go back, but I can't go back the same way I left."

"I'm stopping you, Cora. I didn't stop you in Detroit, but I'm stopping you here."

"This is six months of my life."

"And you are eight years of mine."

In that moment she softened. She was going to leave this all behind; I saw it in her eyes.

She whispered, "Not many people have the chance to see this much money at one time. This is enough money to run away and start a new life. I could be whoever I wanted to be."

Then she shook head again, her breathing thickened, and her anger returned.

She snapped, "I'll tell the FBI, Dmytryk. I'll go to them and list every crime you have committed. I will tell them about the murders. I'll cut a deal with them. I know how to play my cards. I'll tell them that you forced me to become a stripper. I'll tell them about the bank jobs you did, every last one of them. And I'll tell them about the dead bodies that you and Eddie Coyle left by the Uniroyal tire. I'll tell them about you and Rick and Sammy in Los Angeles."

"I'll tell them about your involvement, Cora. Our electric chair will be a love seat."

"I'll tell them that you killed Jackie, then you killed Bishop and Eddie Coyle and I was too afraid not to help you because you had threatened to kill me too. Do you understand? I'm the victim in this. Not you. You can't win. You forced me to do this. So ask yourself, how much is your life worth to you? Go get in your old car and drive away while you can."

Without warning, as we both stood wounded, drowsy, and covered in blood, Cora raised her gun again. She was dizzy and nauseated, and maybe that ringing inside her head was driving her mad. She gritted her teeth and I knew that she was done talking. I saw it in her eyes.

Until death do us part.

My body was racked with pain, but I raised my gun as fast as she had raised hers.

She released a blood-curdling scream and shot twice.

As hot lead entered my flesh, I screamed and pulled the trigger three times.

Then our marriage was over.

25

The FBI questioned me about my estranged wife.

One of the men was younger, looked like he was fresh out of college. He wore a new wedding ring and he reminded me of myself six years ago. The second agent looked seasoned, like he had worked for decades and was on the verge of becoming burned out. He looked like a man who was twice divorced and was still paying alimony for both marriages. He looked like he hated his job and didn't want to be in Detroit. He looked like he would rather have been somewhere drinking away the evening.

We sat in the living room and I told them that my wife had left me last summer. They asked me why and I shrugged, took a deep breath, and told them that our situation was a long story. They nodded like they had time to hear my tale. So I told them that Cora and I had been laid off from the auto industry. Things had become hard on us. We'd gone two years without any real employment. We'd exhausted our savings and retirement money, lost two new cars and a town home. We'd both taken on a handful of part-time jobs. I'd even delivered pizzas. I told them that she had become a dancer, without my knowledge, and had protested when I told her to quit. She had promised that she would. She had met a man at the place where she was dancing, a man of apparent money and means, and her loyalties had shifted.

They told me that my scenario wasn't new to them. They said that women left their husbands to be with their boyfriends all the time, some abandoning their children in order to chase their dreams.

I defended my wife.

I emphasized that my wife was a good woman and pointed at pictures that were up around the house, pictures that showed us in a state of bliss. For four years she had been dutiful, reliable, trustworthy, and loving. She had been my Sistine Chapel. I defended her honor and said that even though she had stayed out all night, then come home drunk and wearing a brand-new fur coat, we were trying. Had tried. We'd argued about that fur coat and she left me the next summer.

They told me that they already knew Cora had left me, and I asked them how. They had talked to the neighbors, who had seen her take seven suitcases and leave with two men in a Cadillac SUV. The FBI had their descriptions. One sounded like Eddie Coyle. The other fit the description of his brother. I shook my head and told them that Cora hadn't contacted me since she'd left. She had left me.

One of them asked me, "Are you okay, Mr. Knight?"

"I'm fine. Considering the fact that the FBI is sitting inside my home, I'm fine."

"You keep looking toward the kitchen."

"I'm sorry."

I asked him where Cora was. I asked for the details of what Cora had done. They told me that she had been involved in bank robberies. Then they told me that she was dead. When they told me that she was dead, I felt a thunderclap inside my heart. Suddenly the air in the room felt heavy, like I was in a room filled with smoke. For a moment it felt as if my head was going to explode. My hand shook and a few tears fell.

"Why are you just getting here? If this happened weeks ago, what took you so long?"

The married agent said, "We extend our apologies."

I extended my sarcasm and said, "Or maybe there were cases with higher priority."

The other agent said, "I can give you a number to call if you want to file a formal complaint."

I sat and shook my head over and over.

I nodded, wiped my eyes with the back of my hand, and asked them to continue. They waited a moment. The pain inside my head subsided and I managed to put on my corporate face and repeat that I was okay. They told me that they had found her DNA at the scene of a crime, a church in the heart of Alabama. They had found her DNA there, but they had found her charred body a few miles away.

I said, "Charred?"

They both nodded.

There had been an explosion where Cora and her friends were hiding out. Everyone inside the hideout was dead. He told me that they had robbed a church, but all of the money had been recovered. Cora's personal belongings had been found in the city of Rome, Georgia, at the home of a man named Lew Hunter. That was Eddie Coyle's real name.

The neighbors in that small town had verified that Cora had been living there for a while. She was the mysterious girl in Rome, the woman who lived in a friendly town and never talked to anyone, but she dressed nicely, went shopping often, and drove a fire-engine-red convertible Mercedes.

The younger agent looked across the room and saw stacks of books, most written in Neo-Latin languages. In a voice that was more personal than professional, or maybe it was just the intonation of a rookie who hadn't learned all of the ropes, he asked me if I spoke all of those languages. I told him that I did. I was rusty, but I was still proficient and I was a tutor. He acknowledged that it might be a bad time to say so, but he informed me that the FBI was looking for contract linguists. U.S. citizens only. No benefits, but the job paid between thirty and forty dollars an hour.

He said, "You can apply online."

I had been the wheelman, the unseen villain in a string of bank robberies that spread from L.A. to Texas, and now a representative of the government was showing me kindness and steering me toward gainful employment. As the winds began to pick up, I appreciated the moment of irony. His partner stared across the room, evaluating my modest lifestyle, his unimpressed eyes settling on my fedora. Then he looked down at my wingtip shoes. His attention rested on the same style of shoes that the Johnston & Murphy Bandits had worn. The look in his eyes told me he suspected something, but it was nothing that could be proven.

I was a man who had an American flag waving in front of my home.

I had an American-made 1969, green, four-door, hardtop Buick Wildcat parked out front.

I was sure they had already probed my bank accounts, but the money in those accounts was modest. They probably knew every Web site I had surfed. They knew every job I had applied for online over the last two and a half years. Big Brother was always watching, but I didn't appear to be a scapegrace.

Maybe they thought that Cora and Eddie Coyle had had a shoot-out over the money, but I doubted that. They knew a person was missing. There was always a driver. Always a wheelman. And the older agent's eyes told me that he suspected the missing somebody was a man who wore a fedora. But a hat wasn't enough to convict a man.

The older agent motioned at my hand and said, "You still have it on."

I raised my left hand and stared at it, gazed at that endless circle on my finger.

He repeated what I had already told him. "Mrs. Knight has been gone since last summer."

I nodded. "She left then."

"You're still wearing your wedding ring?"

"It's never been off my finger, not since I put it on."

Legally I was still Cora's husband. Her life had been her own, her heart had been given to another man, but her remains, by law, belonged to me. There was a joke in there somewhere.

I could hear God laughing as he slapped his knee and high-fived a few angels.

I asked the agents, "What if I don't claim her remains?"

The man who looked twice-divorced said, "Up to you, sir."

"I'd rather remember her the way she was, before she left here."

They stood and stared at me in the awkwardness.

Men being emotional around other men always generated awkwardness.

They gave me their final condolences and the men in black headed toward their dark sedan.

I left the porch light on.

I stood in the window and watched them saunter down my driveway. When they made it to their car, I returned to the kitchen and searched for Cora. I called her name. I whispered her married name. No one was there. No one answered. I went to the back door and looked out into the yard. She wasn't there either.

I went inside the bathroom and pulled my shirt back. My left shoulder had a wound that was healing. Cora had shot me with her nine-millimeter. Maybe she had been dizzied by her concussion, and maybe that had spoiled her aim and saved my life.

I inspected my body. My left leg was healing as well, the bullet having gone through my leg the way a slug had spiraled through Rick's body.

I could've had it all. Even after all had been said and done, even after the last words I'd said to Cora, the temptation to take that money was magnetic. But I'd made a choice. I left Cora's dead body on the floor next to Eddie Coyle. Then I put the money on the ground beyond the garage and left Trussville alone and bleeding.

But Cora's soul had run and climbed inside the car with me. She had possessed the glow of an angel. She had been as beautiful as she had been on the day I had met her. It was as if my wife had returned to me. If not my wife, then the love she'd had for me had wanted to come back home.

I shook my head, felt a wave of guilt coming, felt a panic attack.

Cora was dead. My wife was dead.

Cora and I had been in a standoff. I felt the weight of the nine-millimeter in my hand. I felt its kick when I pulled its trigger. It had been deafening. My finger squeezed the trigger as I screamed in pain. I saw the bullet hit Cora in the center of her chest. Then, as she staggered, the desire to stay alive made my finger tighten around the trigger and the gun kicked inside my hand again. Her head exploded the same way Sammy's had exploded. I felt the untamable anger and wailed in madness.

My fingers loosened and allowed the gun to fall from my hand. I ran to her. The boom from the guns left me deaf, unable to hear my own screams, pleading, crying that I wanted it undone. I had wanted to be the one to die so that Cora could go on living.

I'd put her life in front of mine. But I had pulled the trigger.

It had come as a surprise to me. I didn't think that I'd be able to pull the trigger, but the fear of death had taken control. Either that or I had changed. I knew that I wasn't the same person anymore.

The woman whom I loved had tried to kill me.

And I had killed the woman whom I loved.

A few nights after I'd returned to Detroit, I grew restless. I'd left home at three in the morning and driven for six hours, crossed the state line, and pulled up into a small Midwestern town the next morning. Spending months with Eddie Coyle and his friends, breaking bread with Rick and Sammy, all of that wrongdoing remained in my blood. I sat in front of a bank and wrote out a short note for the teller. *Stay* *calm. No alarms. No dye packs.* But I never stepped out of my Buick Wildcat. I'd always look in the mirror and see Henrick's face. Still, I sat in front of the bank with my fedora at my side and my pocket watch in hand. I let two minutes go by. For one hundred and twenty seconds, in my mind, I was inside that bank. Then I pointed my car in the direction of the house that had been the home of my father and mother. They had loved there. That had been good enough for them. That was good enough for me.

I drove back to Detroit. I drove back home and missed Cora every mile of the way.

The FBI had told me what I already knew. Today I missed Cora more than I could bear.

It came in waves. I didn't miss her every day. Some days I resented her. Most days it was the opposite. Today, after I had visited my parents' gravesite, the wave of love had been like a tsunami.

Over the past few weeks, I've had visions of Cora, the way she had been when she first ran to me in the falling snow and asked me my name, a beautiful autoworker who was dressed in blue Dickies and steel-toed boots, the Brooklyn-born woman I had cooked for and had taken on dates, the woman I had asked to marry me, the woman I had carried across the threshold as she wore her beautiful wedding dress, the woman I had promised to love and honor and cherish and respect until death did us part. That woman was gone, gone forever, but I knew how to make her return to me, if only for a few hours.

As a breeze kicked up and the moment sighed across the barren trees, as I heard my neighbor's kids laughing and passing my home riding their skateboards in the cold, I looked at my wedding ring.

Heat rose and warmed my throat.

I wept.

Then I whispered, "Tomorrow. I'll take it off tomorrow."

I opened the medicine cabinet and removed the bottle of prescription medicine I had been given by a heartbroken and terrified woman named Abbey Rose. A moment passed before I shook the bottle. There was only one pill left. The medication had helped me through pains and helped me cope with a mountain of guilt, a weight that only a man as strong and powerful as Atlas could carry. I had been Atlas for a long time.

I popped the final pill and washed it down with tap water, and then I thought about Abbey Rose Brandstätter-Hess.

One day I might send her a note on Facebook. Or maybe I'll just remember that day in L.A. That would be best. Just remembering that horrible day, as I knew she would, would be best. I was her bogeyman. The man who wore the wingtips and the fedora would always be her bogeyman. Just as it was a day best remembered, it was also a day best forgotten.

The pill took effect and a gentle haze covered my world. This would be the last pill before truth. This would be the last pill before denial subsided and reality took root.

When I stepped out of the bathroom and walked into the living room, I gazed toward the kitchen and Cora was standing there. Her skin glowed and my wife was beautiful and ethereal. She lifted her blue dress and offered me a glimpse of her legs up to her thighs, teased me, winked at me, and then she smiled. This time her hair was longer. Much longer. She tousled her mane and laughed. Her hair was dark brown with golden highlights. It was the way I liked it the most.

She asked, "What's the matter?"

"Nothing's wrong."

Her soft, youthful features, round and doelike eyes, making her appear childlike and seductive all at once.

She was my wife. I was her husband.

Cora turned around and walked back into the kitchen and continued washing dishes.

I went into the kitchen and helped her, shared love as we partook of the division of labor.

She asked, "What did those men want?"

"Nothing. They were looking for somebody who used to live here."

My wife turned and kissed me. As we kissed, my home lit up with the glow of love.

I held her face and asked her, "What do you want to do now?"

She smiled. "We struggle and we overcome and we make this one of the greatest stories of survival and love that . . . we make it a great love story . . . that's what we do."

Acknowledgments

Hey, everyone! *¡Señoritas y señores! ¡Hola a todos!* It's me again. *¡He regresado!*

Acknowledgments

Years ago I had wanted to do a road story—well, sort of. I've always wanted to have a story that moved from one city to another and used as much of the terrain in the USA as possible. I never got around to writing that book, and if the creek doesn't rise, I will. This novel isn't that novel, but it has brought back that desire. While working on *Tempted by Trouble*, the novel you're holding in your hands (or listening to on tape or CD and enjoying the voice of the narrator, Dion Graham), I did drive back and forth across the Land of the Free, starting in L.A. and ending up at the Home of the Braves. That was a long ride and I made that trip three times. I didn't use the trip the way I had desired because the characters needed to get to their destinations, but it was worth the experience—I guess from an actor's POV—to understand what the trip was like and be able to write it correctly. I've done the same thing for all of the books, whether they were set in Pomona, California, or Argentina. I have to make that trip and walk that walk. In this case, I had to drive that drive. Damn gas prices. Anyway. I will tell you this: Once you get out of the concrete jungle called L.A., the topography is beautiful and for about two thousand miles—I kid you not—there are more Dairy Queens than there are stars in the sky. On that long stretch of I-10, there were almost as many DQs as there were those bright yellow billboards with the blue writing, the ones that announced that the Mystery of the Desert was at exit 322. Yup. As I passed through the Texas Canyon, I stopped there too. I have my beer mug and a cowboy hat to prove it. As I have done with all of my fictional novels, whether the setting is a small town called Odenville or in the West Indies on the island of Antigua or in London in the shadows of Parliament, I broke out the charge card and slapped down the passport, packed a carry-on bag, took an electric toothbrush, and visited all of the locations in the name of research.

For a tourist, some places are more exciting than others. But to a writer, they are all worth the trip. There are no dull places. Even a ride down Highway 11 in Trussville, Alabama, can spark my imagination.

Now, a few words about the novel you're holding. (I won't give away any plot points.)

I love stories and films that are noir, stories that are gripping journeys through secrets, lies, and, of course, murder. If there is a gun in act one, by act three there had better be some blood on the dance floor. The characters in *Tempted by Trouble* are, at times, disturbing, and for the duration of the novel, regardless of where they came from, they are all connected. From the onset I had viewed Dmytryk as a dark and broken man who was born thirty years too late. He was made for the era when movies were still being shown in black and white. That thought might be embedded in the dialogue of the novel. Crossing paths with Eddie Coyle and falling into a dubious occupation as a means of survival, for me, creates hair-raising tension as well as subtle complexities. Then toss in some real-world problems and . . . bam.

Before I ramble on too long, or before Gideon or Hawks or the Man in the White Shoes comes knocking at my mental door, let me hurry and get to the most important part of the acknowledgments, the part where I name and thank all of the usual suspects. They are indeed my partners in crime.

Book 'em, Danno.

Acknowledgments

*   *   *

I want to thank Tiffany Pace for her initial edits. Thanks for the assistance. The check is in the mail. LOL. Has it been twelve years? I hope the next twelve go by as smoothly.

Of course, with all of the traveling I do, I have to thank the people who have kept my life in order for the last decade, Karl and Tammy at the Planer Group in Los Angeles. Thanks for everything.

Quiana London and LaToya Lemon in Detroit, thanks for driving me around Motown when I was up for the event at the public library. I'd already started the book, but I hadn't decided where Dmytryk was going to rest his fedora. Being in Detroit a few days, watching CNN, chatting with people in crisis, walking around the Ren Center, riding the DPM, it all helped in the creation of this fictional tale.

Natalie Godwin, thanks for taking a few moments out of your busy schedule and showing me other parts of Detroit. The same thanks and appreciation goes out to you. Thanks a zillion.

On the storytelling front, Sybilla Nash, thanks for the feedback and input. Tell Kortney "Yo!" and that I look forward to seeing her in more Hollywood blockbusters.

Mo in Germany and Kayode in the UK, once again a thousand thanks to my intellectual crew. LOL. You guys read parts, if not all, of this, from the first word. You saw characters added and deleted, and you survived the confusion that came from reading a new chapter where names had been changed midstream. Apologies and no worries. Names still might change before this hits the press. I hope you enjoy the gifts that I sent you. LOL. If Dmytryk Knight can wear a pocket watch, dagnabbit, you can too.

*   *   *

Acknowledgments

I think the difficult thing for me, creatively, was that after writing two Gideon books back-to-back, it was hard to get out of that hit-man frame of mind and not create another character that would fit perfectly into that world. Dmytryk had to have his own personality. His own sensibilities. His own history and motivation. Giving a new character his own voice is the fun part and the hard part. This character reminds me more of someone that character actor William H. Macy would play. At times, he brought to mind Billy Bob Thornton in *The Man Who Wasn't There*. Or Bill Paxton in *A Simple Plan*. (Loved that novel too. It's another that I could read again.) *Double Indemnity*, *The Postman Always Rings Twice*, *Inner Sanctum*, the rich and dark mood from a few novels and more than a dozen noir movies comes to mind as well. Okay, I'm going on a tangent. Mork calling Eric, come in, Eric. Where was I? Oh, yeah. Out of that long list of works in that dark genre, the one that will always stand out is *Chinatown*. There was no fantasy ending and I applaud its depth and grittiness. It had a shocking yet logical ending that showed that money and power rule the real world. That powerful conclusion of *Chinatown* shook up both Hollywood and storytellers alike. Good guys do lose. Bad guys do win. The latter fly to Washington in private jets while the former struggle to get enough change to buy a bus pass to ride MARTA.

And, on a side note, as the world of graphic novels pops inside my brain, maybe that's part of the reason why I'm drawn to Ed Brubaker's work in that wonderful arena, especially *Coward* and the Criminal and Incognito series. His work is gritty and he does not hold back. So far as my works, I'd already written *Thieves' Paradise* and *Drive Me Crazy* before I discovered the work of Eisner Award–winning American cartoonist Ed Brubaker. A few of my characters—maybe Driver,

Gideon, Dmytryk Knight, and the crew from *Thieves' Paradise*—I hope that they all end up in the graphic novel medium at some point.

Anyway. It's getting late, so I'd better get to the part where I thank a few more people.

Lolita Files, thanks for the notes early on. You are, as the Brits say, brilliant.

John Paine, once again, thanks for looking at this book as I was working on the project.

Tyrone Fance, my favorite comedian in the whole world, big ups and high five for allowing me to borrow your book *The Myth of Male Power*. Much love to you, Delia, Taylor, and Devin.

Dana Wimberly, thanks for reading this as a WIP and in its roughest form.

Mrs. Charmont Young, *hola señora! ¡Y gracias!*

And my Facebook homies and fellow writers Robert Carraher and Amaleka McCall Brathwaite, thanks for getting back to me on the questions I posted at the last minute.

Thanks to all of the hardworking people back in New York at Dutton, the best publishing company from coast to coast. We've been rolling since '96. Thanks for years of support. Brian Tart, thanks a zillion. Erika Imranyi, o ye magnificent editor, thanks for your patience and understanding. And thanks for bringing the scissors. You're brilliant. I think we've cut close to 40K words from this baby. I loved the cuts! And while I'm shouting, shout-outs to Ava Kavyani and everyone in publicity and to copyeditor extraordinaire, Aja Pollock. Wait . . . uh . . . do people still say *shout-out*? LOL. I have no clue.

Acknowledgments

Sara Camilli and everyone working at the Sara Camilli Agency, thanks for over a decade of hard work and support on . . . how many novels? I've lost count. It's been a while since Chiquita and Tyrel and Kimberly and Vince and Chante Marie Ellis were created. Seriously. I did an interview and they asked me how many books I'd written and I shrugged. LOL. And I couldn't name them all in order. I guess all that matters is the next one. What's done is done. (Joking.) But seriously, how many trees do I have to kill to make it to one hundred books? Gideon will have cataracts and be wearing Depends by then. . . .

Now, as usual, if I have omitted anyone, by accident or intentionally, here's your chance to shine.

Saving the best for last, I want to thank _____ for all of their help while I was working on this novel. They brought me chicken soup when I had the flu. They gave me brilliant ideas when I had none and was sitting in my office staring at that demon Writer's Block. Yessireee! They were better than spell-check, a dictionary, and a thesaurus. I'm sure that they will tell you all they did to make this novel pop. Feel free to believe all that they say. Just don't buy the bridge in Brooklyn. It's mine.

Sunday, April 25, 2010. 10:26 P.M.
33.43.22 North 84.28.15 West
70°F
Current: Cloudy with scattered showers
Wind: SW at 4 mph
Humidity: 56%

Gray sweats, black T-shirt from W Hotel in San Francisco, locks pulled back into a ponytail.

I'm on a horse. ☺

Feel free to stop by www.ericjeromedickey.com. From there you can link to other sites and see how to find me on Facebook and Twitter. Oh, yeah. Stop by and join the fan page on Facebook.

About the Author

Originally from Memphis, Tennessee, Eric Jerome Dickey is the *New York Times* bestselling author of eighteen novels. He is also the author of a six-issue miniseries of graphic novels for Marvel Enterprises featuring Storm (*X-Men*) and the Black Panther. He lives on the road and rests in whatever hotel will have him.